C000216601

Unequal
By
Birth

The second novel in the
Tales of Flynn and Reilly

Rosemary J. Kind

Copyright © 2019 Rosemary J. Kind

All rights reserved. Any unauthorised broadcasting, public performance, copying or recording will constitute an infringement of copyright. No part of this book may be reproduced or transmitted in any form or by any means, electronically or mechanical, including photocopying, fax, data transmittal, internet site, recording or any information storage or retrieval system without the express written permission of the publisher except for the use of brief quotations in a book review.

Printed in the United Kingdom

First Printing, 2019 Alfie Dog Limited

The author can be found at: authors@alfiedog.com

Cover design: Katie Stewart, Magic Owl Designs
http://www.magicowldesign.com/

ISBN 978-1-909894-43-3

Published by
Alfie Dog Limited
Schilde Lodge, Tholthorpe,
North Yorkshire, YO61 1SN
Tel: 0207 193 33 90

DEDICATION

To my wonderful parents who brought me up to believe
everyone is equal, regardless of race, gender, occupation,
or any other factor.

INTRODUCTION

Whilst much of this writing is based in historical fact, I have taken liberties with some elements of time and place to serve the needs of the story. Examples of this include it being unclear what some of the early women's groups were called and the fact that the first bank in Pierceton did not open until 1876. I hope the reader will forgive me. I have also, on one occasion, chosen to use a song which was not written until three years later. Sadly, it can be hard to come by all the songs which were in use at the time.

None of the divergences are material and, at its heart, this really is a work of fiction.

NOTE:
The characters are all fictitious and any resemblance they may have to persons alive or dead is entirely coincidental. This book is not intended to suggest that the events portrayed happened in reality. It is purely a work of fiction, rooted in elements of real history.

PROLOGUE

Pierceton, Indiana,
November 1863

My dearest William,

I can only thank God that Daniel is now released from prison and safely here with us in Pierceton. It will take many years for him to leave behind the way that Mr Hawksworth treated him in Iowa and his bodily scars will always remind him. I hope they may heal a little in time. Miss Ellie has given him salve to apply to them, which we hope will assist in that process. He is settling well and gaining weight again now he has more to eat than prison food. Please thank your father for all he did to defend him when he was being tried so unjustly. I remain in awe of Mrs Hawksworth being prepared to testify against her husband and sincerely hope that she has found a place of safety for her home.

It still seems strange to call you by your new name. Give me time and I am sure William Dixon will be as closely etched on my heart as was Thomas Reilly. I am only sorry we had to part so soon after being reunited and I can but hope and pray that it will not be long until we see you again.

As we had so little time to speak on our departure from Iowa, I promised that I would write to you with news of all that has happened since we were children together in New York, although I will spare you some of the more mundane details.

When they would not allow me to travel on that first train from New York with you and Daniel, I was sent instead to a children's home for girls. It was not a bad life and certainly easier than our days on the streets. Matron was strict and I found that strange after the independence we had known. I became good friends with a girl called Sarah Duggan, she's Sarah Spencer now, but more of that later.

Sarah and I travelled out on a train about a year after yourselves and were brought to Pierceton, where thankfully we were given a home together by Miss Ellie Cochrane who of course you've met. Miss Ellie didn't adopt us legally as the Dixons did you, but she did in all except paperwork. She has been as much a mother as a guardian and is very dear to me. Sarah and I have worked with Miss Ellie on Cochrane's farm, but were at the same time given a home life, an education and treated as family. When I see what happened to Daniel, I can only be grateful that my life has been as good as it has and pray that now he has joined us here, he too will benefit.

I mentioned that Sarah is now a married woman, having married Joseph Spencer the younger of the sons of Mrs Spencer who runs the general store here in Pierceton. For a while, I was walking out with Joseph's elder brother Henry, but sadly he was taken from us during the war. It was following the loss of him that I felt the need to see if it was possible to find you and Daniel. Both of you are so dear to me and losing someone close one is a strong reminder of how precious those we love should be. It was then I determined to travel in search of you in Dowagiac, but that part of the story is familiar to you.

Miss Ellie, as you know, decided to accompany me on the journey, which, given the events that unfolded, was indeed appreciated. She has given me wise counsel over the years. Although in a very different way, I think Ben, the farmhand who helped me to find Daniel, has been of great support to him too. He even allowed his little dog, Duke, to stay on the farm with Daniel to give him some company in the bunkhouse when Ben himself had to move on. Ben returned to Hawksworth's farm each harvest for a while, as much to see Daniel and ensure his safety as for the work. I earnestly wish we had been able to find him again before we left Iowa. Miss Ellie would be delighted to give him a place of ease here on Cochrane's Farm, that he might have comfort in his old age. Her cousin, James, also lives in semi-retirement here, although he did look after the farm while we were away.

Although the court said that Daniel must stay here at Cochrane's Farm for at least two years, I can see no reason he should ever go otherwise. Miss Ellie has taken him into her home as she did me and already Daniel is beginning some education as well as learning farm management. I am more happy than you can know to have him here and our childhood bond is as strong as it ever was.

Please write to update me with all your news.

Your ever-loving sister,

Molly Reilly

#

Pierceton, Indiana
April 1865

Dear William,

I hope this letter finds you well. Writing still does not come easily to me, so I will keep this short and leave other news for Molly to tell you when she next writes.

The last eighteen months have been the happiest of my life. Miss Ellie has given me a home the like of which I have never known before. Between them, Molly and Miss Ellie have taught me to read and write more completely than I could previously and to manage much of the farm and I am the better for it.

Molly is, as indeed she has been since the day I met her, the dearest person in all the world to me. I cannot imagine a day without her by my side. I do believe that no man could love Molly more than I do. I'm not a man who finds words easy, but what I'm trying to say is, I hope that I might have your blessing to marry your sister. It would be my dearest wish that you could be present at the ceremony and, as soon as the date is fixed, I will write to you again with the details.

Your sincere friend,

Daniel Flynn

#

Dowagiac, Michigan
April 1865

Dear Daniel

I would be delighted for you to marry Molly and become my brother-in-law as well as my brother by blood. I wish you both every happiness and will write separately to my sister.

Maybe one day I will find a love of my own, though I own I'm the more interested in Jeanie since her father forbade her seeing me. The truth is that I never really loved her and it has taken all that has happened to show me that. She has other suitors and I'm sure she will be happy with one of them soon enough. For my own part, I am satisfied to learn the practice of law and may take up a place to study at university later in the year. Ma and Pa Dixon have forgiven me, which is more than I deserve, and I still look forward to taking over the family business in the fullness of time.

Your brother in all but birth,

William

#

Pierceton, Indiana
October 1865

My Dearest William,

What a delight it was for us to see you all once again and have you present for our wedding. I guess a secret is easy to keep over such a great distance as the one at which we find ourselves. We are indeed grateful that you could act on our behalf in the matter for which Miss Ellie summoned you. I had no notion that she intended to transfer the farm into my name and I am still overwhelmed by the gesture.

I cannot believe all the good things which have happened over the last two years. That Daniel is now my husband is my greatest delight and we are very happy together. It is strange to find myself all of a sudden with such great responsibilities. Whatever would Mammy think if she could see us now, me a farm owner and you a lawyer? We have come so far from the wretched life she was forced to lead. I think she would be very proud of the both of us, God rest her soul.

Well, dear brother, I was indeed happy to hear that your life is progressing well in Dowagiac and I am mighty proud of the achievements you have made. There will always be short-sighted folk who do not see the people we are now, rather than the life we once led. That Congressman Makepeace would not allow his daughter to marry you will only be to his detriment and not yours. You will make a fine husband when the time comes. Even here in Pierceton I have faced some degree of prejudice and mockery, as has Miss Ellie for taking Sarah and me into her farm. In our case it is the result of being women, but prejudice is prejudice whatever the cause. Miss Ellie bought land that came to market when old Mr Reese couldn't pay his debts. He'd deserve pity if it weren't the result of his drinking and idling and his sons are no better. They resented Miss Ellie's success, which they wrongly saw as being at their expense. People can be strange creatures and no mistake. I fear they will not appreciate the fact that that land has now been passed to me. Those around me here say I should be watchful of them.

I know that Miss Ellie will be with you herself shortly. I will miss her while she is gone. Please take care of her for me.
Your ever-loving sister

Molly Flynn

CHAPTER 1

She was lovely and fair as the rose of the summer,
Yet 'twas not her beauty alone that won me;
Oh no, 'twas the truth in her eyes ever dawning,
That made me love Mary, the Rose of Tralee.
The Rose of Tralee - Edward Mordaunt Spencer, 1846 approx.

August 1866
The worn leather boots felt heavier to Daniel than they had
done that morning, as he set them by the door to the
farmhouse once again. At last his day's labours were done.
He stretched his back and bent from side to side, then he
straightened up and sighed. Having positioned the kettle
on the range, he took the letter from the table and started
to read what was written in Miss Ellie's fine scrawling
hand. Then, frowning and shaking his head, he turned the
paper over, as though the blank reverse might make more
sense. Turning it back he read it once again.

My dearest Molly and Daniel,
  *I hope this letter finds you both well and that, Molly, you are
resting. I dare say that Daniel will be only too happy to work all
the harder for as long as you need him to. I know you've another
four months before your time, but farm work can be heavy and
we wouldn't put a cow to the plough when she was in calf, nor a
milking cow come to that.*
  I am sorry to hear what those Reese boys have been a-doing.

They can't see their problems are from their own laziness and not the hand of another. If their dear mama were alive today, she'd be giving them such a hiding for troubling you. I don't suppose it would do any good for me to go reminding them of that. If their daddy hadn't been just the same, their mama would have had a much better life, which brings me to the main reason for my letter...

Daniel looked up to check the kettle was yet to start steaming and realised Molly was watching him intently. He went back to the letter trying to take it all in.

...I know you will understand why I needed to show my support. The Suffrage Movement here in Dowagiac is much ahead of our own in Pierceton and they have been petitioning for the right to vote alongside their menfolk for some time. It is a fine thing that our country at last recognises all men should be considered as like, but I've worked all my life until now and pay my taxes as any other. Well, I'm sorry to say that whilst I was cheering my support for the speech being given, by no less a person than Mrs Dixon herself, a gentleman of the law took hold of my arm, at which point I spoke to him quite sharply with my demands that he unhand me...

As Daniel read on, he began to picture his wife's feisty guardian and what lengths she might have gone to. He looked up and said, "It would be a brave man who tried to argue with Miss Ellie, and I'm mighty surprised to find that such a man has even tried."

He read on.

...It was at that point I found myself being led to no other place than the Courthouse, whereupon I was taken to a cell. I

thought only of the other women who are standing together for our cause, as I hear they are doing right across this great country, and not of my own discomfiture at the situation I found myself in. As I sat on the wooden bench waiting to find how long I should be held there, I thought also of your Daniel and what horrors he withstood…

Daniel shuddered at the recollection and took a deep breath before being able to read further.

…I'm pleased to say that it was Mr Dixon who attended the Courthouse and spoke with the Sheriff on my behalf. However, I'm sorry to have to report that due to the Sheriff's misguided view of our Constitution, I have been granted bail on condition I appear in the Courtroom itself on Thursday week. Whatever would my poor daddy have to say about that? Mr Dixon says that I should avoid attending any further demonstrations, though I do believe he was looking at me with mock seriousness as he spoke.

Your brother, William, sends you his best regards and has asked me to tell you that he will do all in his power to ensure I am back with you safely in time for your confinement, although I assured him I could take good care of myself.

Your ever-devoted guardian,

Ellie Cochrane.

Daniel let out a low whistle. "If I hadn't known you all these years, Molly Reilly, I'd swear she was your kin and not your guardian."

Molly stood before him, hands on hips. "And how do you make that one out, husband of mine?"

He laughed heartily and took her in his arms. "Oh, I can see a similarity or two between the pair of you." He brushed her lips with his own, then pulled back. "Though I daresay you would have given the Sheriff's men even more to think about."

Molly raised an eyebrow and looked at him sternly, although with the dancing light in her eyes the effect was somewhat spoiled.

Daniel began to massage his wife's shoulders. He could not be more proud of all she had achieved in the last year and, whilst of course he had played his part, he counted himself a lucky man for so many reasons. Remembering back to the first time he'd met Molly in New York, he began to sing to her.

As I was a walking one morning in May,
I saw a sweet couple together at play...

"It's about time you were learning some new songs there now, Daniel Flynn. Ones that belong to our new country."

"I know them already, you know I do, but I need to be singing to little Michael the songs my da sang to me."

"And how do you know it's not going to be Mary, after my mother." Molly rolled each shoulder in turn, in time with his singing and the movement of his thumbs.

"Because that would be a funny name for a boy, so it would." As he said it, he was jolted by a recollection of his uncle Seamus so many years ago in Ireland saying something similar and he smiled.

"I despair, Daniel Flynn, to be sure I do. It's men like you..." Molly reached forward and took another look at the letter. "'Granted bail', indeed." She sat back in the chair, resting her hands on her ever-expanding girth.

"You'll be telling me Miss Ellie's calling for you to join her next." Daniel refilled the kettle from the tin pitcher on the bench near the door.

"You know I can't go now. We've work to do. Harvest is far from over and if you're to learn all there is to know of farm management, we need me to be working. You're going to have to be ready when my time comes."

"Well, if the new calf was on his feet in hours, I'm reckoning you and young Michael won't be much longer."

Molly sighed and shook her head, the edges of her mouth twitching as she tried to resist the smile playing across her lips.

"You're the one who really understands it all, Molly. I'm just as happy to do your bidding when it comes to the farm work. I'd rather be in the fresh air than doing sums and numbers."

"You'll not be saying that when we've no corn for sowing…"

As Molly paused, apparently ready to continue to berate his tardiness with the books, a scratching at the door caused them both to turn.

"Daphne? Gerty?" Daniel pushed his feet into his boots and opened the door to find, as he thought, the chickens strutting up and down the yard, pecking amongst the dust for any imagined nourishment.

"Oh my!" Molly jumped from her chair. "What are the chickens doing out? They should be safely away in the hen house. I'm quite certain I closed the coop after I fed them."

Daniel stayed her arm as she reached the door. "You rest a while. I'll go."

Molly bristled beneath his touch. "You think I'm becoming as chicken-brained as Daphne, like any other woman with child might."

Molly flushed, whether through annoyance or embarrassment, Daniel could not tell. He'd heard talk of how her condition might affect a woman, but he hadn't been about to suggest that now. "I just meant you need to rest, for young Michael's sake."

"Oh, will you just stop with the Michael thing? I know I closed the coop. I'm going to get our hens in before darkness starts to fall." And before Daniel could say another word, Molly marched past him into the yard.

He shook his head and followed. It would not be like Molly to leave the hen house open. He knew that. Pregnant or not, she was meticulous in her farm work. He went around the other side of the yard, driving the chickens ahead of him back in the direction of the coop. It would be dangerous for them to be out as evening fell. With foxes and coyotes about anything could happen. Quite apart from that, it was harder to find their eggs whenever they chose to lay them around the yard. He was looking down as he walked, carefully watching to ensure none of the hens doubled back and, at the same time, trying to count them as he went. He heard a shriek from Molly.

The noise was followed by the booming sound of Molly's voice at full, but controlled, volume, "Jacob Reese! Reuben Reese! Never mind your poor mama, you might be a good deal older than me, but if I prove this was you, it will be me who tans your backsides."

When Daniel caught up with his wife, she was holding aloft one of their chickens, its neck broken and the head hanging limply down.

"It might have been an accident. There's many a hen has got her head trapped…"

"This! This was no accident, Daniel Flynn. This was those Reese boys again. Same as the hole in the bucket was the Reese boys and the well cover was the Reese boys. Miss Ellie bought their daddy's land fair and square and now they don't like that it's me who's farming it. They wouldn't do anything while it was Miss Ellie here, except for name calling, but that didn't get them far and neither will this." She whirled around as she said that last part as if declaiming it to the brothers, wherever they were at that moment.

In truth, Daniel knew which place they were likely to be right then. The same place they spent most every evening and many days besides, with a pitcher of beer for company.

He took the dead chicken from his wife's shaking hand, as, with the other hand she wiped a tear away from her eye.

"Now will you just look at that. I must have got some dust in my eyes as I came across the yard." She sniffed, took a deep breath and marched across to the coop rounding up the remaining chickens as she went.

Daniel knew better than to interfere and took the dead chicken back toward the house to pluck ready for the pot. At least the brothers hadn't stolen the bird. For that he was grateful.

But then, there was a pattern to the things the Reese boys were doing. Everything could be seen as an accident. Who would believe Daniel and Molly if they went to the sheriff and claimed their farm was under attack? Besides, neither he nor Molly nor any of their farm hands had seen anything. He believed that of their permanent hands, but he was not so sure where the loyalties of the casual farmhands lay — the family who'd been around the area since the town began, or the incomers, even if those incomers were the ones paying the wages at present. He sighed. There must be something they could do.

He looked carefully at the hen's wing feathers. It was

Gerty. He'd had a soft spot for her, as much as you could for an animal which did little more than cluck. She'd been a good layer and more than earned her place in the brood. There was an injustice to her death that struck him as going further than the life of one poor chicken. He felt a wave of anger rising as he thought of what Gerty represented. He laid her on the kitchen table, took a spill from the pot on the mantle and used it to light the lantern. He wasn't going to let this injustice pass.

Molly was just coming in as he turned back to the door.

"And where are you going at this time of day, might I ask?"

"I need some air, Molly. I'll just take a walk for a while. You eat and I'll have some bread when I'm back." He couldn't meet her eye. She knew him too well.

"That's not the answer, Daniel." Her voice was softer. "They'll not take kindly to any words from you."

He wanted to say it wasn't words he was thinking of, but thought it better unsaid. He kissed her lightly on the forehead and strode off into the gloaming. He'd been bullied too much of his life to sit back and let it happen again. If he thought too long, he'd be afraid to go. Confronting them in a bar might be asking for trouble, but this time he meant to stand up for himself and his family.

CHAPTER 2

Oh father dear, the day will come when in answer to the
call
Each Irishman with feelings stern will answer one and all,
I'll be the man to lead the van, beneath our flag of green,
And loud and high we'll raise the cry, "Remember
Skibbereen!"
Skibbereen - Patrick Carpenter - attributed

Daniel knew the road to Pierceton well enough by now,
though seldom walked it in darkness. He would have
ridden the mare, but the track from the farm was rutted
and in need of repair and they could ill afford the cost or
problems of an injury. The trees overhanging the lane on
either side blocked much of the light from the stars and he
was glad of the little illumination the lantern cast ahead of
him. His temper was cooling to a controlled state as he
listened to the comforting sounds of the night creatures
accompanying his boot steps.

He knew the risk of any trouble with the law and had
no wish to find out what might happen if he took matters
into his own hands. The Civil War might have ended and
the army was in less need of men, but he didn't imagine
Pierceton would think twice about sending him away, in
the same way that Iowa had the last time he'd acted
without thinking. He certainly didn't want to be sent back
to Iowa. Not even the Reese brothers were worth that risk.

As he approached the edge of the town, Daniel began to wonder at the wisdom of any confrontation, even verbal. But he'd wasted too much of his life thanks to people like Jacob and Reuben Reese and he wasn't about to see the same thing happening again. He was no callow youth now and he'd have his own child to protect soon enough. Besides, he was as strong as any man around this area, of that he was certain.

He paused as he approached the start of First Street and drew in a deep breath. The railroad was at the far end and the clapboard structure of Marsh's saloon rather nearer. He knew exactly what he was going to say when he did see those Reese boys and that thought reinvigorated him as he continued to walk.

There were a number of bars in town but it was Marsh's where the farmhands often gathered. Daniel himself had drunk there more than once but entering alone was strange to him. He swallowed hard as he opened the saloon door and then his fists tightened as he dropped them to his sides. The Reese boys were where he expected to find them. The self-same place he'd last seen them, propping up the bar as though they may have been there the entire time.

Silence fell as he moved forward and as he felt his heart pounding, the bar seemed to take on an expectant air. Daniel stood a little way behind Jacob and Reuben Reese, but could see in the mirror that they knew he'd entered. "Jacob! Reuben!"

The boys didn't so much as look up from their beers. Not a muscle twitched.

Daniel drew a deep breath and began. "You may be older than my da would have been now, God rest his soul, and I'm reckoning those years should have given you time to learn some manners."

"I'll have no trouble in my bar." Franklin Marsh leaned his hands on the long counter, which ran the width of the saloon, and with eyes narrowed, stared intently at Daniel.

"I'm not here for trouble, sir. I just came to give these here boys a warning." He looked back from the landlord to Jacob and Reuben before continuing. He could feel his cheeks burning as he spoke. "My wife owns the whole of Cochrane's Farm justly and you'd better get used to that idea. When Miss Ellie bought that land from the bank it meant she was free to give it to whomever she pleased, and it so happens that, together with her other land, she's given it to my Molly. You don't mess with my family or our property and if I so much as find you setting foot on our land..."

Daniel was focused on the bar ahead of him and saw only a flicker of movement in the mirror above it. He became aware that three men had entered the bar behind him when two of them spun him around and the other punched him, sending him sprawling across the floor. It was then Marsh intervened. But it was Daniel he took hold of, hauling him to his feet and hurling him out of the bar. The landlord rubbed the palms of his hands across each other as if getting rid of dirt. "As I said, I'll have no trouble in my bar. These boys here are regulars, the likes of you can take your custom elsewhere."

As the landlord returned inside, Daniel brushed himself down as he wondered if any of the other drinkers would come out after him. He'd be prepared this time and stood his ground waiting but, while he could hear loud jeering voices from inside, the door remained closed and still. His face was in searing pain where the fist had landed, but as he gingerly ran his fingers over the cheek it was at least clean to the touch and nothing seemed to be bleeding or broken. He was grateful for the good sense to have left his lantern out of harm's way and he took it up again. Shoulders slumped and eyes cast down, he began his trudge back to the farm.

Whilst he still had the night creatures for company, they offered less comfort now and it seemed a much longer path. He began to wonder what other action he could take against those boys. Maybe retaliation was closer to the language they spoke, but he'd probably made things worse already. Molly had been right that he should not have gone, but what man wouldn't take action to protect his own? He hoped she might be sleeping when he returned, but the sight of the candlelight as he approached told him otherwise. He was careful to keep his face away from the light as he entered. He didn't need to be explaining what had happened now.

"Are you hurt bad?"

He shook his head and winced at the pain. "How did you…?"

Molly rushed to him, taking the lantern from his hand. "Come, sit by the fire. I've a bowl of water and a sponge ready."

Daniel dropped his head as he sat. "How do you know me so well, Molly?"

"You've the voice of an angel and a heart of gold, Daniel Flynn. I've known that a long time. I saw you tend to Mammy before she died." As she gently dabbed his face with a herbal mixture, she continued, "Some days I'd come back from gathering rags and watch you a while from the doorway." A tear ran down her cheek. "Now will you look at me." She sniffed and took the bowl over to the sink. "You'll be fine, but for some bruising. It looks as though you got away lightly there, but I'm doubting that will be the end of it."

Daniel sighed. She was probably right, but short of calling in the Sheriff's men he'd little idea of what to do. "What would Miss Ellie do?"

"I don't rightly know. Perhaps we should ask her." Molly perched on the edge of a chair by the table.

"If we do that, knowing Miss Ellie she'll be on the first train home, as long as Mr Dixon has kept her out of jail. There must be something we can do."

"I've a mind to visit Sarah and see if her Joe's mother has any ideas. Running the general store gives them a pretty good insight of what's going on and happen Mrs Spencer might know a trick or two. Come now, Daniel, we've both got an early start in the morning. There's nothing more we can be doing now."

Before he followed Molly up to bed, Daniel went out into the yard and listened. Nothing sounded amiss. He hoped the chickens could sleep easy in their hen house. He closed the door again and took the candle to light has way upstairs.

Daniel was awake long before the cockerel the following day. He lay in the darkness waiting for the bird to crow. If he got up too soon, he'd disturb Molly, so, instead, he thought about the day ahead and the areas of farm management he still needed to learn. He was happy with the heavy work, there he knew what he was doing, but the dairy was mostly a mystery.

Molly stirred just as the cockerel announced the new day. "Oh my, this baby does want to sleep."

"Then stay here a while. I can get things started until you're ready."

"And who's going to have breakfast ready for you all if I do that? No." Molly sat up. "Besides, I want to be finished by lunchtime so I can be away to town to see Sarah."

Daniel nodded. He could finish off what needed doing in the afternoon. He readied himself for work in quiet contemplation, breakfast would be ready by the time he'd milked the cows and collected the eggs.

"What's this I've been hearing, Master Daniel?" Ed, an old farmhand who'd worked for Miss Ellie shouted to him as he passed the bunkhouse. "You don't want to be taking on those Reese brothers. They're no good those boys and their kin with 'em. They've a big family in these parts and no one's come off the better for taking them on. If Miss Ellie were here now, she'd tell you to leave it be. They be just like a thorn in the side of an ox, more annoyance than anything, until they's turned bad."

Daniel was not best comforted by Ed's words. He could see without another's eyes that he may have made the situation worse, but it was too late to undo what was done. As the morning wore on, he worked twice as hard at the corn to take his frustration out in his labours. He tried to sing as he worked, but for once his heart wasn't in it and instead, he thought back to his times in Iowa, working alongside Ben, with Duke at their heels. He missed the wisdom and counsel of his old friend and wondered how time might have treated them. He wished he could return the money Ben had given him too. Now he and Molly had the farm, he figured that Ben's own need must be by far the greater for the use of the sum.

He'd taken a hunk of bread and a piece of cheese out to the field for noon time. He could get water from the stream to wash it down and was heading that way as Molly approached.

"I'm away to town. It's not so warm as the dairy orders will spoil on that short journey, so I'll take them out now to save time in the morning and call at the store as the last point."

Daniel wiped the sweat from his face with a rag and kissed his wife's cheek. She laughed in response and his heart missed a beat. He would never tire of seeing her smile. "Take care of the both of you."

She nodded and headed away up the field back to the yard.

As he watched her walking away, he could feel that, at last, he had a song in his heart and, for all the hours he'd already worked that day, his toil was the easier as he sang.

... And it's no nay never, no nay never no more,
will I play the wild rover, no never no more.

But even as he sang, he couldn't get rid of the nagging doubt that until someone stopped those Reese brothers Molly would be in danger.

CHAPTER 3

As the cart bounced over the track, Molly could feel the baby shifting position and she smiled. For all she'd said to Daniel, she was glad to be sitting down for a while. Standing in the dairy that morning had left her back and legs aching and she was happy to rest, even with the jolts of the cart. She'd be glad now when the baby arrived but with months still to go, there was no point thinking like that just yet.

She drove the cart first to Conant and Moore's works. It was useful to have business with the factory. Bartering for the goods they couldn't produce themselves was always helpful. It would not take many more pats of butter and blocks of cheese before she could order the new door they had need of for the farmhouse. She continued then to the sawmill with their orders, before working her way back toward the town delivering as she went. Despite the better roads in this part of town, she would have sworn that the roll of the cart felt a little different than it had done at the start of the journey. She put it down to her own discomfort and the day catching up with her.

Most of her orders had now been delivered and where she'd not been paid for her goods, she'd exchanged them for other necessities. Her return load included a skein of wool and some cloth for the baby's clothes. Whether it be boy or girl, it would make do with the same colours. It would be a while before baby was in a position to complain. She grinned at the thought. Michael Flynn indeed! Oh, she'd nothing against naming a child after Daniel's father, but she would love to have a daughter to share her life with. Mammy had been a good mother for the few years that Molly had spent with her and she longed to have a daughter of her own to bring up as best as she was able. Of course, she'd love a boy no less than a girl and if he was half the boy that Daniel had been then they'd both be exceedingly proud. Her reverie was halted by the cart bumping left in a peculiar fashion and she ceased her dreaming to concentrate again on where the horse was trotting.

She called the horse to a halt outside Spencer's General Store and stepped down from the cart. Then she started to lift down the goods for this final delivery.

"Here, let me." Joseph had already been outside when she pulled up and was there in an instant. He was an attentive man and he and her childhood friend, Sarah, seemed happy enough together.

Sarah had come out of New York with Molly and the other orphans and they'd both been given a home by Miss Ellie.

As Joe opened the door to the store and held it for Molly, Sarah came out and greeted her.

"Well, will you just look at you?" Sarah kissed her friend and led her inside. "Ma, look who's here." Sarah led Molly through the depth of the store, past the neatly stacked shelves and the sacks of cereals and flour, and through the back of the store to the light airy parlour. Mrs Spencer was working on some darning. Molly blinked adjusting to the light again after the relative cool darkness of the store.

"Molly, dear." The older lady put down her sewing and

came to greet her daughter-in-law's friend. "You're looking very well."

Just then, Henry Jnr, Sarah and Joe's son, walked falteringly into the room to join them and sank to the floor clutching Molly's leg.

Molly picked the boy up and sat him on her knee, running her fingers gently through his tangled curls.

"Will you join us for some tea?" Mrs Spencer went out as she was talking and returned soon after carrying a tray of cups and a pot of tea. Sarah followed with a plate of biscuits fresh from the oven.

Although Joe joined them, whenever the shop bell rang he left to serve whichever local customer had stopped by.

After catching up with all of their news, and having listened to Sarah's account of local gossip, Molly searched for the right words to tell them about the goings on at the farm.

Before she got chance to start, Mrs Spencer laid a hand on her arm and said, "Is everything all right with Daniel?"

Molly started and felt automatically defensive. "Why yes, why ever would it not be?"

"Well, it's just that..." Mrs Spencer hesitated and looked to Sarah.

Molly frowned and turned to her friend. "It's just what exactly?"

"What Mother is trying to say is that we heard he had some trouble last night." Sarah leaned conspiratorially toward Molly, appearing eager for more information.

Molly nodded her head slowly in realisation. Close as she was to Sarah, it suddenly dawned on her that whatever she said now would be traded for other information, much as the butter milk might be traded for corn. She wasn't about to have hers and Daniel's business bandied about the town, as it could do no more good than Daniel's actions of the previous evening. She was saved from any further explanation by Joe returning from the shop once again.

"I've just been talking to the town marshal. There's rumblings amongst some of the women of the town wanting to send a delegation to the next Women's Rights Convention. Whatever is this town coming to? You would think that their husbands would make clear where their places are." He looked at Molly rather than his own wife as he said it.

Molly couldn't help but think he'd heard of what Miss Ellie was doing. She frowned, wondering how he might know. She thought better of saying anything further of her own affairs and chose instead to take her leave. Molly wondered what life might have been like for her had she married Joseph's older brother Henry, as they had planned before he died in the war. Whilst she doubted she'd have been having problems with the Reese boys if she had, her life would have been very different and not, she thought, for the better.

Joe loaded the oats and other provisions into the cart for her as she said farewell to Sarah and Mrs Spencer. Then Molly climbed up into the front of the cart, took up the reins and set the horse off into a brisk walk.

They had cleared the edge of the town and the track became more uneven. As the cart jolted over a deeper rut, it lurched and there was a metallic grinding followed by a jerk and a loud crash.

"Whoa there. Whoa, girl."

Molly had been thrown to the edge of the cart and had she not clung to the side, she would have been thrown clear completely.

The cart horse was a placid girl and pulled up without

any reaction. She was used to a range of farm activities and rarely gave much more than an occasional whinny, whatever the circumstance.

"Steady there, girl." Molly made sure they had stopped completely before surveying the extent of the problem. The corner of the cart was now, at its rear, quite close to the ground. "Oh my," Molly said, looking across to the cart wheel which lay to the edge of the track. "Thank the dear Lord that we have a four-wheel cart, or I'd be clean away in the ditch."

She climbed down carefully and, having retrieved her bonnet, she began to gather up the packages which had been distributed across the lane in the accident. She was grateful that the cloth for the baby was well wrapped and would have come to no harm from the mud.

There was nothing else for it, but to tie the mare to a neighbouring tree and finish the journey on foot. She hadn't the strength on her own to both lift the cart and return the wheel to its former position and would ask Daniel and one or two of the men to come back to address the problem when she got to the farm.

She was heavy of foot by the time the farm came into view and pleased to find Daniel near the yard and not at the further end of the fields. When he saw her approaching, he ran across the yard to her. It made her wonder just how dishevelled she looked but, by this time, she was much too tired for any considered discussion, so with the barest explanation she left Daniel to take their other mare and make good the cart while she went indoors.

The next thing Molly knew was the sound of the horses returning to the yard as she woke in the chair to the side of the stove. She took a moment or two to come around and remember what had taken place. She was still clutching her bonnet and her shawl was around her shoulders. She got up and went to the door to meet Daniel. His face was dark and Molly wondered whatever was the matter.

"Is the cart all right? Is the horse hurt?"

"Everything's fine, Molly. You were lucky that nothing worse happened. Those Reese boys have some answering to do."

"Oh, Daniel. Tell me you aren't going into town again."

He shook his head sadly. "If I thought I could sort those Reese boys with my bare hands, I'd probably be there, but no, I'll not be doing that. It looks like I've made things worse already. Do you remember anything odd that occurred while you were out?"

Molly thought back to the afternoon. "The cart was a little strange before I'd got to Sarah's. I can't remember where I was. It was after she was tethered up at the sawmill. I had to step inside to make anyone hear that I was there."

Daniel nodded. "It looks as though someone loosed the bolts to the wheel. As each one worked its way out, the cart would have become more unstable, until the last one could hold no more. We only found two of the bolts nearby. I'm guessing the others had already gone. There's nothing wrong with the wheel or the cart, so it makes no sense otherwise. You could have been hurt and hurt bad."

Molly shuddered. "Surely those boys wouldn't do something to injure my person. They've just seemed mean and stupid until now."

"Stupid's probably what they are, all right," said Daniel, shaking his head.

Molly followed him back into the kitchen and helped

him off with his boots, then after she had put a kettle on the stove, she made a decision. One thing was clear, if they were going to deal with the Reese boys then they were going to need help doing so and, in that situation, there were only two people they could turn to.

CHAPTER 4

William put down his butter knife and looked up at his father.

"How very unusual." George Dixon raised an eyebrow as he carried the letters into the breakfast room. "Something is clearly afoot." He passed the first of the pile to William and the second to Miss Ellie. "You don't normally both hear news from Pierceton by the same post."

"No, sir." William furrowed his brow and took the proffered envelope. Then he looked to Miss Ellie. "Who should go first?"

Miss Ellie sighed. "I don't rightly know. I can't help thinking this isn't going to be good news. They've already told us about the baby." She picked up a letter opener and slit the top of the envelope, then passed the knife to William who followed suit. His letter was in Daniel's handwriting.

"*Dear William,*" he began to read aloud. "*I hope you are all well and that Miss Ellie is comfortable with you there. Molly and I are in good health and, from the amount of kicking of his little feet, the same can be said for the baby.*" He looked up at Miss Ellie, who let out a breath and put down the napkin ring she had been fidgeting with.

"*I am writing this to you personally as I don't want to worry Miss Ellie…*" William stopped abruptly and looked across the table.

Ellie Cochrane grimaced. "Well it's too late for that now, go on."

"Perhaps I should read it first." William could feel his palms damp and wished he had left reading the letter until later.

"Please be so good as to read it to me now, William." Whilst still gentle, there was a steel to Miss Cochrane's voice that would have been the pride of any school ma'am.

William hesitated, looking back at the paper and reading on a little to himself before he continued.

Once William had finished, Miss Ellie gave out a sigh. "So, he's worried my first reaction will be to go running back to Pierceton to whip the butts of those Reese boys. Well I've a mind to do just that, but I'm guessing that's not going to make a mite of difference. It's no good if they only go behaving their sorry selves while I'm around. Besides, I'd be surprised if Molly wanted me to fight her battles. She's a grown woman now and mighty capable of teaching those boys a thing or two." She slipped the letter from Molly out of the envelope and began to read it to the assembled family.

"That's my girl. It's that man of hers she's worried about and not herself and the baby. Happen on this occasion it's a good job that Daniel's doing the worrying for her. I've still a mind to sort it out one way or another, even if that doesn't mean me going in person."

"Madam, would it help if I were involved?" George Dixon wiped his mouth with his serviette and got up from the table.

"Well, I saw you taking on the judge in Iowa and you did a mighty fine job of that, but I'm reckoning on this occasion it's not the law we need involved at the moment, but some practical help. Besides, you've still got the court

30

here to deal with on my behalf, or I'll be going nowhere anytime soon."

"If Pa could spare me, I could go and stay with them for a while." It was a braver statement than William was feeling on the inside, but he owed that much to his friend.

Miss Ellie let out a laugh. "Oh, you sweet child. Those Reese boys would eat you before you'd finished your toast. No, we need someone who can act as eyes and ears for Molly and Daniel without looking any too uncomfortable in the process. If we can catch those boys in the act once, they'll soon go off to look for other sport to hinder."

William relaxed a little. He was too used to desk work to stand well in a fight. His days on the street felt to him to be so firmly in the past that it was almost as though they hadn't happened at all.

Until now, Ma had sat quietly opposite Miss Ellie and not so much as started to eat. She coughed slightly to gain attention and began quietly, "As you were reading, I did wonder whether we might know just the person if he could be found anywhere."

William looked across to see a hint of a smile playing across Ma's face.

"Ma?"

"And in fact, William, you might well be able to assist. Do you remember Daniel talking about the farmhand who helped him escape in Iowa?"

"Ben?" Miss Ellie asked.

"Yes, I think that was his name. He was clearly something of a father figure to Daniel while he was growing up. Well, what if he could be employed to work with them at Cochrane's Farm, now?"

George Dixon sat down once again. "Finding him

might be the hard part. We've no way of knowing where he headed. They did hope he might have joined them soon after Daniel left the place."

"Well, he'd certainly be the sort of person we'd be after." Miss Ellie folded the letter decisively. "Now we just need to work out where he might have gotten to."

"And I could go to try to find him. Maybe that is something I would be good for." William grinned ruefully. Though even for that job he had no idea where he would begin.

"I've an idea on that front as well." Ma looked up smiling. "You boys go on to your business and leave us women to get on with the real work."

George Dixon laughed as he kissed her on the cheek and took his leave. "Come on, William, I'm sure the ladies will enlighten us later."

#

Summer was definitely over and Miss Ellie felt the autumnal chill in the air. The days seemed much the same as back home, but the nights were colder. She and Mrs Dixon walked on toward the town centre.

Mrs Dixon broke the companionable silence they had been walking in. "It should be a good afternoon. There's to be a full report of a meeting that Mrs Abigail Rogers spoke at just recently. Her college sure has been a blessing for those women who want the opportunity to study."

"I'd have liked Molly to have had that ahead of her, but she's doing well nonetheless. Which reminds me, what was the idea that you had which might help us finding Ben? I've been racking my brains for an answer, but I sure haven't come up with any ideas yet."

"Well." Margaret Dixon's face was beaming, "I was just wondering whether our speaker this afternoon might not have a part to play."

Miss Ellie stopped walking. She shook her head. "How could Mrs Davy of Battle Creek have any knowledge of a farmhand from Iowa City?"

Mrs Dixon's smile broadened. "Because, that same Mrs Davy has been travelling around more than just our state, talking to women's groups about the work that's taking place. I don't know that she's been to Iowa City itself, but I do know she was in Des Moines just a short time ago."

Miss Ellie sighed. "Well, a state might be a big place, but there's no telling where she wandered while she was there. Even if we find a woman we can write to, we know precious little about Ben himself to find him."

"Except for his dog. It's funny how the little things like that can stick in the mind. We can but ask." They walked on into the centre of Dowagiac.

Miss Ellie felt a thrill of excitement as she saw the little crowd gathering outside the hall. They might be slow in making ground towards equality, but little by little the movement's numbers were growing as women started to question what had been the accepted norms of their lives until then. With no man in her own life, it was easy for Miss Ellie to see the injustice of paying taxes on her own labours whilst getting no say in how that money was spent. For other women, their marriage vows seemed to have brought with them complacency, or at best resigned acceptance of how things were. That George Dixon positively supported his wife's involvement had been a blessed revelation to Ellie and made her thankful for their friendship and support.

"... and that is why, sisters, it is of grave concern that every woman should be able to continue with her studies if she so chooses. Our great nation can only be made stronger by hearing the voices of all our people and by harnessing the talents we all have. It is to this end that the Michigan Female College has been working and has already educated close on a thousand women. We hope that the work can continue to expand and call upon colleges and universities across our land to open their doors for women to come forth."

As one, the women rose and applauded and continued to do so for some length of time. Miss Ellie felt the keen buzz of excitement as chatter broke out around the room. A crowd soon gathered about the platform with many women wanting to express their appreciation for the work that was being done on their behalf.

"We'll have a bit of a wait before we can get to talk to Mrs Davy," Mrs Dixon said as she handed refreshments to Miss Ellie. "We'd be best leaving it until the general throng has died down if we want the chance of her full attention."

They talked to other women who were lingering in the hall, discussing whether any progress could be made on education for women there in Dowagiac and about the rallies for women's rights that were taking place in many cities. Eventually the crowd began to thin and Miss Ellie followed her companion who was moving purposefully toward the staging and the speaker they had just listened to.

After Mrs Dixon had completed the basic introductions, she asked, "Is the movement strong in Iowa, where I believe you were visiting just recently?"

Mrs Davy's face creased in a resigned expression. "There's more work to be done there than there is here in Michigan. The university in Iowa City is advanced in its thinking, but I wasn't able to visit there on this occasion."

Mrs Dixon's shoulders dropped slightly. "Were the meetings well attended?"

Miss Ellie shifted position and tried to feign interest in the general chat. She wanted to move things along, but realised that Mrs Dixon was far more experienced in the ways and manners of small talk than she ever would be and her own blunter style might not get what was wanted on this occasion. She smiled ruefully, nodded at appropriate points and clutched tightly to the edge of her shawl. She found her mind drifting to other matters and had to bring herself back to the conversation. She'd spent too many years with cows for company to be ready to ask after the health of people she'd never met.

"Well, if you could put me in touch with the ladies of Des Moines, I'd be mightily grateful to you. Thank you." Mrs Dixon at last seemed to be wrapping things up.

By the time they left the hall, Margaret Dixon had the address of the chairwoman of the group who had hosted Mrs Davy in Des Moines and the assurance that there were women in that group who were originally from Iowa City itself.

"I still don't rightly see how you're planning to find Ben." Miss Ellie walked slowly alongside her companion who was clearly lost in thought.

"I'm not absolutely sure that I do, either. I'm hoping, after an initial exchange of greetings, that might be where William comes in. However fast our postal service is, we don't have time for lots of to-ing and fro-ing by letter. If I can effect an introduction for William to the women's movement in Iowa City then it is just possible that one of them might know on what farm Ben can be found. It may not be straightforward, but it's got to be worth trying." Margaret Dixon grinned. "I know what you're thinking, they may not entertain a man, but Molly is his sister and I'm hoping if I explain enough about her owning the farm and your involvement here, then it will be enough to give him safe passage through their numbers."

Miss Ellie laughed. "You've got this all worked out. I do hope for Molly's sake that you're right. From what was said before, I thought he planned to move clean away from Iowa, city and state."

"And go where exactly? The poor dear man lost his wife and child while living in that area. He won't stray far without good reason from the place he last had a mite of happiness. I'm just hoping that Daniel's need of him will give him reason enough to move now."

Miss Ellie had known her companion sufficient time to realise she was usually a good judge of human nature and the chances were she was right in this matter as well. Miss Ellie certainly hoped so. "By all accounts, he's a good man and I'm happy to make recompense to him to move, a sort of pension if you will. I know rightly the farm is now Molly's but that doesn't stop me from employing someone who might help them." Realising there was little more that could be done on the subject just then, Miss Ellie added, "I still have a goodly sum of money in the bank that I saved in the better years. I was wondering about endowing a scholarship at the ladies' college that Mrs Davy was speaking of."

Mrs Dixon stopped and turned to face her friend. "You know, I was wondering if there wasn't something we could be doing along those lines closer to home."

CHAPTER 5

If anyone can save me it's my brother in the army
I think that he is stationed in Cork or in Killarney
and if he would be here we'd be rovin' in Kilkenny
I know he'd treat me better than my darlin' sportin' Jenny
Whiskey in the jar - traditional

"Bertha and Candice are loose in the corn field. They been spooked and they sure are causing some damage."

Daniel sighed at the news the farmhand brought him. The cows shouldn't be anywhere near the corn field, even if they'd got out of their own enclosure. He walked across the yard and took the long stick that they used for guiding the cows, then set off down the farm. Bertha and Candice should, by rights, be in the small meadow close to the house with the rest of the cows. The grass was lush there and they were close by for milking. The only corn field they had not yet harvested was some distance off and an unlikely place for them to have wandered without encouragement.

When he got to the field, he surveyed the extent of the damage. This was no accident. Even if the cows had made their own way down there, they were unlikely to have forced their way into the middle of the crop. The only way they had got there was by being led and no one on this farm was likely to have done that. What made matters worse was that they'd panicked. Being stuck in the middle of a crop much taller than yourself was bad enough as a human, but it was clear the cows hadn't liked it at all and had rushed around in all directions looking for a way out.

As far as Daniel's view allowed him to see, there was flattened corn. Bertha and Candice were now huddled together near the fence, recovering from their trauma. It was a shame that recovery would not be so easy for the corn. Daniel wondered how much of it could be salvaged. Half a ton of cow was less than helpful if you wanted to leave food unspoiled.

"Easy there, girls." He tried to soothe the cows as he approached. He had no wish to have them panicking again. They were normally very gentle, but any animal would fight its way out of a corner and these girls were no exception. He walked around behind them in a large arc, before calling to them to, "Move along there. Let's get you home and back to your friends and some nice grass." He held the stick wide to discourage them from doubling back and step by step moved forwards toward the field entrance.

"Now what are you doing taking some of my girls for a walk there, husband of mine?" Although her voice was light, Molly's face was serious.

"The girls are fine, it's the corn we need to worry about." He indicated with a shake of his head in the direction of the far field.

"The Reese boys?" As much a statement as a question, Molly stood with her back to the hedge, hands on hips, waiting for the three of them to pass before walking away down in the direction from which Daniel had just come. He continued his steady progress back towards their meadow, not wanting the cows to change their minds and take a different route.

"Even with all the extra workers we've got in for harvest, the Reese brothers aren't letting up," he called back to Molly. "How do they keep managing to do things and no one sees?"

Molly soon caught up with him. "I prefer to think our farmhands saw nothing, but the Reese family is well known around these parts and there's few who'd talk against them. Some keep silence through family loyalty and others by fear. We're not the only ones who've suffered at their good-for-nothing hands. I guess it could have been a lot worse. At least no harm came to those two or the other girls. A dairy with no cows is a pretty sad affair."

"A corn farm with no corn is not a whole lot better!"

"Oh come now, Daniel, it's not the whole crop that's ruined, just the corner of one of the fields. We might even save some of that. They might have trodden on some of it, but they haven't eaten it."

Daniel loved that Molly could always see the positives. It reminded him of the time she'd pretended to be a boy and gone off to sell newspapers, when they and William were penniless children, with no one to rely on but themselves. He wondered what would have happened to the three of them if it hadn't been for Molly's fighting spirit. He smiled, determined to be more like her if he possibly could be. What he was really struggling with was the thought that it was his job to protect Molly, especially with her expecting their first child, and yet time and again the Reese brothers were getting through. Being an incomer was all well and good, but on occasions like this having better local knowledge and support would be worth its weight in corn.

He wondered if there was more he could have done to

become part of the Pierceton community. He would have felt uncomfortable in the company of the 'right' people, if he'd even had the chance to be introduced to them. His years of isolation had left him ill prepared for social situations. Here with Molly on the farm he felt safe and content. So what, that Miss Ellie had bought the land which old Mr Reese had to sell when he was bankrupt? It wasn't Miss Ellie who'd put him out of business and it certainly was nothing to do with Molly. Those Reese boys just couldn't bear to watch a young woman succeed when their own family were such failures. He shook his head sadly and returned his attention to the cows.

Bertha and Candice seemed perfectly relaxed now as they ambled their way back into their own field. Their day's adventure was at an end. Daniel hoped that might be the case for all of them. He was surprised not to have heard back from William and the more so as Molly had received no word from Miss Ellie. He hoped that all was well with them in Dowagiac and, not for the first time, wished they were nearer. The old William would have told him to retaliate, but that was no more Daniel's nature than mixing with local bigwigs. Daniel wondered what the new William really thought. Maybe there was something in the way of legal action he could help with.

"Yesterday's trouble had more impact on the girls than we realised." Daniel dropped his hat onto the side as he came into the kitchen for breakfast. "Candice is not so bad, but Bertha's milk was still low this morning. Let's hope she recovers quickly. Thankfully the other girls are doing fine. We can ill afford to lose dairy business as well as corn."

"I'm in hand with the butter and cheeses, so a day or two won't cause a big problem." Molly wiped her hands on her apron before picking up their plates to take to the table. "Oh, Daniel, whatever are we going to do to stop all this?"

Daniel hated to see the frown on Molly's gentle face or to hear the worry in her voice. "We'll do what we've always done and get through it." His words were more confident than he was feeling. Truth be told, he had lain awake much of the previous night thinking over the self-same thing. Talking wasn't getting them anywhere and he knew fighting would never be the answer. He'd got a family to care for now, though, and he couldn't just sit back and do nothing. He'd even wondered if they should sell the farm and move elsewhere, but Molly wasn't one to give up and he knew she wouldn't welcome the suggestion.

"I thought maybe this afternoon we could take a picnic out and have a break from working."

Daniel looked up suddenly.

"Now, don't you go looking so surprised there, Daniel Flynn, I'm not going soft. I just thought a bit of time to think would do us both good and we have precious little chance when we're working, or too tired from the day. There's nothing that can't keep for an hour or two."

"There's the corn in the end field."

"And that will still be there tomorrow. It's not going anywhere. We don't know how much of it we can save anyway."

He grinned. She'd got it all worked out. "Yes, ma'am."

It never ceased to amaze Daniel how Molly could produce a whole feast out of nowhere. It was a fine afternoon and sitting at the edge of the meadow with a tablecloth covering the ground, Daniel could almost think himself a man of leisure, though his calloused hands told otherwise. Laid out in front of them was bread baked fresh that morning and their own butter and cheese to go with it. It was a banquet when he came to compare it with the days when they had hardly more than a stolen crust between them, back in New York. She might have taken his name when she married him, but Daniel still loved the sound of the name he'd first known her as. "I must be the luckiest man alive, Molly Reilly."

"And don't you forget it, Daniel Flynn."

"Ah, but now you're sounding like my old da." He raised his cup skyward. "I'll never forget." He dipped his head as a moment's sorrow washed over him that his da couldn't be with them now, then took a drink and sighed. He was about to ask Molly for her views on what they should do next, but she beat him to starting the discussion.

"The way I see it, we have some choices to make."

He put his head on one side, listening but not wanting to disturb the flow of what Molly was saying.

"We could sell up and move away…"

He chose not to fill the silence. He knew that was not an option Molly would favour and she didn't need him to say so.

"… But if I were a man and Miss Ellie had been a man, they'd have had no issue with us, at least none that would lead to this kind of behaviour. If I hadn't pretended to be a boy when we were in New York we'd probably still be there now. It's a sad day when a country has no respect for half its population. I'm proud of the work that Miss Ellie is getting involved in and maybe there'll be a time when I'll be able to join her. The least I can do is not run away because the Reese boys say 'boo'." She cut herself another piece of cheese and sat chewing for a moment. "Nor do I plan to go after them with my gun. It's not that I can't shoot straight enough. You know that I can. I'm afeared that if I start shooting at those boys I very well might not stop and they're not worth hanging for."

Daniel smiled at the thought of Molly confronting them like that. She could be scary enough when you were on the same side as she was, without being her opponent.

"They don't have a wife between them that I could appeal to the better side of. I guess there's no surprise there. They've been married to that bar for best part of the time I've lived in Pierceton. Perhaps it's the bar I should be talking to." Molly shook her head and looked away into the distance.

They were silent for a while before Molly continued. "What do you think they would say if I went to Marsh's bar?"

Daniel found it hard not to show his surprise. "You know…" He thought carefully about the words to use. "There's a reason much of the opposition to the women's cause comes from within those walls. Same as they fight against pretty much everything and everyone else that gets in the way of their lazy, good-for-nothing lifestyles. They don't like change. It scares them. Makes them think they might have to do something. Anyways, if you go setting foot in that bar, it would be like sending out a challenge and they ain't going to take it awfully well. Things are bad enough now, and I don't suppose I made them any the better. But if you were to go…" He didn't finish the sentence, just shook his head sadly.

Molly got up from where she was sitting. "What would Mammy have done?"

She clenched her fists as she spoke and Daniel could see the whites of the knuckles. He went to her and took her fists in his larger hands.

"I don't rightly know. I don't know what your mammy would have done, or my own ma come to that. I do know that they were wise women who put protecting their families first. Ma wasn't happy when Uncle Seamus took up with the Irish Republicans. However angry he was about losing his family's home, she made quite clear to him that his priority should be taking care of Aunt Jane and their children." He laid a hand flat across her expanding belly. "We've more than just us to think of in all this. You know I'd never try to tell you what to do, Molly, but I'd be a sight happier if you didn't think of setting foot in that bar. I shouldn't have gone myself, but I couldn't see that then. I can see we could make things a deal worse than they already are."

Molly relaxed her fists into Daniel's hands and looked up at him. "Will you come and take the rosary down from the wall? I want to talk to Mammy."

Daniel knew better than to explain that she could talk to Mammy as easily without it. That rosary had been there for them both at difficult times and maybe it could help them find the answer now as well. He relaxed his hold on her hands to gather up the remains of the picnic and return them to the basket, then, gently, he took Molly's hand once again and led his wife back towards the farmhouse, hoping they might yet find their answer.

CHAPTER 6

"Pardon me, ma'am." William bowed slightly as he addressed the tall, stern looking woman who he'd been told was in charge of the Iowa City women's movement. Used as he was by now to business meetings, he rarely found himself in the company of quite so many women and, for all his past bravado, his palms were damp and clammy as he clutched the letter from Mrs Dixon.

The woman looked at him over her half-glasses and raised a quizzical eyebrow. "And you are?"

It was not quite the greeting that William had been expecting and for a moment he had no idea how to start to introduce himself. Then an image of Molly dressed as a newsboy in New York came into his mind and he smiled. He was here on behalf of his brave and feisty sister and was proud to be so. "William Dixon, ma'am." He would have raised his hat had he not already taken it off on entering the hall, so he nodded. "I come on behalf of my sister, Molly." Then he held out the letter which his mother had given him, but aware that the room was filling with people was unsure what to do next.

The woman took the letter but made no move to open it. "As you can see, we are about to begin. Unless this is urgent, then it will have to wait until after our meeting." She smiled for the first time. "Will you join us?"

William wasn't sure if she intended him to say yes, but as he did not want to leave without knowing that he had

made some progress, he said, "Thank you, ma'am. I will."
Then he moved to a seat indicated to him at the side of the
room and settled to listen to the rousing speeches calling
the women of Iowa City to question the past and demand
representation where it was fairly due.

Despite his misgivings at being almost entirely
surrounded by women, William lost himself in the stories
being told and once again let his thoughts turn to Molly
and the injustice of the way she was being treated. She
worked hard, paid taxes and did no one any harm and yet
not only was her voice not heard, but neither was it
welcome. Were the town's elders not aware of what was
happening in their borough, or were they happy to
countenance the behaviours? There was certainly no sign
of anyone stepping in to prevent the Reese boys in trying
to bring down her farm. Molly might not have been born
in Pierceton, but she'd lived there for enough of her life to
call it home.

The more William listened that afternoon, the more he
realised his parents were right. They believed that all men
and women should not just be born equal, but treated as
such throughout their lives. He'd seen poverty and he'd
seen privilege in his life. He'd also seen the massive
injustices inflicted on both Daniel and Molly and he
suddenly realised that he too wanted to make a difference.

He was one of the first on his feet at the end of the
speeches, his hands raised in applause. Never had he felt
more proud of the work his mother was doing, or of his
sister. The applause died down and the speakers left the
platform. He'd almost forgotten he was waiting for a reply
to the letter and had not simply come to the meeting for its
own sake, when a hand laid on his arm made him jump
slightly.

A young woman about his own age was standing there, her eyes bright and her face flushed. He could only assume she'd been as moved by the speakers as he had been.

"Mr Dixon, my mother, Mrs Hendry, would like to speak with you."

Her eyes were blue, he especially noticed that. He opened his mouth to reply, but fell over the words. "I… you… er, yes."

She smiled and William felt his surroundings melt away.

She indicated to close by the platform where her mother was deep in conversation. He nodded meekly and followed.

It was an altogether different response he received now to the one before the meeting. Mrs Hendry held out her hand to him and greeted him warmly. "We sure will help you if we can, Mr Dixon. Do you know anything more about the man that you're looking for?"

William scratched his head, recalling conversations with Daniel. "Well, ma'am, I know he had a dog with him, Duke I think he was called, but that was a while ago, so I can't rightly say now."

Mrs Hendry pursed her lips and nodded. Then in a decisive movement she marched back to the lectern and brought down the small gavel to bring quiet to the room. "Excuse me, ladies, gentlemen, I'm sorry to disturb your conversation, but we have a visitor here from Michigan." She smiled over to William and then turned her attention back to the room. "He'd like to say a few words to bring greetings from our sisterhood there and has an unusual request. Mr Dixon, would you like to come to the podium?"

William looked around, before taking in the full import

of what Mrs Hendry was saying. He was expected to speak. He had never addressed a meeting of any sort and was completely unprepared. In his head he started to repeat, 'This is for Molly, I'm doing this for Molly.' He took a deep breath and moved slowly forwards. There was a quiet air of anticipation in the room as he reached the front.

"Ladies and gentlemen, thank you for the warmth of your welcome. It is my pleasure to bring to you greetings from my mother, Mrs Margaret Dixon in Dowagiac, Michigan and from Miss Ellie Cochrane of Pierceton, Indiana and of the whole of the women's movement that they are working with. Listening to the speakers today, it is important to remember that this is not a cause of one woman or even one group of women..." He lost himself in the moment as he warmed to his subject. He felt a thrill of excitement run through his body and in that instant William was certain where his future lay. It was a career in politics which was his vocation. "... and so, it is my earnest hope that one of you might have news which could help my sister in her work as she so ably runs the farm that has been put in her capable hands, while the farms former owner works tirelessly for the cause. Thank you."

There was a ripple of applause around the room, not the volume there had been for the earlier speakers, but enough to make him smile as he stepped back. He saw Miss Hendry smiling and watching him move from the podium and felt his heart miss a beat. As he moved away, conversations around the room began tentatively at first, but then gradually the hum of voices increased in volume and William was left wondering whether his plea would be in vain. He felt slightly awkward and wondered what he should do next.

He was pleasantly surprised to find women

approaching him to shake his hand and ask him to return with their greetings. Still others, who had travelled a distance to the meeting, offered to share his plea in their own towns when they returned. His request seemed set to go out to the four corners of the state, and possibly further still. However, William began to realise that any answer might come after the night itself and that patience was going to be required.

He was surprised to find himself happy to be wondering if that might give him some excuse for a return visit, given that he was due to leave the following morning. He looked across the room to where Mrs Hendry's daughter was holding an animated conversation with a woman at least twice her age and sighed. He would certainly appreciate the opportunity to get to know her better.

He was still watching Miss Hendry when a voice said, "Now don't you go getting ideas, young man."

He started and turned to find the girl's mother smiling at him. William grinned. "You must be very proud of her."

"I am indeed and I'm guessing from your address this evening that your parents would say the same of you."

"Thank you." William suddenly started to feel a little shy under the gaze of this woman.

"Will you join us for some supper this evening?"

"I had been expecting to go straight back to my lodgings. The thought of company would be a very pleasing one, if it is not too much trouble, ma'am."

"No trouble at all. Now tell me about how your sister comes to be living so far away from you."

William wondered how much of his past he should tell, but something about this forthright and determined woman made him think that nothing short of the truth would be adequate, so began to tell her about his and Molly's lives before they had been mercifully given homes by the kind, good people who they now called family.

They walked as he talked and lost as he was in the story, William had not been aware of Miss Hendry joining them until they had gone some distance and his tale, in its briefest form, was all but told. For reasons he could not explain, he felt no need to hide the worst of events from these people as he might have done in the past, but was comfortable to bear his soul, whatever they may think.

"That really is quite a story, young man. You were very lucky to find Mr and Mrs Dixon." Mrs Hendry touched his arm gently to indicate they were turning into the gateway of the house.

"Yes, ma'am," he said quietly, "I most certainly was."

They talked at length over supper about the actions being taken by the women's movement in the area and he learned that Miss Hendry, Cecilia, had the same ambition which had come upon William that evening.

To even his own surprise, his candidness continued over supper, "My only experience of politics until now was a brief time engaged to the daughter of Congressman Makepeace." It was only when Cecilia looked taken aback that he realised it may not have been the thing to mention. "I'm sorry. Sadly, it was she who saw no future with me. I learned a great deal from realising that her family did not consider my background good enough for her."

Mrs Hendry nodded sympathetically. "There are many people in our Government who see themselves as being above the people they serve. It's a sad fact."

Throughout the meal, William had wondered about the absence of Mr Hendry, for whom a place was clearly laid at the table, but thought it inappropriate to ask. The meal was almost over when an energetic man with a shock of white hair bounced into the room and pecked his wife on the cheek before proffering his hand to William and shaking his hand warmly.

"And who is our young visitor, my dear? An admirer of our daughter I'll be bound."

"Father!" Cecilia blushed a dark pink and looked away from William.

"Herbert!" Mrs Hendry pursed her lips and gave her husband a stern look. "Mr Dixon attended our meeting this afternoon. He's visiting from Michigan. In fact, it's possible you may be able to help."

"Might I indeed. And how could I do that?" He began to take some food from the bowls on the table and add it to his plate. He waved his fork in the direction of the plate of bread and butter in a distracted fashion as he waited for his wife to answer.

As she passed the plate to her husband, it was William who Mrs Hendry addressed. "My husband is a doctor. He gets to visit many of the houses and farms around the area."

His lateness and the lack of comment on it suddenly made sense to William and he nodded.

Mrs Hendry had stopped talking and William became aware that both she and Dr Hendry were looking at him expecting him to explain.

"Sir," he began.

"Good heavens, man, don't call me sir, it makes me feel ancient. I'm Herbert."

William saw Mrs Hendry sigh. He couldn't help but think that Dr Hendry was really one of the most extraordinary people he'd ever met. "Herbert," he began again tentatively, feeling a little uncomfortable. "I'm trying to find a farmhand called Ben. He's an older man, that much I know, and black skinned. He has a dog, called Duke, or leastways he did a couple of years ago."

"Does he have a family?" Dr Hendry looked intently at William.

"No, sir, er Herbert. I believe him to be alone in this world."

Dr Hendry nodded and looked thoughtful as he continued to chew. "I don't often get to see farmhands in my line of work. No one's willing to pay the bill. If they come to me I won't turn them away, but I'm rarely called out. Ben, you say?" He put his head on one side and looked away into the distance.

"He used to work for a man named Hawksworth."

He saw Mrs Hendry start.

"Do you know him, ma'am?" William was eager to know more.

Mrs Hendry nodded slowly, a light of comprehension dawning on her face. "Well, I'll be. Your childhood friend, was that the boy who worked all those years for Mr Hawksworth and ran away because of the abuse?"

"Why, yes indeed, ma'am. And now he's married to my sister."

A wide smile broke across Mrs Hendry's face. "Well I'll be. Just wait until I tell Annie."

"My dear," Dr Hendry waved his knife in an expansive gesture, "perhaps you should explain a little more to William."

Mrs Hendry pushed her plate away from her on the table. "Annie, that is Mrs Collins, is Mrs Hawksworth's sister. She and her husband took Mrs Hawksworth into their home. That was after Mrs Hawksworth testified against her own husband at Daniel's trial. Herbert," there was pride in her voice as she said Dr Hendry's name, "treated the many injuries which Mrs Hawksworth had sustained at the hands of Hawksworth, quite without charge."

"And Mrs Hawksworth is well, ma'am? This is such good news. I must write to Daniel immediately to tell him. We were all so worried about her."

"She's had a hard time, and those things take a lot of getting over. It's a blessing that Mr Collins, her sister's husband, was as supportive as he was and not afraid to set himself against the farm community here. I know his business suffered, but they've got by and there's many who have shown their support."

"Might Mrs Hawksworth know where I could find Ben?" William felt a thrill of excitement that his mission might be successful.

"There's only one way to find out," Dr Hendry said, getting up from the table and leaving his meal half finished. He moved swiftly to the door and left the room.

William turned to Cecilia who smiled, clearly used to her father's behaviour.

Moments later the doctor returned carrying a quill, ink and paper and with great ceremony handed it to his wife. Mrs Hendry nodded her thanks and set about writing a letter.

CHAPTER 7

At the rising of the moon, at the rising of the moon
For the pikes must be together at the rising of the moon
The Rising of the Moon - John Keegan Casey - 1865

"Molly! Molly!" Daniel headed out of the back door towards the dairy in search of his wife.

"Whatever is it?" She'd come rushing out at the sound of his cries, a buttermilk streak across her cheek where she'd wiped her sleeve across her face.

He momentarily forgot that he'd been calling for her. "Are you all right?"

"Oh, don't mind me," she said waving her hand, "these were happy tears. I could feel the baby move as I worked and I was singing to her."

He reached out and took her hand. "Well I've got more news that will make you happy." He held out the letter for her to read.

"You read it to me," she wiped her eyes again. "I don't seem to be able to stop the tears today."

"William has found Mrs Hawksworth and she's quite well."

"Oh, Daniel, that's wonderful news," Molly said as the tears flowed openly down her cheeks. "Now, will you look at what you've done." She laughed and he led her back to the house so they could sit and read the rest of the letter together.

As they sat by the kitchen stove, having by then read the letter through a couple of times, Molly said, "There is one thing in all this that's rather troubling me."

Daniel laughed. "Well I think it's quite clear that William is sweet on this Cecilia."

"No, silly, not that. And yes, I do believe you're right about that. But what was William doing in Iowa in the first place?"

"Oh, no!" Daniel was on his feet and pacing the room. "He's our lawyer. You don't think... I've not done anything that could..." He knelt beseeching in front of his wife. "Oh, Molly tell me I won't have to go back there."

Molly stroked his hair and brushed her fingertips across his forehead. "Hush, my darling, I didn't mean that. There's nothing you've done that could make anyone call you back there. I don't suppose those Reese boys even know there was a court condition, and I was certainly never going to tell them."

"Did you tell Sarah?"

"Why yes, but..." Molly hesitated, she knew her friend, but she was less sure of Joseph. "No," she said decisively. "I don't believe it's to do with that. William would have said something in his note and if not then I'm sure Miss Ellie would have written to me, or more likely been back here before we could know of it."

"But we don't know of it. We only have this letter from William."

"And I say that he would not have written it if there was other news to bring us." Molly stood up. "He's up to something, I just don't know what."

It took most of the evening before Daniel was able to convince himself that Molly was right. Despite his labours, sleep did not come easily to him that night and by the time the cockerel crowed the new day he was already up and writing a reply to William by candle light. Of course, he would send greetings to Mrs Hawksworth and was indeed delighted to hear good news of her, after all she'd been through for him, but the purpose of his letter was clear and he demanded of William to receive any news, however bad it might be, about his own situation. It would be several days before he might gain a reply and all Daniel could think to do was occupy himself with more work than could leave him time for worrying.

Whatever Daniel did over the next couple of days, the thought of Iowa was never far from his mind. He reasoned that the condition had been to join the army, not to return for further punishment in Iowa City, but that thought never went through his mind without being chased by the doubt it might not be so. He was having one such argument with himself, while taking his boots off in the kitchen when his reflection was interrupted by shouting in the yard and then hammering at the farmhouse door.

"The hay's ablaze," shouted the out of breath farmhand before turning on his heel to head back across the yard.

Daniel thrust his feet back into his boots, all thoughts of Iowa gone. He turned to Molly who had come in from the dairy just ahead of him. "You stay inside. Let me go," but Molly was already running ahead of him and despite the fading light of the day, the unnatural orange light from the nearest field told him all he needed to know. At least with haymaking only just past they still had all the workers on site, but no amount of passing buckets of water was going to stop this fire.

"Get the forks," Molly shouted, taking up a pitchfork as she went past the old barn. "We need a break."

Daniel followed his wife's instructions and took up one

of the forks resting against the inside of the barn. As he did so he was surprised to find other farmhands taking the remaining forks. Daniel had little idea of what Molly intended them to do, but trusted she had her reasons. To his mind, it was water they needed to put the fire out, he was sure it was.

By the time he caught up, Molly was already climbing a ladder against a neighbouring stack to the one on fire. As soon as she left the ladder she started tossing hay into a waiting cart.

"If we can clear this stack we might save the others." She wetted her finger and held it to the air. "It's only a light breeze but the wind's against us." He found it hard to make out her words as she shouted to him in gasps, coughing away the smoke that surrounded them.

"But Molly, you can't…"

"Don't you go arguing with me now, Daniel Flynn. It's my farm and there's work to do." She threw herself into the work and there was little point in Daniel remonstrating further. He climbed the other side of the hay rick and began to copy the actions his wife was taking. A horse was being readied to take the cart load of straw away from the fire and a second cart was already being brought to replace it.

Daniel realised how inexperienced he still was in farm work, when he saw the other workers automatically falling into their roles to deal with the emergency. He was also amazed to see other workers from the surrounding farms arriving unbidden to help, and he felt humbled by the sight.

Following Molly's instruction, Daniel worked furiously, tossing hay from the higher parts of the stack. As he worked it was far too dangerous to take his focus away from what he was doing. He could hear shouts around as others worked nearby, each seeming to know what was expected, but all he could think of was Molly and the need for her to stay safe.

His heart was beating heavily and he paused for a moment to wipe the sweat from his eyes. It had dawned on him what Molly was trying to do, but he could see no way they could succeed, they simply couldn't get the hay away fast enough. He carried on throwing forkful after forkful down to the cart below. It was hot work but there was no relenting. The wind had now picked up and the direction of the smoke was clear, making their work all the harder. If this failed they'd lose all the hay for certain. It was then he realised the heat was not just from his working, but the fire had spread and the rick they were working on was now alight.

"Molly! Molly!" He had no choice but to work his way down the ladder, there was no more he could do where he was. He'd be roasted alive before the rick was moved. He went to help the others down and find his wife. "Molly!"

As he rounded the end of the rick he saw her, the flames were almost engulfing where she was standing and she had no option left but to jump.

"Molly!" He ran the last few yards to where she was, but by the time he got there Molly was already lying on the ground at the base of the stack and Miss Ellie's cousin, James, was pulling her away to a safe distance before they could begin to assess if she was all right.

Daniel froze. He couldn't live if anything had happened to his beloved Molly.

James shook him forcefully. "Goddamnit, Daniel, she needs you. Pull yourself together and let's get her up to the house. She's breathing, that's something at least." James's voice was little more than a croak and Daniel knew how parched he must be feeling.

Daniel gave a shake of his head and focused his thoughts on what needed doing. He supported Molly under her other shoulder and between them they carried her limp figure. Daniel felt as though he were somewhere distant to everything else that was happening around them. At least the breeze was carrying the smoke away from the buildings. He could hear the shouts and was aware there were people running in all directions, but he was not part of it. All he could think of was Molly. Molly and their baby.

They got Molly through the farmhouse door and laid her gently on the floor in front of the stove.

"You stay with her and try to bring her round. I'll take charge of the men."

Before Daniel had time to ask any more, James was gone from the kitchen and he was left to care for his wife. He took a cushion and put it under her head and pulled a blanket from the chair to wrap around her. Then he took the rosary down from the wall and pressed it into her hands. Once she looked a little more comfortable, he fetched a cloth and cold water and began to dab her face with the compress, hoping it might revive her. As he watched her, Daniel's tears fell on Molly's cheek and he prayed the words of the Hail Mary quietly as he worked.

It felt as though he had been watching Molly for hours, though he suspected it had in reality been only minutes, when she coughed and groaned then half opened her eyes.

"Oh, Molly, can you hear me? You stay still now and rest."

Molly screwed up her eyes and frowned.

"Molly, what is it? Are you in pain?" He wanted to

draw her to him and hold her, but needed to wait until she was ready and to see what harm had been done.

"Dan…" Molly coughed.

It was plain to Daniel that the smoke had affected her throat and he rushed to fetch water for her to sip, then raised her head a little as he put it to her lips.

She took a little and swallowed then coughed again and lay back on the cushion. After a moment she screwed her face up again and groaned. Then when whatever spasm of pain had passed, she raised her head for another sip. She smiled weakly at Daniel and his heart missed a beat.

"I'm still here," she said quietly.

"Thank the dear Lord for that. Oh, Molly, you're everything to me. Where are you hurt?"

"I don't know. I think I need to sleep." Then Molly lay back onto the cushion and closed her eyes.

Daniel watched her once again, and as her chest gently rose and fell, he breathed a little easier with it.

His reassurance was short lived as Molly suddenly cried out and opened her eyes wide.

"Where, Molly? Where are you hurt?" It was a few moments before her face ceased to be contorted with pain and as she lay back exhausted. Daniel very gently ran his hands over first one of her legs, then the other and then her arms. It was clear her ankle was sprained, he realised that from the swelling, but he found no broken bones as far as he could tell. He took up the cool, damp cloth to mop the sweat from her brow and as he worked bit his lip, fearful of the next spasm of pain coming and wondering what the cause was. He wished James would come back up to the house, or better still that Miss Ellie or Sarah were there to help, but he couldn't leave Molly's side to call for assistance or send word to Sarah. Everyone else was occupied with the fire, it would be a while until anyone was free to offer help.

When the next wave of pain engulfed Molly, Daniel was almost frantic with fear. This time, as before, the spasm passed and Molly fell back onto the pillow exhausted.

CHAPTER 8

I would swim over the deepest ocean
The deepest ocean, my love to find
But the sea is wide and I cannot swim over
And neither have I the wings to fly
Carrickfergus - Traditional

Daniel held Molly's hand around the rosary. 'Please, God, let nothing happen to her.' He almost held his breath waiting to see if pain swept through Molly again. As he waited, he became aware of the sound of running feet coming across the yard and voices getting closer.

"Just go straight in, Miss Sarah. Don't disturb Daniel to come to the door."

Daniel recognised James's voice and felt gratitude that someone had thought to send for Sarah. "Help's here, Molly. Help's here."

Sarah came rushing through the door, throwing off her bonnet and shawl as she came in. She came straight over to Molly and knelt beside her. "Is she conscious? Molly are you there?"

"She comes and goes. She seems to be having waves of pain, but I can't find what's causing them."

"How often are they?"

Sarah looked up at Daniel with an intensity that startled him. He felt flustered as he replied. "I don't know. They've happened several times." Before Daniel had chance to say anything further, Molly was overtaken by another wave of pain.

The colour drained from Sarah's face. "I think it's the baby coming. Oh my, it's way too early. We need to get her upstairs to somewhere more comfortable. Help me take her up."

"No, Miss Sarah," James stepped further into the room. "I'll take her up with Daniel, you go ahead and get things ready. I'll come back for water and towels."

Sarah seemed reluctant to leave her friend's side, but did as James suggested and went to the upper floor. By the time James and Daniel had supported Molly up the stairs Sarah had already stripped the covers, except for the sheets, from Molly and Daniel's bed and laid them to the side of the room where they'd come to no harm.

"I can boil the sheets if needs be," Sarah said while trying to settle Molly into a comfortable position. "Can someone be sent to bring my mother-in-law? She's a deal more experience when it comes to being a midwife than I ever have."

Daniel thought how pale Molly was looking and didn't want to leave her side.

"Yes, ma'am," said James turning on his heel, then turning back to Daniel, "While I'm gone, you'll need to get the necessaries ready for them."

Daniel nodded. That was something he could do without going too far from his Molly.

He was only part way down the stairs when he heard another cry. He turned and went straight back. Her eyes were open and she was clutching Sarah's hand.

"The baby?" Sarah asked gently and Molly nodded, tears starting to fall down her cheeks.

Daniel came to her side. "You'll be all right. I know you

will. You're strong, Molly. We can do this." Then as her eyes fluttered closed, he went back down the stairs to bring water and whatever towels and linen he could find.

It seemed to take an age to warm the water and Daniel fretted as he waited, not sure whether to go to the well to fill another pail or stay close by in case he was needed. His decision was eased when there was a knock at the kitchen door.

One of the young farmhands stood there, black streaks across his face from where he'd been dealing with the fire. "Pardon me, Master Daniel, but Master James said I should come and see if you needed any help."

"Oh, indeed I do, thank you." He thrust the pail at Nathan. "Please fill this and bring it back to the house. Wait…" Daniel went back into the kitchen and found the largest pan hanging on the hooks. "Fill this too, please. Thank you, Nathan." Then as Nathan took the empty pail and pan and went back across the yard, Daniel took the already warm water up the stairs to Sarah.

Sarah had removed Molly's lower clothing and covered her with the second sheet. "Her waters have broken, the baby's coming. It's much too soon, Daniel. She still has two months or more until it's due. You know the baby's not likely to live being so early, don't you?"

Daniel nodded and sighed. "Just help my darling Molly. I couldn't bear it if I lost her now."

Sarah put her hand on his arm. "I'll do what I can, but I'll be mighty glad when Ma Spencer gets here."

Daniel went back to heat another pan and to occupy himself as best he could. If he hadn't gone to confront those Reese brothers maybe none of this would have happened, but it was no good thinking like that right now. It had happened and all they could do was deal with it.

As he watched the stove in the kitchen Mrs Spencer knocked and then came straight in.

"Am I ever glad to see you, ma'am," Daniel said, leaving the stove to take Mrs Spencer's coat and hat." Let me show you where they are."

He'd hardly taken any steps from the kitchen when Molly let out another shriek from above.

"I think I can probably find them," Mrs Spencer replied, quickening her step, but Daniel still carried on ahead of her, wanting to look in on his wife for his own peace of mind.

As they went in, Sarah got up and ran through with her mother-in-law how things seemed to her so far. She finished by saying, "There's no sign of the baby's head yet, so I think we've a while to wait."

Daniel moved to Molly's side and she smiled at him weakly. "Oh, Molly, am I ever happy to see your smile," he said bending down to kiss her. "I love you, my brave, brave Molly." Then he turned to Mrs Spencer and said, "Ma'am, may I sit with her awhile?"

"Well, Daniel that's most irregular, but I can't see it doing any harm, but we'll stay nearby so we're here when we're needed."

He nodded and knelt by Molly's side, stroking her hair and holding tightly to her hand.

The spasms of pain engulfing Molly were starting to come more frequently and after one yet more forceful than the ones before Mrs Spencer came and gently touched Daniel's shoulder.

"It's her time, we'll call you when there's news."

Daniel looked up and nodded. He knew he'd be in the way if he stayed and they'd be happier with him downstairs, but this was his Molly, his beloved Molly. He got up slowly, kissed his wife and, with faltering steps, walked from the room.

Daniel paced the kitchen. He opened the outside door wide and breathed deeply. He'd welcome being in the fresh air, but he wanted to stay close enough for them to call him. He heated more water, but they didn't call for any. He could hear nothing of what was happening apart from the intermittent screams from Molly. After one particularly piercing cry Daniel dropped to his knees in front of the stove the rosary clutched between his hands as he prayed. Tears were streaming down his face and he could wish only that he could take the pain instead of Molly.

As time passed, he realised that the screams from Molly had stopped and he could stand to wait in the kitchen no longer. He took a deep breath before heading towards the stairs.

Sarah was just coming out of the room as he reached the landing. She was clearly upset and Daniel stopped in panic.

"Oh, Daniel, I'm sorry."

"Molly?" He could feel his heart racing.

"Molly's fine, but your son..." Sarah burst into tears and could say no more.

"May I go to her? She'll need me."

Sarah nodded and turned back to the door, opened it and spoke quietly to Mrs Spencer between her sobs. Then, putting her hand to her face, she nodded to Daniel and moved aside for him to pass.

Molly was sitting supported by the pillows, holding the infant wrapped in cloth and laid against her chest. Tears were coursing down her face and she looked older than she had done only that morning. She reached her free hand out to Daniel.

"You were right. Will we still call him Michael?"

Daniel drew close to the pair and looked at them both. He could only see his son's tiny face. His eyes were closed and his skin almost translucent with a reddish-purple tinge. His lifeless body looked quite unreal and Daniel found it hard to imagine that such a short time ago he had been alive and unborn. "Michael," he said, reaching across and putting his arm around the one of Molly's which held their son. "Our boy."

Then he and Molly held each other and together wept over their departed son.

When they eventually broke apart, Daniel said, "Why don't I let you rest a while. I'll go to find out the extent of the damage to the hay."

He'd barely finished speaking before Molly's eyelids had fallen and he gently moved his arm to let her rest undisturbed. Then he gave Michael one final kiss on his tiny nose and quietly left the room. Before he went anywhere, he planned to write a letter to Miss Ellie to tell her all that had happened and ask her to return.

When he got down to the kitchen, he found Mrs Spencer and Sarah cooking breakfast for the workers. As events had progressed Daniel had had no notion of what time it was, nor whether it had been light or dark outside.

"You'll need to eat too," Mrs Spencer said, placing food in front of him. "Molly is going to need you to be strong. Today's going to be hard for all of you. Many of the men have worked all night to quell the blaze and once they've eaten you need to let them all get to their beds. It would do no harm now for you to do the same. You've no mother of your own to take care of things, so if it's all the same to you I'll stay a day or two until Molly's back on her feet."

Daniel sat in awe at the transition in Mrs Spencer. Suddenly, when the need arose, she reminded him more of Miss Ellie than he would ever have thought. "Yes, Ma'am." He had no idea what else to say, but had no time for more as Mrs Spencer continued.

"Sarah has already milked the cow, so there's nothing to worry about there. I shall send her back to town to see the Pastor and to tend to the shop. I'm guessing you'll want the baby buried close by and the Pastor should be here to attend to it."

Daniel of course knew they'd want a Christian burial for their son, but had given no thought to what might need to happen with him being so early and managing hardly a breath. "Thank you. I'll talk to Molly when she wakes."

"I've made up a bed in your old room for you for the time being so you don't disturb Molly and until I can get everything sorted in there and I shall take Miss Ellie's until she's home. I've already sent word to her and happen she won't be long in coming."

Daniel felt overwhelmed. Had this kind woman thought of everything? He tried to eat, but was in no mood for food.

Mrs Spencer came and stood by him. "Now I've brought up sons and you need to eat, boy. You get some of that food down you and then go and sleep."

Daniel almost laughed at the way she could read him. Slowly he ate a little bacon and then, more eagerly, the hunk of bread. His stomach growled as he did so and he realised it had been a good while since he'd last had food. Mrs Spencer was no doubt right that he needed it.

By the time he woke it was long after noon and having washed and dressed he went to look in on Molly. Michael was no longer in the room and Molly was washed and wearing a clean night gown as she lay resting in her bed. When she saw him come in, she held out her hand to him. Neither of them spoke but they fell into each other's arms and shed the tears of the loss they shared. When they had both wept tears enough, they moved apart and simply held each other's hands.

"Is it the wrong thing to do to ask you how you're feeling?" Daniel asked.

Molly shook her head. "I'll be ok in time. What about you?"

"I guess that's a measure of it. I've still got you and as long as I have, I'll deal with all else that's thrown our way."

"I've worked on a farm too long not to know how closely life and death are linked. We'll always think of what might have been, but there's work to do and when I'm rested that is exactly what I shall do."

"Was the birth awful bad? Are you hurt from the fire?" Daniel stroked Molly's hair and looked at her in wonder, ready to face what lay ahead. She was his strength and no mistake.

"Not so bad I wouldn't do it again. I guess I'm bruised from the fall, but I don't think I came to much more harm. It's Michael who took the worst of it and that's something I will never forgive those Reese boys. We need a new plan, Daniel, before worse comes to happen."

"I know, but I've no mind to what that might be." As he spoke, he could see how tired Molly was.

"Then tell me the worst of it for the farm."

Molly looked determined and whilst he was reluctant to burden her, Daniel knew she wouldn't take silence for an answer. If he didn't give her the whole picture then she'd be out of bed and finding out for herself and it was too soon for that.

"We lost all the hay. Every last straw of it, except for the few cartloads they brought away to the top end of the farm. We were lucky the wind was blowing down toward the stream and not in this direction. The men stopped it spreading any further, but it's still smouldering and will be hours before there's no risk at all."

"No one hurt?" Molly asked, looking anxious.

Daniel shook his head slowly. "Except for you and Michael everyone got away from it in time. The animals are safe too, they were upwind of the smoke and are showing no distress. The mares will be upset if we don't get them some hay from somewhere, but we're all right for a few days and there's folks around who've broken ranks with the Reese boys and are saying they'll help us. Maybe this is a turning point and will be the last of the problems."

"Daniel Flynn, you always did look for the best in people and you're the better man for it. I sure do hope you're right, but we're going to need to be watchful. If I were to take to gambling, I'd say those boys will be back but I hope you're right, indeed I do. Now, will you pass me the clothes over yonder so I can get out of this bed and get on with some work?" Molly threw the sheet away from her and moved her very swollen ankle to the edge of the bed.

Mrs Spencer knocked and came in as she did so. "Now what have you been telling her, Daniel? You're staying there today, my girl, make no mistake."

Mrs Spencer spoke with such force that even Daniel who had already seen her in action downstairs was taken aback. He could have almost laughed as, without protest, Molly moved back onto the bed and meekly pulled the sheet back up.

"You've had a very difficult night with the birth of the baby…"

"Michael." Both Daniel and Molly said at the same time, then Molly reached for his hand and smiled.

"Well, yes," continued Mrs Spencer. "In my book it doesn't do to name those whose recollection can only bring you grief, but as you wish, Michael. Anyway, with that and the fire and the state of your leg, you're going nowhere until I say so. Now sit yourself up and have something to eat."

Mrs Spencer laid the tray down to Molly's side so she could take the plate which was laden with food as soon as she was ready. "You don't have to eat all of it, but I'm not taking it away until you've had your fill."

Daniel couldn't help but think that Mrs Spencer would have made an excellent school mistress had she not married and supported her husband in the store. He kissed Molly and made his excuses to leave before Mrs Spencer had chance to give him instructions as well. There was work to do on the farm and if Molly was to follow Mrs Spencer's orders she'd need a full report of progress so she could relax. Besides, something needed to be done to stop those Reese boys causing any more harm.

CHAPTER 9

"But how, when you don't yet have the vote, do you expect to enter Congress?" William was astounded as he listened to the hopes Miss Hendry outlined for her own future. She was unlike any woman he had ever met. He'd known enough strong women in his life, but it was the ambition that took him by surprise. It had never occurred to him he might find a woman whose own dreams came close to his own.

"Are you saying that you don't think I could do it?" Miss Hendry's eyes narrowed as she looked at him intently.

William shifted uneasily. "No, miss, I most certainly am not. I think I'm rather in awe of your dream and it sets me to thinking of my own. Until I attended the meeting a few days ago, I'd no notion to go on to do anything more than take over the law practice from my father. Now, I have my sights set on an entirely different goal. Though I've no idea, even in my own case, of what it might mean or where to start."

They were sitting in the parlour of the Hendrys' house where they had been reading the latest newspaper reports.

William had asked leave of Pa to stay on in Iowa until he heard news of Ben, a decision which even he recognised as not being entirely altruistic.

"Why don't you go to university first and take the chance to study?" Cecilia asked as she carefully painted the words on a poster for a rally being held the following weekend.

When William had spent time walking out with Congressman Makepeace's daughter in Dowagiac he had been used to her having little else to do with her time and she in turn had been delighted by the least suggestion of entertainment. Cecilia Hendry was an altogether different matter. Cecilia was busy it seemed almost all the time with preparing for, promoting or attending meetings of the women's movement, and while she herself did not speak at those meetings she did spend her remaining time reading letters and reports of such speeches and work elsewhere.

For want of any other idea of an approach William found himself starting to read what he could and offering his own time to help if they would have him. The more he read, the more he realised how strongly he agreed with all they were working for.

"Pa has offered that I could go to any university I choose, as long as they'd have me. I could ask the same of you?" He looked at her scowl and realised he might once again have said the wrong thing.

"Do you have any idea how few universities have places open to women? It's one of the things we're fighting for." Then to his surprise she smiled. "Iowa was the first to become co-educational a little over ten years ago. Alas, they don't offer the course I wish to take."

William was reluctant to ask what course she wished to pursue as he couldn't help feeling another pitfall might lie ahead, but he was intrigued so was careful to make no assumptions. "And what might that be?"

"Law," she said, looking at him defiantly.

William responded without a second thought. "And a

very fine lawyer I think you'd make." He could see Miss Hendry sizing up his reaction and could only conclude that she had found him genuine as from that point on she seemed to thaw a little and began to discuss things with him more as an equal.

It was a further couple of days before William received a letter sent to his lodgings by Mrs Hawksworth. It contained as much information as she had yet been able to glean.

'… It is my understanding that Ben moved out to the farm of Mr Dansworth to the north of this city, where he was until three months ago. It is of interest to Mrs Dansworth to find Ben as it seems that Duke had a liaison with their dog, Jessie, and she has recently had puppies. Mrs Dansworth was hoping that Ben might give a home to one of the pups…' William had a sudden crazy thought as he read the letter and chuckled to himself before reading on. 'Mrs Dansworth had a notion that Ben planned to visit his wife's sister, but regretfully had no information on where that woman might reside.' William sighed. How could he find one man in an area so very large? Especially one of no fixed abode. He decided to go for a walk to do some thinking and set off into the chill of the October day.

William tried to think how his father might address the problem. He knew very little of Ben's background, save what Daniel had relayed to him. If he were to guess, he'd say that Ben's sister-in-law might live in the same area where Ben's wife and daughter were buried. Although William knew that was somewhere not far distant from where he was now, it could be fifty miles in any direction of the compass and he knew not which.

Instead he found himself returning to the thought

which had so amused him earlier and to that end made enquiries as to where he might find the Dansworths' farm. That proved a straightforward task and so he went once again to the Hendrys' house to speak with Cecilia and explain his plan. He rather hoped she might be willing to accompany him on his visit and was pleased to find her seeking her mother's permission to do so.

Of course, it would not have been seen as proper for the two of them to go alone, although that would have been William's preference, but when she heard of William's scheme Mrs Hendry smiled more broadly than he had seen before and agreed to accompany them without further delay.

It turned out that Mrs Hendry was already acquainted with Mrs Dansworth, so effecting an introduction would be made all the easier by her presence. They took a carriage out to the farm, which turned out to be a rather bumpier route than William was used to. He was more than glad to get out at their destination and take a few deep breaths of air. Thankfully, Mrs Dansworth was home, as it was not a journey he would relish doing often, leastways not by cart. He thought riding might be decidedly preferable.

Once Mrs Hendry had made the introductions and they had been ushered into the parlour and drinks served, William began to explain.

"Madam, it is I who am searching for Ben who used to work here. You see… "and he explained the situation in which Molly found herself and the hope that Ben might be of help to them there. Then he continued. "When I received the letter from Mrs Hawksworth earlier today, I set to wondering about the puppies…" Here he blushed and faltered in his story. "Well, I had a mind that maybe I could take one of the puppies to Daniel to remind him of his dear friend. I shall of course still look for Ben, but I thought that at least…" As he said it out loud, he realised how ridiculous it must sound and ran out of further explanation.

Mrs Dansworth was already on her feet and smiling. "Come with me, young man." And she headed toward the door, beckoning for them all to follow.

In the farmhouse kitchen, close to the range, Jessie was curled up with a large litter of sleeping pups.

Mrs Dansworth stood back and smiled. "What do you think?"

The pups were clearly very young, although William had no experience in such matters. Before he could speak, Cecilia knelt down close to the bitch and was gently stroking her and speaking to her softly.

"How old are they?" she asked.

"They're a little over five weeks old now. They're a whole bundle of trouble when they're awake. Five boys and three girls and we need homes for them all. We may keep one of them ourselves, but we certainly can't keep all eight."

Now that Jessie seemed to trust her, Cecilia gently lifted the pup nearest to her and it was not long before it was nestled against her neck sleeping once again. "Mama, could we keep one too?"

"Oh, mercy me, whatever will your father say?"

But Mrs Hendry was smiling in a way that made William think he had a pretty good idea what Dr Hendry might say, if he were given any choice in the matter.

William knelt down next to Cecilia and copied the approach she had taken, first befriending the mother dog before approaching the puppies. He was still stroking Jessie when one rather plump little puppy waddled over to him and began trying to pull himself up onto William's leg.

"Looks to me like that one's chosen you," Mrs Dansworth said and laughed. "They need to stay with their mama a little longer, but I'll be very happy for you to take them after that."

As they left, William began to think through the practicalities both of collecting the puppy if he'd already returned to Dowagiac and of delivering it to Pierceton. He began to realise his plan may not have been thoroughly thought through.

Cecilia was, by way of contrast, highly animated. "Oh, what shall we call her? She's such a pretty little thing. William what will you call your dog?"

"Mine?" said William, suddenly taken by surprise. He hadn't thought of the pup as being his, but only that he would be giving it to Daniel. "I had not thought that I needed to name him. I guess there's more to this than I'd considered."

Cecilia laughed. "I think I will call her Cady."

William looked at her quizzically, but felt certain that asking why she chose that name was going to be the wrong thing. He hoped that her purpose might become clearer to him if he bided his time. Then it came to him. "There's only one name I can give him. He will be named after his father and called Duke junior."

Later, in his room, he was reading one of the newspapers he had managed to find and from which he was trying to learn about the current politics of the country. As he did so, he came across the name of women's rights campaigner and slavery abolitionist Mrs Elizabeth Cady Stanton and smiled. Cecilia's puppy would have a lot to live up to.

He went back to his reading, continuing as he did so to note down questions he wished to ask Pa on his return. President Johnson's approach to Reconstruction following the Civil War was certainly one thing he was struggling to comprehend but there were also more basic questions. The elections to the House of Representatives were due to take place early the following month and William wanted to be clear on what the Republican Party, who held the Michigan seats, stood for. He set to thinking about the changes he'd like to see in this great country and wished Pa were there to discuss them with. He had not the least idea of where he should start if he wanted to be elected himself.

CHAPTER 10

The following morning at breakfast, William was surprised to see another letter from Mrs Hawksworth waiting for him so soon. His hand trembled as he took up the letter opener and slit the envelope. Surely, it could only mean one thing. He read the page rapidly and broke into a broad smile.

Mrs Hawksworth had succeeded in obtaining an address for Ben's sister-in-law and had been assured that he was still in residence at the address as she wrote. Mrs Hawksworth asked William if he would like her to write to Ben on his behalf. The letter was brief and to the point and gave no detail on how she had achieved what had seemed to William to be impossible.

"You're looking mighty pleased with yourself," the landlady placed a plate of eggs and toast in front of him.

"Thank you, ma'am. I think it's fair to say I am." He tucked into the food hungrily as he formulated a plan.

William decided it would be best that he should see Ben in person and would write back to Mrs Hawksworth immediately after breakfast to thank her and tell her of his intent.

Ben's family were further out of Iowa than William had supposed and he concluded that his best approach would be to ride out there over the coming days. It was still too soon to collect Duke Jnr, and, in any case, the little fellow was in the opposite direction, but if Ben could be persuaded to move to Pierceton, perhaps he could then be the one to take the pup to Daniel and Molly when he went. That thought came as a great relief to William.

William's excitement at tracking down Ben was tinged with regret that his time in Iowa would soon be at an end and, with the great distance between the places, he had no notion how he might see Cecilia Hendry again once he left. He would however seek the Hendrys' advice both on where he could borrow a horse and what he might need for the journey.

It was a little over a good day's ride to Fairfield had his horse been a fit one, but the only one William could find to borrow was happier to walk than to build up any speed and plodded her way out of Iowa City toward Washington County, where William had been assured he'd find lodgings for the night. The horse seemed to want more breaks to rest than William might have taken himself and he wondered whether the journey might have been achieved faster on foot. It was a long time since he'd had need to walk any distance and he thought ruefully that even a slow horse might be better for the job than he was.

Washington was well established and he had little difficulty in finding a suitable resting stop. The horse was only too happy to reach stables. William smiled, realising he was developing an affection for the stubborn animal and admired her steadfast intent to do things only at her own pace. He just hoped that Ben had not chosen that day to move on, having stayed in one place a while.

Once both William and the horse had had their fill of breakfast the following day, they set out along the road to Fairfield. The weather was cold but thankfully dry and the horse plodded, as she had done the day before, without undue protest. It would be only a short time until temperatures remained steadfastly below freezing and by then William hoped to be back in Dowagiac with the comforts of home.

He had little notion of where in Fairfield the address he was looking for would be found and could think only to ask directions once he reached the town.

Eventually he dismounted from the horse in the town centre and went to make enquiries. As it turned out, the house was set back from the road and he'd already passed it on his way to the centre. Having booked himself accommodation for the night William prepared to remount the horse, but she immediately showed her displeasure and intention to take a longer break. William smiled ruefully. He never would understand how to get the best out of women. He gave her a further half hour to rest and munch her way through a net of hay and then tried to mount once again. This time the horse stood firm and allowed him to sit comfortably in the saddle.

At Ben's sister-in-law's house, William dismounted a little way up the track and led the horse the last few yards where he found a convenient tree to tie her to, before he went to knock at the porch door.

A black woman, in her mid-fifties he guessed, with an apron strung around her wide girth, came out onto the porch and William presumed this to be Ben's sister-in-law, Maisey.

"Well I'll be. It's not often we have visitors calling on us out here. I ain't done nothing bad, mister, and no one can tell you otherwise."

She was smiling as she said it and William didn't know if she was being serious or teasing him.

"Excuse me, I'm mighty sorry to bother you, but I'm looking for Ben." The sound of a dog barking and scampering toward him made William smile as he immediately saw the resemblance to Duke Jnr, "And if I'm not mistaken, this must be Duke," William said, leaning down to greet the excited dog.

"And who be you, as already knows my family, but doesn't know me?"

"I'm sorry." William was mortified that he might have caused offence when he was so desperate to make a good impression. "My name is William Dixon, ma'am and I come in search of Ben on behalf of a dear friend of his, Daniel Flynn." He took a slight bow to Miss Maisey, who nodded and curtsied in return.

"Well, it looks like you've come to the right place. He's out back in the yard. Duke'll show you the way." Then Miss Maisey turned and went back into the house, leaving William to follow his four-legged guide to find Ben.

Ben was feeding some chickens when William arrived. "Good day, sir." William called, raising his hat in greeting.

"And who in the name of God raises their hat to old Ben?" Ben replied, carrying his bucket over to the edge of the coop to address William.

"I do, sir, and mightily proud I am to meet you."

Ben shook his head in apparent bewilderment and William thought he'd best explain quickly.

"You were friend to my dear friend Daniel Flynn when he had no other and for that I will always be grateful to you."

"Well, I'll be," said Ben, scratching his head. "You wouldn't be Molly's brother Thomas, would you?"

"I am indeed, sir," William replied excited that Ben already knew of him. "Though I'm known as William now, sir, but let me explain."

"Let's go on up to the house. There's a chill in the air

and my old bones don't take it so well now." Then Ben led the way back where William had come from and took him through the screen door into the parlour.

"We've a visitor, Maisey and a rather special one at that."

Maisey was already prepared and tea was laid out ready for them coming in. They all sat down and William realised that Maisey was as ready to hear the tale as was Ben.

William began the story with Molly finding Daniel in prison, which was the point at which Ben had met her and last knew what had happened. Then he ran through the court case and told proudly of how his father had arrived to defend Daniel and how Mrs Hawksworth had testified against her husband.

"And you says Mrs Hawksworth had been hit by that man too?" Maisey sucked on her remaining teeth and shook her head. "And you wonders why women all over wants to see things changed. There ain't no man as has a right to strike a woman, wife or no wife."

William nodded his agreement and tried to bring Ben back to the story of Daniel so he could build up to what he needed to ask. Then he realised that the point Maisey was making could only help him if he could move forward to telling them about Miss Ellie and what was now happening on the farm.

William continued the story as best he could until he'd covered the events which he knew of up to his leaving Dowagiac. "Miss Ellie had hoped you might have gone out to work on Cochrane's Farm when Daniel first moved there and left word for you to that effect. I guess it never reached you. In any case, Daniel would be mighty glad if you would choose it as your home for the future. He needs a friend and no mistake."

"Now let me get this straight." Miss Maisey stood with her hands on her buxom hips. "You come all this way to offer my brother-in-law a home, when he's already got one right here in Fairfield with me and Clement. Isn't my home good enough?"

"Now, Maisey," Ben lay a placating hand on her arm. "Settle yourself. He ain't said there's anything wrong with your home. You and I both know I'd never planned to stay here. I'm no good indoors and there's not work enough here to keep me busy." Then he turned to William. "I'll need to think on it. My Esme and Flora are buried here and I've never been away from them for long, or too far to come back to them when I need to. Can I give you my answer in a day or two?"

"I'm returning to Iowa City tomorrow, or at least starting the journey if that old nag wants to take me. I'll stay on there until I hear from you." William wrote out his lodgings' address and passed it to Ben. Then he realised that he had no idea whether Ben could read and so told him what it said so he could remember. "Oh," said William smiling. "There was one other thing, Duke is a father." He waited for the words to sink in. "I went out to Mr Dansworth's farm to see if they knew where I could find you and met the puppies while I was there. I'm sending one of them out to Daniel to remind him of Duke. I've named him Duke Jnr, and he sure does resemble his father."

Ben looked proudly down at Duke. "Well who'd have thought it? You old rogue. Now I know where you kept disappearing off to. And at your age! Well, I'm glad you're still having fun at your time of life." Then he looked up at William and smiled broadly. "What is it they say? You can't keep a good dog down."

William thought from the look on his face that Ben might just have made a decision and took the opportunity to take his leave. "I'll look forward to seeing you in Iowa City, Ben." He shook the old man's hand warmly. Then carefully took his leave of Maisey who was grumbling, rather less under her breath than might have been considered polite and went to persuade the old nag to take him back to Iowa City.

William was glad that the weather held for his return journey and was very happy to return the horse to her owner who declared her to be a 'fine animal' leaving William to wonder how bad the ones were that he was comparing her to. Then he called round to see Miss Hendry and tell her family about his travels. He was surprised to be greeted by a letter sent to him there from Miss Ellie.

My dear William,

I can only hope that your journey is a fruitful one. I have received most distressing news from Daniel and have no choice but to return to the farm immediately. It seems the Reese boys have not been content with the chaos they have caused so far, but have now led to Molly losing the baby. Daniel says she is well, but she fell from a hay rick while trying to save the hay from fire caused by those brothers and as a result gave birth much too soon.

I will stay at the farm until Ben can join them, as I have every faith that you will not have rested until you have found him and that even as I write he might be coming with you to the farm. Your humble servant,

Ellie Cochrane.

William stared down at the letter aware a tear was rolling down his cheek and not wanting to look up lest Mrs Hendry and her daughter should see.

"Is it terrible bad news," Cecilia asked coming to his side.

William nodded and swallowed hard. His hand shook as he passed the letter to Cecilia to read for herself.

"Oh, the poor child," Mrs Hendry said once she too had read the letter. "And will Ben go with you?"

William recovered his composure and tried to find words. "I think he will, although we might have Duke to thank if he does." And he told them about Ben's pride in his dog and how it made Ben remember there was more to life than growing old quietly.

CHAPTER 11

"Now don't you go getting ideas of going half way across the country when you've a family and a home here with us."

Maisey seemed determined that Ben should stay in Fairfield. He sighed heavily. "Maisey, you know as well as I do that I'm in the way here. I've nothing to do but think of what might have been and that's no way to live."

"Well, all I'm saying is those folks ain't family and we is."

"Daniel was the closest I had to family working out on that farm and it feels pretty good to be useful and important to someone again, after all these years. You and Clement don't want me under your feet here." He looked down at Duke and couldn't help but think he should take a leaf out of the dog's book and take opportunities that came his way.

"And what is going to happen to Esme and Flora I might well ask if you up and leave them?"

"Maisey," Ben said as gently as he could. "You and I both know that they wouldn't want me festering away here with nothing but their graves for company. Your sister was a good woman, and there ain't no one who'd say otherwise. She was taken from us way too soon, but she wouldn't want us all being miserable because of it."

Maisey looked him steadily in the eye and with a mouth screwed tight in resignation she nodded slightly.

Ben sighed. He couldn't have gone without Maisey's blessing and whilst that might be stretching her agreement so far, he knew the worst of the battle was over.

It was too late in the day to walk to the graveyard in Fairfield. He'd need to do that the following morning before he set off. There was little else for him to sort and he travelled light wherever life took him. He picked up the small box that sat by his bed and opened it. He stared at the simple necklace that had been his wife's up to the point they laid her in the ground and which he'd treasured ever since. Esme had died giving birth to their darling Flora. Everyone said that the girl was the image of her mother, right until she burned up with fever when she was near on five years old and the good Lord had taken her to join her mother. Ben sighed heavily again. Maisey had stepped in when Esme died and helped him raise Flora. Time hadn't so much healed the pain as numbed it. If you pressed hard enough, it was as sharp as the day it started.

Duke barked and nudged Ben's leg.

Ben smiled and closed the lid. "If anyone knows how to live for the day it's you. Puppies indeed. No wonder you were so secretive about where you were going to all those times. Well, it's time we had an adventure together and I reckon you'll be mighty pleased to see Daniel when we get to the end of it." Ben wrapped the box carefully inside his spare shirt and laid it in his pack.

"Now you just make sure that poor girl's safe when you get there," Maisey said when they sat to supper later that day.

Ben smiled hearing Maisey giving him her support.

Clement as always sat at the head of the table but said barely a word. He had little need of speaking when Maisey said it all for the two of them.

"She's having a hard time and it's not right. You heard what that young man said and her being Daniel's wife."

Ben grinned to himself. Once Maisey came around to supporting an idea there was no stopping her. This was the blessing he'd been hoping for.

"And don't you go worrying none about your Esme's and Flora's graves. Clement and me will make sure they're clean and tidy won't we Clement?" Maisey didn't stop long enough for Clement's reply before she continued. "Now I've packed some things together that you can be taking on the journey, so don't you go going hungry, I tell you."

She was a good woman, but Ben wouldn't be wholly sorry to be moving on again.

Ben had still been a young man when he'd lost his wife, but his heart ached for Esme in a way that made it impossible for him to think of taking another and he'd nursed her memory ever since. As for Flora, the good Lord had more important places for her to be, so Maisey said, but they mourned her loss as much for her likeness to Esme as for her own life and it had felt like losing Esme all over again.

Meeting Daniel had been like being given the chance of being a father in a quite unexpected way and it had meant a great deal to Ben as he'd grown older.

It was early when Ben and Duke set off the following day. He'd walk for the whole of daylight and rest when it ended. He turned his steps first toward Fairfield and the goodbyes he needed to make. Once he got there, he ran his hands over the gravestones as though he were caressing his wife's face. He'd no words to say, but in the weary sadness of the morning he nodded silently to himself and prayed they'd be reunited one day in a better place.

He walked away slowly, not daring to look back in case his courage failed him. He'd left them often enough, but always to return soon after and he could only hold in his mind that this time might be the same, though he knew it was not so.

He had no notion of how much time had passed while he'd stood close by his wife and daughter, but the sun was rather higher in the sky than he'd been expecting as he turned away from Fairfield and headed north toward Iowa City. He almost thought he'd be best to stop back at Maisey's and leave the day following, but he knew if he took that course his courage would be gone and he'd never leave.

Daniel needed him and that was the thought he held on to. It was a long time since old Ben had been needed by any folks. Teeth gritted and hands clenched, being needed was enough to drive him on as he walked.

CHAPTER 12

William paced the sitting room of the guest house. Two days had passed since his return and there was no word from Ben. He was starting to think he'd misread the man and that Ben would be happy to sit out his retirement feeding chickens. Whatever Ben's decision, he'd given his word that he'd contact William with an answer and if Ben was half the man that Daniel had said, then William could not believe he'd keep him waiting long.

He decided to take a walk to the Hendrys' house to see if he could be of assistance to them, both to fill his time and of course to give him the further opportunity to see Cecilia. He was barely out of the gate of the guest house when a dog ran up and panted by his side. His first thought was irritation, but on looking down William immediately recognised Duke. He turned to find Ben coming along the road behind.

"You look exhausted," William said, taking in Ben's appearance.

"It's a long walk and has taken a while on these old bones." Ben rested against the fence.

William started to wonder what real difference this old man could make to Molly and Daniel on the farm and felt more than a little guilty for not thinking about his immediate need for transport for the fifty-mile journey to meet him.

"If you still want me, then Duke and I would be

honoured to come to Pierceton."

"That is very good news," William said. "Come, let's find you some food and a place to rest." William suddenly felt uncertain whether the guest house would be prepared for Ben to stay and decided instead to continue to see Mrs Hendry who he felt sure would be willing to assist.

Once again, he was grateful to Mrs Hendry who read the situation perfectly and without fuss had a room made ready for Ben with sufficient water for washing and a good meal besides. William remembered the thoughtfulness of his father in finding clothes for Daniel, which whilst clean and new were still suited to his daily life and ones he'd accept willingly. While Ben was resting William went out to find something similar.

When he returned, Ben was talking earnestly to Mrs Hendry and William slipped quietly into the room trying not to disturb the flow of what was being said.

"It's all very well staying here to be near the graves of my Esme and our Flora, but there's a boy out there as close to a son as I'll ever have and his need of me is the greatest thing in my life. Family ain't always the ones born to us."

William smiled. He couldn't have put it better himself.

The following day, they took the cart out to the Dansworth farm once again. William would rather have been on horseback, but after his recent experience thought there may not be a horse available which would make that a pleasure. The road was as uneven as it had been before and the ride was less than comfortable. Duke had the right idea, leaving the jolts of the cart, he spent part of the time running along at the side of the horse and William wished he had the same level of fitness so he might join them.

Jessie was delighted to see Duke and clearly the arrival of the puppies had done little to dampen his ardour. As

Jessie sniffed around him, their puppies trailed behind her and were soon playing and rolling with Duke. He seemed delighted by the whole situation. Cady had separated herself from the pack and wandered over to sniff Cecilia, and Duke Jnr wasn't far behind.

William watched Ben as he smiled, so clearly proud of Duke's achievements and thrilled by the likeness between Duke Jnr and his father.

William was more distracted on the journey back from the farm. Cady was asleep in Cecilia's lap while Duke Jnr was making bids to escape at every opportunity.

"I'm guessing you're not so used to dogs," Ben said, grinning at William. He picked the little dog up and nestled him inside his jacket where he immediately began to settle.

William sighed. "No, I've never had one to look after at all. I don't know the first thing about them. I guess we're going to have to feed him with something."

"Don't you worry." Ben was stroking the little chap as he now quietly snoozed. "I'll take good care of him until we get him to his new master."

They spent only another day in Iowa City before commencing their journey back to Pierceton. It took them several days to cover the distance and whilst William was now used to such travelling, it was the first time Ben had ventured out of the state of Iowa. He was anxious as they travelled, but soon began to enjoy the changing scenery.

At the end of their first day's journey, they left the train and enquired of the Station Master for nearby lodgings.

"I don't know as they'll have a room for a nigger, but you can try this one." The man wrote an address on a piece of paper and pushed it across the counter to William.

William bristled at the man's words, but bit back his

93

instinctive response. "Thank you," he said simply and moved away from the office window. It seemed that whatever the Constitution had to say, not all men were equal. Having Ben as a companion was giving William an insight into the prejudice that was unlike anything he had encountered, even as an Irish immigrant when they first arrived in America.

Ben shook his head sadly, but said nothing.

William was relieved that the guest house was as happy to find a room for Ben as it was for him.

It was their second night that the problem became most starkly apparent.

"We don't have rooms for no blacks here," the landlady said when William enquired.

"Why ever not?" he asked, the anger rising in him as Ben had already turned from their building. William found himself facing a closed door and thumped his hand against the gate post.

"There's no point you doing nothing like that," Ben said with a deep resignation in his voice. "I'm best finding me a ditch for the night to sleep in and can meet you in the morning."

"You will do no such thing." William strode to catch up with Ben. "Daniel would never forgive me if I didn't treat his friend with the respect he deserves. If you have to resort to sleeping in a ditch, then I shall be next to you." They were courageous words, but William really hoped it wasn't going to come to that. He shuddered at the thought of sleeping rough after all these years. He went in search of another lodging and was ready to offer more money on condition that a room would be provided. Thankfully, this time he was successful and Ben was treated with due respect.

William began to shape his views for entering politics based on a broader fight for equality than he had previously realised was necessary. He didn't know what shocked him more, that people could still refuse entry to Ben because of his colour, or that Ben accepted it with such benign resignation. He was clearly so used to such rejection that it no longer came as any surprise. William longed to be back in Dowagiac and able to discuss some of what he had learned with Pa.

They were still two days short of reaching Pierceton and the journey had been an education to them both. Ben had never travelled so far and William was learning as much about dogs as he was people. Even the horses back home had needed little care from William. He talked to them when he was riding, but he'd rarely spent time in the stables feeding and caring for them. Duke Jnr was a complete revelation to him and after his initial reluctance to manage the pup, he was now enjoying every lesson Ben was giving him on how to train and care for the dog. It was going to be much harder to say goodbye than ever he'd imagined.

He wrote to Miss Ellie to send word of their expected arrival and hoped it could still be kept secret from Molly and Daniel.

"It's going to be a mighty fine surprise to them when we all turn up," Ben said as they started the final leg of the journey.

For a moment, William hesitated, anxious in case he'd done the wrong thing, but he felt sure that all parties would be more than happy with the arrangement.

When they finally arrived at the station in Pierceton, it was James who was waiting for them with the cart.

"I'm mighty happy to see you again, Master William."

Then he shook William by the hand and made his introductions to Ben. "You're going to be most welcome indeed," he said to Ben. "Now get out if it." He batted Duke Jnr away as he scrabbled up onto the seat next to him and began to chew on the reins that James was holding.

William took firm hold of the pup before he could get into further trouble and they made their way back to the farm.

It was only Miss Ellie who greeted them in the yard.

"I've packed the others off for a walk in the fresh air, seeing as the weather's so good and Molly needs to build her strength. They'll be back soon enough and the surprise will be the better for it." She had laid out quite a spread on the kitchen table and there were places enough set for all of them, including James.

"I'll not show you your lodgings until after we've eaten. I wouldn't want them to see us before they come in." James put Ben's bag out of the way at the side of the kitchen, where Duke Jnr promptly set to chewing on the strap of the bag. "We'll have none of that, young man." James lifted the dog and carried him back to the hearth where a bone was waiting on a piece of cloth so he could chew in comfort.

William smiled as it seemed that Miss Ellie and James had, between them, thought of everything.

They heard voices out in the yard and Miss Ellie shushed them to silence. Only Duke Jnr didn't understand the message and began to yap and run to the door as though he already knew the people arriving. William held his breath as he watched. As the kitchen door opened, it was Molly at whom the little dog threw himself and she scooped him up as though it was the most natural thing in the world.

"Duke?" Daniel said, with doubt in his voice. Then Ben let go of Duke senior and he ran to Daniel in much the same manner as his son had done with Molly. Daniel dropped to his knees. For a moment he took no notice of the others assembled in the room, but simply held the dog as though nothing else in the world were important.

William ushered Ben forward out of the shadows. "We thought you could use a friend or two," he said greeting his sister with a kiss.

"Ben!" Daniel let go of Duke, stepped forward and clasped Ben's hand. "How did you…? Oh, am I ever glad to see you! Welcome. Welcome to Cochrane's Farm. Molly," he turned to his wife. "This is…"

"I've already had the pleasure, when I sang for you outside the Courthouse in Iowa, what seems like a lifetime ago," said Molly, a tear rolling down her cheek. "Duke here seemed to recognise the song, being one of the ones you used to sing when we were young." Then Molly turned back to address Ben. "I'm so happy that William found you. You are staying, aren't you?"

"As long as you'll have me, ma'am. I'm here to stay."

Duke wove his way between Daniel and Ben as though he couldn't believe his luck.

Once they sat to eat, William recounted the whole story of his search for Ben and Daniel in turn told of the recent happenings on the farm.

"And if you're really sure you can stand to stay here, we'd be mightily glad of a friend," Daniel finished his story and looked to Ben.

"You can count on me and Duke, though it's too soon to say about the little fellow," Ben said looking across to where Duke Jnr was contentedly asleep on Molly's lap.

"Now, I don't think we'll be having too much trouble

from this little chap." Molly stroked his tummy and he snuffled in his sleep.

"How is it you get that sort of response from him so easily and I don't know where to start?" William shook his head.

"Maybe if you spent less time wearing a suit and more time mucking out animals then it wouldn't seem so strange, brother of mine."

William grinned. "And maybe you should try your charms on those Reese boys as well as the dog."

"Ah well, if only that were true. There, dear brother, is where your skills might just be more use than mine. Is there any action we can take against them ourselves, without needing to go to the sheriff?"

William scratched his head. "I can certainly talk to my father, when I return, but it may be easier to teach me to care for the puppy, unless we can get some clear evidence against them."

CHAPTER 13

If you get there before I do
Coming for to carry me home
Tell all of my friends, that I'm coming there too
Coming for to carry me home
Swing Low, Sweet Chariot - Wallace Willis 1860s

"Where is Ben to sleep?" Molly asked Daniel once they were alone. "He sure deserves to be some place better than the bunkhouse, but I don't know as he'd be happy here in the house."

Daniel smiled, appreciating Molly's sensitivity to making sure Ben was comfortable with what was provided. "It seems Miss Ellie is already ahead of us on that one. You know the old log cabin down by the stream?"

"The one next to where James lives?" Molly sat down and looked attentive as Daniel set to explaining.

"Yes. Well, over the last few days Miss Ellie and James have not only cleaned it out, but made it rather cosy. It means Ben has got a home of his own and a neighbour in James whenever he needs one. I think it suits them both rather well."

"And how did they do all of that without us having any idea?" Molly shook her head.

"I guess we've been so busy with our own problems we just didn't see." Daniel went across to the doorway and looked out. "It's hard to know which young Duke will choose as his home, but as long as he's in one place or the other we'll all be happy."

"It's too confusing having them both with the same name. When you call one, they don't know which you're after. Why don't we just call him Junior?" Molly picked a bowl up from the side.

"We could change his name to something completely different," Daniel said, turning to face her.

She turned the bowl around to him sheepishly. "It's a bit late for that now." She held out the bowl on which she had painted his name. In small letters it said 'DUKE' and then in much larger script she had painted 'JUNIOR'.

"Molly Reilly, you're as devious as your guardian!" Daniel laughed. He jumped as Miss Ellie came into the room behind him.

"And what's that I'm being accused of?"

Molly showed her the bowl. "Daniel here was just accusing me of being as devious as you are. I'd painted Junior's name on his bowl before telling Daniel that's what we'd call him. He'd been telling me all the arrangements you've been making for Ben arriving that we knew nothing about."

"Ah, yes," said Miss Ellie. "There might have been one or two things I needed to sort without you knowing, but it's all worked out well from what I can see. Now you've got Ben to keep an eye on the pair of you, William will be escorting me back to Pierceton so I can continue in the work there. We're rather hoping that one of other of the dogs will alert you if there are any more visits from those Reese boys. If that doesn't work, then it may be time to resort to the law. William is going to discuss possible action with his father when we get back."

"Oh, must you go, Miss Ellie? I sure do like having you

around." Molly took both of Miss Ellie's hands in hers.

"Now don't you go getting all sentimental on me, child. There's important work to be done and you love birds don't need me around the place. You know I'm not far away if you need me."

"Couldn't you just stay a few weeks? It will be Christmas soon and it would be so much the nicer if you were here."

Daniel smiled watching Molly plead. He knew when Miss Ellie's mind was made up there would be no point trying to change it. But still, Molly insisted on trying.

Two days later, Molly and Daniel took William and Miss Ellie into town in the cart and waved them on their way back to Dowagiac.

"And, child," Miss Ellie called as the whistle blew, "next time I come back I want it to be for happier times, do you hear?"

Daniel slipped his arm around his wife's waist and they both waved for as long as they could still see the smoke as it swept its way back to them from the departing engine.

When they returned to the farm, Daniel found Ben throwing a stick for the dogs to fetch.

"I do believe this here pup is making me younger." Ben stopped throwing the stick and Junior barked excitedly at his feet.

"There's not much more that needs doing today. Molly's working in the dairy and will soon have that back in shape. I'd wondered about walking into town and showing you around."

"What do you think, boys?" Ben turned to the dogs now jumping up to try to reach the stick which he was still holding. "I think they reckon that's a good idea if I'm not going to throw this stick all day."

As they walked, Daniel told Ben of all that had happened to him since they were last together and Ben in turn talked of his own times.

"It was hard to leave the graves of my family back in Fairfield, but Maisey will tend to them. They wouldn't have wanted me festering away getting under Maisey's and Clement's feet and I ain't so much use around a farm these days." He spoke apologetically. "I've spent all the years since Flora died wandering. I never set down any roots except where the two of them were laid and where you were. I guess it's time these tired old bones felt at home in some place at least."

"It's a friend I need, not a worker."

"Well I'm sure happy to oblige in that one." Ben clapped his hand on Daniel's shoulder and smiled.

"We've enough farmhands to keep things going. Most of them only come in when the work's busy, but a couple stay on through the year. The problem with them is they're local folks and while they're loyal enough, they've no appetite to stand up to the Reese family. There's more than just the brothers belong to that clan around here. When it comes to working, you only need do what you want to do. You gave me half of everything you had when I needed it. This is the least I can do in return." Daniel waited for Ben to retie the lace of his boot and then they continued their route into town.

He showed Ben where the main landmarks were, including those to avoid as well as those they had business with. He stiffened as they were passing Marsh's and the saloon doors swung open and emitted a staggering Reuben Reese.

Daniel swallowed hard and tried to keep walking without paying attention to them. Duke to his surprise started growling and Junior backed away, keeping his eyes firmly on Reuben.

"Got yourself a nigger have you, Flynn? Even an old nigger's fitter to do the work than you are." Reuben spat into the gutter and staggered toward them.

Ben rested his hand on Daniel's arm, but Daniel was bristling with anger, not at any insult to himself but for the way his friend was being treated. Despite his senses telling him to simply walk on, Daniel wheeled around and stood firm facing Reuben Reese.

"This man is a good friend of mine. He's a better man than you will ever be and an honest one. I don't expect anyone to address him in such terms and I won't stand by and hear it from you."

"Is that right?" Jacob Reese had now exited the saloon and was standing next to his brother. "Well I don't expect…"

At that moment, Duke lunged forwards and bit Jacob Reese firmly on the leg, before immediately backing off and returning to his masters. Whilst the Reese brothers were taken up with Jacob yelping and assessing the extent of his injury, Ben took Daniel's arm with a firmer grip than Daniel might have expected and guided him away from trouble and put some distance between them.

"While it's mighty kind of you to stand up for an old man, I've learned from years of dealing with boys like that to keep my mouth shut and walk on by. There's no point arguing with an idiot, they don't know their tongues from their muck heap and are liable to get the two confused."

Ben did not loose Daniel's arm until Daniel started to relax, by which time they were well out of sight of Marsh's and making their way back towards Spencer's Store. They called in at the store so that Daniel could introduce Ben and make sure that Mrs Spencer knew that Ben could charge things to their account.

"Well look who's here." Sarah was just coming out of the store with little Henry as they arrived. "How's Molly?"

Daniel filled Sarah in and introduced Ben, then they turned to see a giggling Henry sitting on the floor being licked by Junior while Duke rested his head on the boy's leg.

"Well, it looks like these boys have made friends." Sarah laughed as she watched her son. "He's going to be asking me for one of his own before I know it."

"What's that?" Joseph asked coming out to join them.

"I was just saying that Henry is going to be wanting a puppy of his own if this is anything to go by."

Joseph smiled indulgently at his son, then shook both Daniel and Ben by the hand. "It's a pleasure to meet you, sir. I hope you'll be very happy living here."

Daniel was pleasantly surprised by the warmth of the welcome but, after what Molly had told him about their gossiping and attitudes, he did wonder what would be reported back to others visiting the store later in the day.

Once they could tear the dogs away from their new admirer, Daniel and Ben continued their way back to Cochrane's Farm. The welcome that Ben had received at the store had lightened Daniel's mood and he put thoughts of the Reese boys out of his mind.

By the time they got back, Molly was just finishing up in the dairy. "Well it's a good thing I wasn't laid up any longer." She stood hands on hips grinning at Daniel. "You've still a way to go before you become the finest dairy maid we've got.

"And what's wrong with my butter?" Daniel kissed his wife.

"It's not your butter that's the problem Daniel Flynn, it's your cheese that still needs working on."

"Oh, does it now. Well it's a good job that I'm happy to eat it then." He went into the dairy and came out with a truckle of cheese. "What do you think?" He asked Ben, cutting a little with his knife and passing it to him.

Ben took the slither of cheese. He first sniffed it solemnly, then bit a corner off and chewed on it for a moment. Finally, he raised an eyebrow before saying, "I do declare it to be the finest cheese I've ever tasted." Then he passed the remains to Duke who sniffed it and walked away, leaving Junior to run off along the path with his new prize.

CHAPTER 14

'Fear not,' said he,
For mighty dread
Had seized their troubled minds
'Glad tidings of great joy I bring
To you and all mankind.'
While Shepherds Watched - Nahum Tate - 1702

The weeks leading up to Christmas were quieter ones on the farm. The weather had turned cold and Daniel spent many evenings sitting by the fire with Junior lying at his feet. Some evenings Ben would join them in the farmhouse and others Daniel and Molly might go down to the cabin to visit Ben. Molly worked long hours developing ideas of how they might make improvements to the farm and although she tried to include Daniel in the plans, he was happier to accept the decisions she reached than to make those decisions himself.

Christmas was marked much as any Sunday might be. Although Molly worked hard to make the house seem cheerful, none of them felt much like celebrating so soon after losing Michael. Ben and James sat down to a meal with Daniel and Molly, but it felt to Daniel to be as much about those absent as about those present.

What Daniel really wanted to do was focus on Molly and the farm and stop worrying about what the Reese brothers were up to, but he doubted that would be wise and never quite relaxed.

With the snow thick on the ground in January, journeys into town were less frequent. They'd laid by enough provisions to get them through, but they still had surplus from the dairy to sell and some goods they needed to buy. Daniel took the mare into town, preferring to leave the cart at home. He made his way to the far end of town to deliver the orders that Molly had listed for him. At his first address on the list, he dismounted and went to deliver the cheese and butter he was carrying.

"Why, Mr Flynn, I'm dreadful sorry, we cancelled our order a few days ago. Didn't your wife receive our note?"

Daniel shook his head. "And will you be wanting your delivery next week as usual?"

Mrs Sanders looked uncomfortable. "I'm real sorry, Mr Flynn, but we're buying our cheese from another farm now."

Daniel's shoulders slumped. "And might I ask why that is ma'am?"

"I'm sorry, Mr Flynn," was all Mrs Sanders would say before turning to go back into the house.

Daniel checked his list and continued his round. Of the three other deliveries he needed to make, only one was pleased to see him and take their order. The other two both claimed to have cancelled and Daniel began to have an uneasy feeling. He stopped at Spencer's General Store as he passed, wondering if they might have need of additional stock. If not, he at least hoped they might tell him what they'd heard of the reason for the cancellations.

He tied the mare to the post and carried his saddle bag into the store.

"Daniel!" Mrs Spencer sounded surprised to see him.

"Good day, Mrs Spencer. Wherever I go today, I get the

feeling there's something someone isn't telling me. What is going on, ma'am?"

"Joseph, mind the store. Daniel, you'd best come through." Then Mrs Spencer led him through to the back of the shop and into the sitting room.

"Sit down, Daniel."

Daniel was beginning to feel a little uncomfortable. "Mrs Spencer, what is this about?" He sat on the edge of the chair and held firmly to the saddle bag which he was still carrying.

"There's a rumour going around the town," Mrs Spencer hesitated and looked down at her hands. "We haven't added to it you understand."

"What rumour?" Daniel was trying to control his temper and he spoke in a very flat voice.

"That the fire affected your dairy and that your butter and cheese aren't fit to eat." Mrs Spencer continued to look away from Daniel as she spoke.

"But you know that's not true." Daniel was on his feet and pacing the room. "The fire was three months ago. You were there. It came nowhere near the dairy, or the cows. How exactly is it supposed to have affected what we're making now?" He wheeled around to face Mrs Spencer balling his fists. "And why, when you were there and saw for yourself, haven't you told people that they're wrong?" By now Daniel's voice was raised and Joseph came through from the store.

"I'll ask you to leave, if you please, Daniel. I won't have you talking to my mother like that."

Daniel deflated. "I'm sorry. I spoke out of turn. But Joe, I thought you were our friends. Why haven't you explained to people that the rumours just aren't true?"

Joseph Spencer at least had the decency to look

ashamed. "They're good and long-standing customers, Daniel. What were we supposed to say?"

"The Reese brothers!" Daniel snorted. "They're not good customers. They haven't paid their bill with you, Sarah told Molly as much. You're afraid of them. You're scared if you don't go along with them they'll do the same to you as they've been doing to us and you're afraid." He shook his head in disbelief and disappointment. Then he looked Joseph in the eye and with a steady voice said, "I didn't know your brother, but he went off to fight to make sure that bullies don't win. He gave his life to defend the rights of his countrymen. And you," he paused trying to find the right words, "you won't even stand up to the playground bully in your own back yard." He picked up his saddle bag from the chair. "Good day to you!" Then strode back to the door through to the shop and out into the street.

"Wait. Daniel, wait."

He heard Mrs Spencer calling after him, but he took a few deep breaths, put the bag back onto the mare, mounted and rode off toward the farm. At least with the weather cold, the butter and cheese would last longer while they tried to find new buyers. They needed to show people that their dairy was as good as any around and he could only hope that Molly might have some ideas of how to do that.

He was forced to slow the horse to a walk as they came to the deeper snow. The rhythm of the gentle ride gave him time to calm and to think. Somehow they needed to get more of the town on their side, but compared to the Reese boys they were newcomers and led a very different life. Daniel guessed this was the sort of place a family would have to have lived for generations to truly belong. He wondered if there was anything that could be done about it or whether the battle was lost.

Daniel returned the butter and cheese to the cool of the dairy store before going into the farmhouse. With so many troubles to address over the hay and losing the baby, Daniel was reluctant to add another worry to Molly's shoulders, but he had no choice.

The kitchen was warm and the smell of bread cooking met him even before he'd opened the door. Both James and Ben were at the table and Daniel sank gratefully into his usual chair.

"And whatever is wrong with you, husband of mine?" Molly asked putting a plate of fresh bread down in front of him.

He looked up at her. "Whatever did I do to deserve such a wonderful wife?" And he felt a tear trickle down his cheek.

"Now, we'll have none of that, Daniel Flynn." Molly took his face in her hands and gently kissed him. "I'm guessing we've more trouble than I already know about, but whatever it is, we'll get by."

Her no nonsense approach was exactly what he needed right then and he pulled himself together and sighed heavily. He told them the whole story, including walking out of Spencer's Store. "So now what are we going to do?"

Molly looked thoughtful. "I've got me an idea…" but before she'd gone any further, there was a quiet knock at the kitchen door. Molly was already standing, so went across to open it.

"May we come in?"

Given the weather conditions, Daniel was surprised to see Mrs Spencer and Sarah enter the kitchen, both of them looking anxious.

It was Mrs Spencer who spoke. "I've come to apologise." She looked down and picked at a thread on her gloves. "You were right. I don't know what I was thinking. I'm sorry. I knew their Ma you know. She was a good woman, and she wouldn't have stood for this nonsense and I shouldn't be doing so either."

Daniel got up from the table and went to her with an outstretched hand. "Thank you. That means a great deal to us. We were just discussing what we could do. Won't you come in to the warm?"

"And your arrival is just perfect," said Molly who was positively beaming. "Now sit yourselves down and I'll explain what I was thinking." Once they'd made themselves comfortable, Molly continued. "We've got spare cheese and butter and we can't eat it all. I'm not expecting people to just start buying it again, even you telling them the rumour's wrong, won't change that immediately. What if we were to give it away for free through the store when people made other purchases? Then people could see for themselves how good it is without having to pay?"

"But what if they don't eat it?" Sarah asked.

James laughed. "Folks around here won't throw something away that they're given for free. If it saves them spending money that could be spent on beer, they'll eat what they're given, I'll be bound."

"And what if they don't buy yours next time they come in?" Sarah still didn't look convinced.

"Well," said Molly clearly still thinking it through. "We know our cheese and butter are as good as anyone's and better than most. What if we sell it at half price for the next couple of weeks, so they choose ours rather than any other and then put the price back to normal when all this is forgotten. Selling at half price has to be better than not selling any at all. What do you think Mrs Spencer?"

"I think," she looked up from her hands for the first time, "it might just work." She looked across at Sarah for support before saying, "On that basis we'll increase our order for the shop and see what happens." Then she turned to Daniel. "What you said about Henry…"

"I'm sorry, ma'am, I spoke out of turn."

"No, Daniel, you spoke the truth." She hesitated. "I do believe he loved Molly, but I also think he would have been pleased that she'd married you now. I didn't stand up to the Reese boys, partly, I think, because I felt that Molly had betrayed Henry by marrying you. What you said, it made me think about what Henry would have done and what he would have wanted. He wouldn't have wanted this. I'm sorry. You can count on our support from now. You have my word. We should go. Shall we take the cheese and butter with us now, or will you bring it tomorrow morning?"

Daniel looked to Molly.

"Daniel will bring it tomorrow. It will be awkward for you to carry."

Mrs Spencer nodded, then took her leave of all present and she and Sarah went on their way, leaving Daniel to sit down to his food once again, far lighter in spirit than he had felt the first time.

CHAPTER 15

William took the letter from the table and began to read. He was the first down to breakfast so for the time being was undisturbed.

Cochrane's Farm
Pierceton
Indiana
April 1867

Dear William,

I hope this letter finds you well. Things are, for the time being a little easier here. Our wonderful Molly never ceases to amaze me. Her idea for sales of our dairy goods has worked. It is a little over three months since we began to put the plan into action and more people are buying our cheese than ever they were before.

Folks seem to have completely forgotten the things which were being said and now oddly speak of it as being better quality, so much so that we have been able to price it a little higher and still sell all we can spare. Mrs Spencer has reported back to us what customers to the store are saying and we are happy to hear it.

Ben has settled into his cabin as though it has always been his home and I'm mighty glad to have him here…

"Good morning, William."
William had been so engrossed in the letter that he had

not heard Miss Ellie enter the breakfast room and he started slightly. "Ah, Miss Ellie, good morning. I was just…" He raised the letter so she could see who it was from.

"And how are those Reese boys, might I ask?"

"Spitting tacks, I'll not wonder, if what Daniel writes is anything to go by." He grinned. "My sister takes some beating and at the moment she seems to have them under control."

"Those boys won't give up easily, but if all's quiet for now that can only be a good thing. And what about your own plans, William? How are they coming on?"

William groaned. "I don't rightly know where to start, if truth be told. Everyone seems to tell me I'm awfully young and need to get experience and standing in the community. It strikes me, by the time I get that experience I'll have lost all the energy I have now."

As William was talking Pa had entered the breakfast room to join them.

"We'll make a president out of you yet," Pa said and clapped William on the shoulder. "You're not yet twenty-four years of age, I think we can do something to get you on the ladder. You've got a few weeks until you can make your first speech here and who knows where that will lead."

William sighed. "On that note, sir, would you mind running through what I'm going to say this evening?"

"Why of course. The more you practice, the more it will sound as though you're saying it for the first time."

"I know, sir, so you remind me for the court work we do. The better I know my facts the harder it will be to wrong-foot me. I have listened, sir, it's just…" William trailed off looking for the right words in addressing his father.

"...hard to know where to start?" his father offered.

"Yes, sir. Indeed so."

Pa nodded. "In my experience, the beginning is pretty much the only place to start. I shall be out of the office most of today, but we can get together this evening when we're both home."

"Thank you, sir." William was grateful for having such a good tutor as Pa and was determined to make the most of the learning.

The weeks passed quickly until William was due to address the Republican meeting in the town.

Ma brushed the shoulder of William's jacket. "I've never been so proud of you."

He looked at his reflection in the hall mirror. His collar felt more starched and the shirt appeared more starkly white. It all served to make William stand taller and with greater dignity.

"Ready?" Pa's face showed as much pride as Ma's, but William knew better than to expect him to say as much. Pa would give his verdict later after the speech had been delivered.

He took one final look in the mirror and nodded. "Ready."

The time for practising was over. Pa had gone over his speech with him so many times that William hoped he would not have to refer to his notes.

All that Pa had taught him was echoing around William's head.

He remembered the excitement he'd felt when called on to make the impromptu speech to the women in Iowa City. It had definitely been easier without any advance warning. This time he had had the chance to prepare and he knew what it was he wanted to say. He wondered why Pa had never followed this route when he clearly knew so much about it. When William asked, Pa had said that the courtroom was as big an audience as he needed. All that William was learning now would stand him in good stead in the courts, whether he succeeded in politics or not.

Over the last few months Pa had introduced William to as many of the great and the good of Dowagiac as he could find the opportunity for and included William increasingly in his legal meetings. Neither one of them expected the Party to adopt William as a candidate just yet, but it was certainly time for him to start making an impression.

When they walked into the hall in which the meeting was to take place, William felt a rush of excitement. He took his seat at the front, alongside the other speakers and looked back to where Pa had found an empty chair three rows behind. As he turned, William smiled at the difference in the audience he faced today. There was not a single woman in the room. Instead of an atmosphere of excited anticipation this room seemed to be filled with self-satisfaction and success. He gave a wry smile to Pa. It was quite possible that his speech might take them a little by surprise and he wondered for a moment if this was the wrong place for him to be.

When William's turn came, he took a deep breath, rose from his seat and walked tall as he approached the rostrum. Once there he looked not at the faces before him, but as Pa had taught him, slightly over their heads so he caught no one's eye.

"Fellow citizens of Dowagiac." The room was quiet except for a little shuffling and William knew that if it stayed that way it would mean he'd held his audience. "I stand before you today with the honour of telling you how I would serve you if you select me as your candidate…"

He spoke well for the next few minutes, outlining what he believed and what he would stand for. He was relieved to find that the audience did stay with him. Eventually, he brought his speech to a close. "…and so, whilst I am younger than the other candidates, I would bring an energy and determination that will not be found wanting. I do believe I can bring about many improvements for our town and for the state as a whole. Thank you, gentlemen."

He returned to his seat to the sound of indulgent applause. There was none of the vibrancy of the meeting in Iowa, none of the glowing faces hoping for a better tomorrow. His speech could only be described as a success and yet he felt deflated. He had an overwhelming feeling that these were not men who wanted a young, dynamic representative. What they really wanted was people who looked just like them.

Afterwards, talking with Pa, many of their acquaintances clapped him on the shoulder and offered words of encouragement for the future, but there were few present who seemed to want anything other than the status quo. The impression William got as he stood there was that anything beyond small steps of progress would be rebuffed. They liked things the way they were. It suited their ends and he would be welcome to represent them only when he'd matured and fallen into line with their stagnation.

"You did a good job," Pa said once they were away from the hall.

"Thank you, sir." William was glad for Pa's praise but disappointed by the reaction of the others present. "Sir?"

"Yes, William?"

"You could have done a mighty fine job going into politics."

Pa laughed. "Thank you, William. Like you, I thought I could change this country of ours. When I was young, I wanted to stand up for what was just, and what was right. I learned one thing early on, it takes a lot of determination and courage not to give up. It takes money and connections too and back then I didn't have a whole lot of either of those. I stood up for the things I could change along the way, but I couldn't do much about the big things. If my money and the connections I've built can help you to do the things I couldn't do then Ma and I will be mighty proud to support you, every step of the way."

William turned to him, blinking slightly as he did so. "Thank you, sir. I shall make you and Ma very proud."

"We already are, son. We already are."

That night William sat down to write the events of the day to Cecilia. He wanted nothing more than to see her again, but the distance to Iowa made that difficult.

He looked at the blank sheet of paper and held the pen ready. He considered what to say for so long that, when he came to begin, the ink had dried and he needed to dip the nib in the ink pot once more. This time he started as soon as his pen was ready.

My dearest Cecilia,

My speech went as well as I could have hoped for, but the reception was disappointing. I do believe that the gentlemen present wish for no more to change than they feel they can control.

He looked out of the window and across to the ridge. He thought about what Pa had said about being prepared to give financial support if that were required and made a decision.

I am determined to use my life for good and to make this a fairer society. It will not be an easy job and not one I shall wish to do alone…

Once he had finished writing, he folded the letter carefully and put it into an envelope which he neatly addressed to Miss Cecilia Hendry. He then put the letter down and went in search of Pa.

William knocked on the door of his father's study.

"Sir, can I ask your advice?"

Pa sat back and smiled. He looked almost as though he had been expecting the interruption.

William was not entirely sure where to start. "I believe, sir, if I am to follow the career we have talked about, that it would be better for me to do so with a wife by my side."

Pa steepled his fingers and looked thoughtful, but remained silent.

"I know that when I was walking out with Congressman Makepeace's daughter, you thought she would make a good match for me and I wonder now, sir, if you have a view on what I should do?"

As William had been silent for a little time, Pa asked him a question. "Are you asking my opinion of who you should choose, or my blessing to ask someone you have already chosen?"

William felt uncomfortable. "I… well… If I had married Jeanie, sir, it would have been better for me entering into politics wouldn't it?"

Pa nodded but said nothing.

Eventually William came to the point. "Sir, I'd like to

ask Cecilia Hendry to be my wife. I don't know that she'll accept me, but I think I love her, sir. The thing is, though, that it won't help me to win support for being selected."

"Sometimes, William, the support you need is having the right person at home. No one knows the Hendrys here and so it won't add to your connections. However, if you are happy and she encourages you in what you want to do, that may be worth more than any connections would be."

"May I have your permission to ask her then, sir?"

"You may indeed, William. I've heard a little of the family from Ma and Miss Ellie and I think she sounds a good choice. She's very independent though, William, so you mustn't be too disappointed if she has other plans."

"Thank you, sir. May I arrange to travel to Iowa to ask her?"

"Indeed, you may, William. Indeed, you may."

William returned to his room and carefully took the letter out of the envelope. He added a brief paragraph to the end to say he would be travelling to Iowa shortly and would let her know when he would arrive.

When William went down for dinner later that day, it was clear that Pa had made both Ma and Miss Ellie aware of his intent.

"William," Miss Ellie paused appearing to choose her words carefully. "It's a mighty long way from Iowa City to Dowagiac."

"Yes, ma'am I know, but I will take several days over the journey."

Miss Ellie coughed. "I know you will, but that wasn't the point I was making. The thing is," she paused and looked pensive. "The thing is, William, Miss Hendry may not want to move so far away from her home. She is already involved in politics herself in Iowa City and may not want to leave what she is helping her mother to build there."

William frowned. It had not occurred to him that Cecilia might want to stay in Iowa City, but now that Miss Ellie mentioned it, the possibility seemed very real. "Surely, ma'am, she could get involved in the women's movement here in Dowagiac? You've said yourself there is plenty of work to be done."

"And so there is," Ma spoke gently as she joined the conversation. "However, do you think that you might move to Iowa City if that's what she prefers?"

Ma looked anxious as she asked and William wasn't sure if she was suggesting he should think that or was worried that he might already have that thought. He got up from the table and walked across to the window to look out. Wasn't it always women who did the moving? He knew Daniel had moved, but that was different. He did that for work and for the courts, not for Molly. In his heart he knew that Daniel would have moved for Molly, if that was what she wanted and began to wonder what he should say to Miss Hendry. He was spared the opportunity to discuss the matter further when Pa came in to dinner and he needed to return to the table. He was certainly going to have to do some serious thinking.

CHAPTER 16

The train journey to Iowa gave William plenty of time to think. He wasn't like Daniel. Of course, he was happy for Cecilia to continue working for the women's movement if they married, but he couldn't just stand in the background supporting her. He needed to achieve his own ambitions. If that meant they couldn't be together, then sadly there was nothing else he could do. It did seem unreasonable, when he thought about it logically, to even ask her to give up what she had in Iowa City to move to Michigan. He began to think of turning around, of not asking the question. But what if she were to say yes? If she did, he knew he'd do everything in his power to support her in her choice and to make her glad she'd made it. He sighed and looked out at the passing countryside. How much had changed for him over the last twenty years. He knew only too well how hard it was to move.

He had arranged lodgings away from the Hendrys' house, even though he had received a note by return saying that Mr and Mrs Hendry would be delighted for him to stay with them. He couldn't help but think if Cecilia refused him that it would be better to be elsewhere.

William was tired from several days of travelling and by the time the train pulled in to the station at Iowa he was looking forward to a wash and a rest. He dropped the carriage window and looked out onto the platform. As Cecilia came into view his heart leapt. She looked utterly beautiful in her long pale blue dress, standing demurely waiting. He could see the gentle smile which played across her lips and hoped more than anything that she would have him. As he waited to open the door, his tiredness left him and he had the urge to run to her and swing her around. The thought of it made him smile as he realised the more open emotions of his street days still lay so close to the surface.

Once he alighted from the train and the porter had taken down his bags, he went to Cecilia and took her hand and kissed it. He could feel the grin which spread so wide across his face and simply looked at her in wonder.

Cecilia in return looked shyly at him. Gone was the feisty look of fire, for only a moment, and instead she was just a girl. He wondered if that were a good or bad sign, but had little time to decide before her mother stepped forward to greet him and he had to try to form a coherent sentence in acknowledgement.

As he stuttered out polite replies to enquiries about his journey he tried to continue to gaze at Cecilia and every so often caught her returning the look.

The carriage took them to William's lodgings and he agreed that he would wash and change and then join them that evening for supper. As he watched them move away, he wanted to run after the carriage to keep Cecilia in his sight. If she did refuse him because of not wanting to move, then leaving again would be far harder than he had realised. For the first time ever, he thought of his mother's wooden rosary which now hung above the fireplace in Molly's home and wished he could be holding it. "Maybe you were right, Mammy," he muttered as he shook his head and proceeded to his room.

William's palms were clammy as he walked to the

Hendrys' house. He was more anxious to ask Dr Hendry's permission than he was to ask Cecilia for her hand. It took him only five minutes to walk from where he was staying, but that was long enough for his mouth to have become dry and his thoughts confused.

"Now, William, do tell us of what is happening in Dowagiac and how your speech went last month." Mrs Hendry took his arm and led him through to the sitting room.

There was no sign of Dr Hendry and suddenly William feared he might be out on a call.

"It went well, Ma'am, though I have a lot to learn. I did rather feel like the new boy, but I have at least made a start. Before I say too much, I must bring you greetings from Ma and Miss Ellie. They are longing to hear of the progress being made here. They asked me to give you this letter." He handed over the letter that Miss Ellie had entrusted to him. "I'm guessing they feared I would forget to tell you all the details of their work."

"Thank you." Mrs Hendry took the letter and picked up a letter opener from the table to slit the envelope. She took it out and began to read. As she did so she got up and went over to the window. William presumed the light would be better there. He turned to Cecilia. "And how is the work here going?"

Before she had chance to answer, Mrs Hendry smiled at him warmly and said, "Would you excuse me a moment, I need to see if Dr Hendry is home yet?" And she left the room, leaving William and Cecilia alone.

William sighed. If only he could ask her now before his courage failed him, but he knew he had to do this all the right way around. He realised Cecilia had begun to answer the question he had asked and turned back to give her his full attention.

"It's so hard. Even when people listen and agree, no change seems to come about. How can we change the way things are when we cannot even vote for those who make the laws?"

"Though it seems unfair," William said, "I guess you have to work through those of us men who agree and will support your goals. I know from my own speech the other day, how little most people want to see change brought about. They like what they have and are fearful of losing it."

They continued to discuss their views on the politics of the land and what steps could be taken to bring about some alterations. It was only when they came to a natural pause in the conversation and Mrs Hendry spoke that William was even aware she had returned to the room. "William, my husband is in the library and wondered if you might be available to talk with him?"

William jumped up. He had not been expecting that. He struggled to find words. Of course, he had been preparing to ask to speak with Dr Hendry but had thought he had a little time to build up to it. "Yes, ma'am. Now, ma'am?" He felt confused and flustered. "Where is the library?" Although he had been to the Hendrys' home a few times, he had never wandered unaccompanied and wasn't completely sure of the layout.

"I'll show you." While Mrs Hendry's voice was matter-of-fact, she spoke kindly and he hoped perhaps his approach would be well received. He took a deep breath and followed her from the room. As he left, he turned back and looked at Cecilia who looked almost shyly in his direction.

"Close the door, William. Come and take a seat." Dr

Hendry got up to shake his hand, then indicated the second of the tall backed leather chairs for William to sit in.

It was a light airy room, and William had enjoyed the time he'd been able to spend in it previously, searching out books on politics and American history to learn what he could when he was here last. As he waited for Dr Hendry to speak, he looked around at the beautifully bound books. These books had been purchased for their content and were arranged by subject around the shelves. Their spines differed in size and were not arranged merely for their aesthetic effect around the room. William wished that he was here now to read rather than to talk to Dr Hendry.

As the older man didn't speak, William began, "You wished to see me, sir?"

"Well, of course I do, but I rather thought that you wished to see me, William?" He looked meaningfully at William and he felt himself blushing.

"I did, sir. I mean, I do, sir, but how did you...?" Then it began to dawn on William that Miss Ellie had not written purely to update Mrs Hendry on the work they were doing in Pierceton. He looked quizzically at the doctor. "Did Miss Ellie...?"

Dr Hendry grinned and looked innocently at him.

William took a deep breath and rose from his chair. He paced across the room and then back to stand in front of Dr Hendry. He didn't know what to do with his hands as he spoke and first put them behind his back and then tried to hold them by his sides, but started nervously fiddling with his cuff.

"The thing is, sir..." He took another deep breath. "The thing is, since I left here a while ago, I've found I can do nothing but think of your daughter. I long for her letters. I hang on every word she writes." He felt slightly foolish saying all of this to her father but knew not how else to commence if he were to convince the man. "Well, the truth is… what I'm trying to say is… I've never met anyone like your daughter. I admire her. She inspires me and… I think I love her, sir." It had been easier talking to a large audience than talking to this one man. "With your permission, sir, I would like to ask Cecilia if she feels the same way and, indeed, to ask her to be my wife." He paused wondering if he'd said enough.

Dr Hendry merely sat quietly, nodding to himself rather than in answer and William waited. The doctor didn't speak for what felt to William like a very long time.

Eventually Dr Hendry began. "Cecilia is our only child. We've brought her up to believe she can do anything. We have given her an education so that she can do as she chooses. What would you give her, William?"

William felt as though he were answering a riddle rather than asking for Cecilia's hand. Then in his mind he pictured Cecilia and the fire in her eyes when she spoke with passion about something in which she believed and he began to understand. "Sir, I would give her the support and freedom to be the person she wants to be. I would protect her and care for her, but I would not prevent her from being her own person. Sir, I have watched your daughter and I would never want her to stop being the person she is now. I hope the models you may see in my parents and in my own dear sister may convince you of that."

Dr Hendry nodded but said nothing.

William waited. He didn't feel that he should say more, but he didn't know what to do in the silence. He shifted to his other foot and tried to stay as still as possible.

Eventually, Dr Hendry rose from his chair and went across to the window. It was dark outside, so even though he appeared to look out he couldn't possibly see what was in the garden. Dr Henry continued to face the window as he began to speak quite quietly. "If Cecilia accepts your proposal, would you move here if that is what she wanted? And if she moved to live with you in Dowagiac, would you bring her here often to spend time with us?" He sounded sad. "Her mother would miss her dreadfully."

William felt winded. Dr Hendry was giving him permission. He wasn't saying no. William wanted to dance around the room and his agitation made standing still almost impossible. "Why, of course, Cecilia and I would need to discuss where we live, sir. If she moves to Dowagiac not only do I promise to bring her to visit as often as we can, but I hope too that you might be able to visit us on occasions."

"With my work, that is hard, but perhaps her mother..." His words trailed off and he waved a hand to his side. "You should go back to the others, William. Ask her with my blessing."

William wanted to shake Dr Hendry by the hand. "Thank you, sir," he said, but realised the other man needed to be alone so he repeated, "Thank you, sir," and slipped quietly from the room.

CHAPTER 17

William took a few deep breaths once he closed the study door. All his nagging doubts lurked in the dark corners of his mind as he stood in the hallway. Was he really good enough for Cecilia? He remembered how Congressman Makepeace had sneered when he had found out about William's background and how Jeanie had so coldly broken off their engagement. Perhaps they were right, but then Dr Hendry knew all that had happened in William's life, even the worst of it, and he had given William his blessing.

What if Cecilia didn't feel the same way? William's heart was pounding and he tried to slow his breathing to take back a little control of his body, which was clearly ready to run. He thought of his talk with Pa before leaving Dowagiac and took bolder strides back to the parlour. He didn't need to ask Cecilia immediately. He could wait a while.

When he opened the door, he saw Cecilia sitting reading a journal. Her hair was bathed in sunlight from the window and William simply stood and gazed at her.

"Is everything all right?" She looked up from her reading with concern etched on her face.

He nodded mutely.

"My mother has stepped out for a while. Won't you come and keep a poor girl company?"

It was then William noticed that the journal Cecilia was

holding was the wrong way around and he frowned. Then he realised, that Cecilia may already be aware of his intentions and that it might not be a coincidence that Mrs Hendry was absent. For a moment it felt like he was the only one on the outside of a secret and he was not sure whether to laugh or simply turn around and leave. Then he thought of Molly and Daniel and how happy they were together and he knew more than anything he wanted Cecilia in his life.

He went across and knelt in front of her, pretending not to notice the magazine. Much like any speech, he'd been rehearsing what he wanted to say in his mind and now, before his courage failed him entirely, he needed to get the words out. "Cecilia, since the first time I met you I have been in awe of your knowledge, your intelligence and, of course, your beauty. I know I am in no way worthy of you. I am but a poor soul by comparison. However, with you by my side, I know I can be a better person. I want to work for change in this country. I want to live in a place that sees everyone as equal and gives them the opportunity to reach their potential. Oh Cecilia, I know I'm not saying it very well, but would you do me the very great honour of being my wife?"

Cecilia tenderly touched his cheek and he felt a thrill run through him, but she said nothing. As he waited his heart was pounding and his anxiety was growing rapidly.

Cecilia got up from where she was sitting and put the journal on the table. She went across and looked out of the window and William didn't know if he should stay on his knee or get up. He felt awkward.

Then after a few seconds she turned around and addressed him. "I had thought I should never marry. As you know, I too would like a career in law and politics. I know that is unusual for a woman, but my parents have brought me up to believe I can do anything. I did not think I could find a man who could share those dreams with me and who would want what I wanted. I could not marry a man who thought to indulge my whims as though they were simply a gentle humour to him. I think, I could marry if I found a man who believed in me as much as he did in himself and could truly see me as his equal, no matter that others may mock him for it." She knelt down in front of him, so they were on the same level. "Tell me honestly, William, in your heart, can you be that man?"

William broke into a broad smile. He was so grateful for the questions that both Pa and Miss Ellie had asked him when he spoke of his intention. It had given him time to think about the implications of a marriage on an equal footing and he felt prepared to answer.

"I do believe I can. I may need you to keep me on the straight and narrow once in a while, but with your help I could do anything. I dare say my sister Molly would have something to say if that were not how I treated you. Dearest Cecilia, will you accept me? Oh, but before you do, I must ask you, where would you want to live? No, don't answer that, if you will be my wife, I do believe I could live anywhere you chose, even here in Iowa if that were your heart's desire."

Cecilia was both laughing and crying now. "You silly man, I don't mind where we live as long as we decide it together. Yes, yes, I'll be your wife."

William's hands were trembling as he took Cecilia's hands in his. He gently raised them to his lips and kissed them. Then sat back on his heels and looked at his bride to be, shaking his head in wonder that she had accepted him.

CHAPTER 18

O Father, o Father, I've got me a man
And he is the one I would wed if I can
As handsome as ever in leather did stand
For my kiss in the morning early
A Kiss in the Morning Early - Traditional

"Daniel." Molly looked over at her husband who was sitting the other side of the kitchen.

He raised his eyes from the basket he was trying to repair.

"How would you feel about going to Iowa?" She looked at him intently.

His eyes widened. Iowa was a place he had never planned to return to. "Ww… why?" Even the thought of it had made him go cold.

Molly smiled. "I'm sorry, I didn't mean to startle you. This would be a good visit." She handed over the letter she'd been reading which was addressed to them both.

Daniel realised it was in William's hand and scanned past the initial greetings and pleasantries until he got to the part to which Molly was referring. He put the basket down, stood up and ran a hand through his hair. "Best Man, me! But I can't hope to dress like William and…"

Molly rested her hand on his arm. "It's not your clothing that William wants. It's you. You are the best man he could have to support him when he marries Cecilia. Oh, do let me read the letter again." She reached out to take it from him.

"Come, sit," he said. "Let's read it together."

I travelled to Iowa City for the sole purpose of asking Cecilia for her hand. I am delighted to say she has accepted me and I could not be more happy. Asking her father's permission turned out to be more difficult than asking Cecilia herself. However, even there, Miss Ellie had already interceded on my behalf and I was a little surprised to find the gentleman quite prepared.

I asked Cecilia later that same evening, before I lost all my courage. Although she had not had a communication from Miss Ellie, I suspect she had guessed the reason for my visit and was eager to hear what I had to say. I did ask if she was prepared to move to live with me here in Dowagiac, or wherever else my new-found political career might need me to be, and I was mighty relieved to find she was. It is more than any man could hope for. In turn I have promised faithfully to support her in continuing to work for the women's movement and do believe that she will make a formidable team with Miss Ellie and my own dear Ma.

The wedding will take place in her home town in three months' time. If I have worked it right, harvest should be complete and winter not yet setting in. It is my sincerest wish that you should both be present and that Daniel might stand as my Best Man. Pa says he will happily meet all the costs of your travelling comfortably and will make the arrangements from here if you agree. I hope we can arrange the journey so that for the most part we can travel together. I think as her father is the local doctor it may be a grand affair with many guests on the side of my darling bride.

Please reply to me at your earliest opportunity...

Molly had tears running down her cheeks when Daniel

looked at her. "Oh, Molly, of course we'll go."

"It's not that." Molly was sobbing now.

"Whatever is it?" Daniel stood up and drew Molly to him. "We can organise the farm being run while we're away. If necessary, I'll stay and you can go."

"It's not the farm, Daniel. It's me. I'm pregnant."

Daniel broke into the widest smile. "But that's wonderful news." He hesitated, seeing that Molly still looked distressed. "Isn't it? Is something wrong?"

Molly shook her head and tears splashed away from her cheeks. She looked up into his face and his heart flipped.

"I'm scared, Daniel. What if something happens and we lose this one as well?" She cast her eyes down and stroked her hand across her still-flat tummy. "I couldn't bear it."

He wrapped his arms around her as he tried to think what to say. He held her, listening to the gentle tick of the mantle clock almost as though it were the baby's own heartbeat. "We won't lose this one. I will wrap you up in muslin like a special cheese and care for you every day. No one is going to take this child away from us." He hoped his words were true. He certainly felt a steely determination, but of course he couldn't know what really lay ahead. He knelt down in front of her and put his ear to her tummy. He looked up at Molly and smiled. "She says she'll be strong like her own dear Mammy."

"Oh, Daniel, do you think it will be a girl?"

"I hope so, for you, my dearest Molly. And I will love her every bit as much as I love her mother." He got up from where he was kneeling and went over to the kitchen table. He plucked one tiny yellow bloom from the vase which stood there, then came back and gently tucked it into Molly's hair. "I used to love to see the meadows around Killarney with their yellow flowers. One day, I will sit her on my knee and tell her all I can remember of the old days and the land we came from." He laughed. "I'll tell her the tales of leprechauns that my Uncle Patrick used to tell to me and I'll take her out into the fields to see if we can find any as far away from their homeland as we are." He had tears in his own eyes now as he gently tucked a stray strand of Molly's hair behind her ear. "You're going to make a wonderful mother, Molly Reilly. But first, we've a wedding to prepare for." He kissed her lightly on the nose. "Shall we wait to tell our news to the others until we can do so in person?"

Molly smiled as she dried her remaining tears and nodded. "Thank you," she said simply and squeezed his hand.

That evening they set to planning how they could arrange things so that it would be possible to be away for the wedding.

"We'll need James to help again as long as he's prepared to," Molly said jotting down some notes. "Do you think the Reese boys will cause them trouble while we're gone?"

"They've been quiet for a while now, perhaps things have turned a corner. I think Mrs Spencer has been as good as her word and that certainly helps."

"Maybe," Molly said thoughtfully.

Daniel sighed. Like Molly, deep down he feared their problems weren't over yet and knew they had to stay alert, but going to William's wedding was something they both wanted to do, Reese boys or no Reese boys.

The following day, Daniel walked around the whole farm with both Ben and James, talking about what would need to be done as they went.

"Never you mind, Daniel. This farm ran like clockwork when Miss Ellie went with Molly and I'll see to it that it does just the same now. I've Ben, Duke and Junior to help this time as well. And, if I'm honest, I've rather missed it." James grinned and lifted Junior up off the ground, his tail circling like a windmill. He looked into the little dog's eyes. "Though keeping him out of the chickens might be half the work."

They all laughed and continued over to the dairy. Ben had been learning some of the dairy work and was to cover much of that for them. He didn't like being idle, but was happier to be indoors rather than out in the fields. Whilst he didn't have Molly's dexterity, he had a flair for cheese making that more than compensated for it.

"If I could have my time over, I'd have me a little dairy farm of my own, or maybe just a cow or two. I've never been so happy as I am making butter and cheese and I'd never have thought on it if Molly hadn't asked." He shook his head in wonder. "So, don't you go a-worrying Daniel. We'll do you proud, won't we boys?" The dogs yapped as if in response.

"We've just harvest to get through first and I'm sure Molly's mind will be as much on what happened to little Michael as it will be on the farm itself." Daniel shrugged his shoulders, trying to keep his own emotions in check. "At least with…" He stopped himself, remembering that they weren't planning to tell anyone about the baby until they could break the news to Miss Ellie and William in person. Molly hadn't even told Sarah, which he was quite sure would cause annoyance on Sarah's part.

The weeks of harvest passed in a blur of activity. From

dawn to dusk there was work to do outdoors and, once that was complete, there was paperwork to be kept up with as well. Daniel tried hard not to fuss over Molly, but he was desperate to make sure nothing untoward happened during this pregnancy.

"If I promise not to climb up the haystack will you just stop thinking I can't do anything?" Molly stood with her hands on her hips and a broad smile across her face. "I'm fine, Daniel, really I am. In fact, I've never felt better."

He looked at Molly's face, tanned and healthy. She always looked amazing to him, but maybe now she did have a certain glow that was hard to define. "Just promise me…"

"Daniel, trust me! You know how I felt about us losing Michael. I don't ever want something like that to happen again. This baby is worth more to me than that. Our baby. Our child." And she grinned so widely that Daniel couldn't help but take her in his arms and very gently start a jig.

Molly laughed. "Now will you stop enjoying yourself, Daniel Flynn. There's work to be done." She handed him a basket and turned him around back toward the orchard.

Eventually the work was finished. Thankfully it had been a good year and would go a little way to make up for the loss of the hay the previous autumn and the cost they had had as a result. As they had gathered this year's hay Molly had arranged for more distance to be left between the stacks. Whilst it wouldn't be certain of preventing a repeat of what had happened, it would go some way to ensuring such a disaster could be contained.

"What do you think?" Molly said, standing back and inspecting their handiwork. She still held a pitchfork in her hand. Her face was stained with dirt and sweat and strands of her hair were falling down from under her cap.

Daniel looked at her carefully. "Honestly? I don't think you've ever looked more beautiful than you do right now."

"I meant the hay." She showed mock exasperation, but her laughter gave away her delight at what he'd said.

They walked up to the house, hand in hand, each carrying a fork in their other hand as they went.

"You two look like some strange warriors about to go into battle," Ben said as he came out of the dairy.

"Going to Iowa feels a lot like going into battle." Daniel held his fork aloft. "Wish us well."

CHAPTER 19

Guide me, O thou great Jehovah,
Pilgrim through this barren land;
I am weak, but thou art mighty;
Hold me with thy powerful hand;
Guide Me, O Thou Great Jehovah - William Williams - 1700s

It was a very different Iowa that Daniel returned to than the one he'd left. Although he was now a man and soon, God willing that this child should live, would be a father again, he still had flashbacks to the orphan boy he had been, tired, dirty and afraid, who first alighted the train at Iowa City. This time he had Molly by his side and was accompanied by Miss Ellie, William and Mr and Mrs Dixon. They made a fine party as they waited for the porter to bring their luggage. Dr and Mrs Hendry, along with Cecilia, were waiting for them on the platform. William rushed forward to greet his fiancée. Daniel smiled and squeezed Molly's hand. He hoped that William would be as happy with his bride as Daniel himself was with Molly.

It was Miss Ellie who took charge of their little group, and made the introductions to Dr and Mrs Hendry, while the young lovers were busy engrossed in plans for the wedding. Mr and Mrs Dixon were to stay with the Hendrys; the rest of the party would stay in nearby lodgings.

There were two days until the nuptials and Daniel was

determined to make the most of them. Cecilia was occupied with preparations, so William was free to spend the time with Daniel and Molly in looking around Iowa City.

"In all the years I lived here, I saw virtually nothing of the place," Daniel said by way of explanation. "I was taken straight from the train to the children's home, where I stayed until I was taken out to Hawksworth's farm. When I next came to the city, I was imprisoned as soon as they found me. Then from the courtroom we left by train the next day. I was here for ten years and I don't know a single road name. Except for our lodgings I've never visited any place here as a free man."

"Oh, Daniel." Molly put her hand to her mouth. "I'd never thought."

"I'm fine. I don't feel sorry for myself. I was just saying how strange it is." He squeezed Molly's hand.

"Where would you like to start?" William asked. "I don't know many places myself."

Daniel broke into a broad smile. "I'd like to visit Mrs Hawksworth. I think I owe her a debt of gratitude."

It was William's turn to smile. "That one is already arranged. She's coming to Cecilia's house for tea this afternoon. Of course, she'll be at the wedding too, but then I think most people in the town have been invited."

Daniel felt a shock wave run through him. "Not quite everyone I hope?"

"Well…" said William, but he was clearly teasing Daniel.

Daniel laughed. "I'm glad to see you haven't changed completely." He turned to Molly. "I'd like to see where you stood to sing the day when Ben found you."

"I don't exactly remember, but I'm sure it will come to

me as I walk." She took his arm and began to promenade along Washington Street toward the Capitol building. Then after some time down by the river they walked back along Iowa Avenue, stopping to take in their surroundings as they did so. They took a turning here and another there, until most of the morning had passed.

"I spend all day outdoors back in Pierceton, but walking along roads is much more tiring than the fields," Molly said as they found a bench to sit on.

"You don't suppose being pregnant has something to do with it, do you?" Daniel asked, knowing she would never admit to being able to do less because of it.

By the time they called at the Hendrys' it was already early in the afternoon and Daniel felt rather more familiar with the town which had been his biding place for more of his life than any other. He would never think of it as home, but it felt better to take some positive impression of the place for the first time, dulling the stark memories that rested in his mind.

On their arrival they were shown into the sitting room to find some of the party had already arrived ahead of them. As they entered a lady who had been seated on the far side of the room rose and came eagerly toward them. She held out her hands to Daniel and after a moment of incomprehension he reached and took both her hands in his. "Oh, ma'am, am I ever pleased to see you. You saved my life." He shook his head, overcome by emotion and struggling for words.

Miss Ellie rose from her seat and came over to them. "Molly, allow me to introduce you to Mrs Hawksworth. I think she may look a little different to the last time you saw her."

Indeed she did and Daniel could only look in wonder

at the confidence and happiness which so clearly shone from her face. "I feared that life would be hard for you after what you had the courage to do, and I should like to beg your pardon if that has been the case."

"It is I who should beg your pardon, Daniel, and thank you in return. You may well have saved my life as much as I yours. Ned, that is, Mr Hawksworth, was becoming ever more violent in his tempers and there was no knowing what might have happened to me in the future. Leaving was hard. I can't say otherwise, and there were many in the town who were against me. But my sister's husband is a good man and he stood his ground in taking me in. The women who spoke against me were those who feared for their own positions and I can do no other than feel sorry for them."

"You look so changed." Daniel was still in wonder at the difference that time had wrought in his dear protector.

"As indeed do you. We've both found friends when we really needed them. Ellie and I have been writing to each other for some while now, but perhaps I should leave her to tell you of our plans."

Both Daniel and Molly looked eagerly to Miss Ellie to explain to them.

"Now, don't you youngsters go worrying that I won't be there for you when the baby comes, but it's our intention to go to a women's rally in New York and then on to Washington. What do you think?" Miss Ellie was finding it hard to contain her excitement. "I never thought I'd get to see those great cities, but now I have the opportunity. We'll be travelling together and staying in the home of a woman who is herself involved in the movement. You have no need to worry about us."

"Indeed, I will worry." Daniel looked across to

William. "There are parts of that city we know all too well and you'd be best steering clear of."

William nodded his agreement, but said nothing.

Before Daniel was able to say anything further, the door opened and a smaller version of Junior came bounding in. Cady's markings made her look as though she wore a patch over her left eye and with her pricked right ear a matching colour, she looked quite comical. Cecilia followed close behind the little dog, together with Mrs Hendry.

Cady ran straight to William and Daniel was amused to see how lost his friend looked as to what to do next. William tried to move carefully forward to greet his bride to be, with Cady all the time jumping up his leg as he tried to glide it forwards. Cecilia reached down and picked up the little dog. She held her close to William's cheek so that Cady could lick his face. Given time, Daniel was sure that William would get used to it, but for the time being he looked most uncomfortable.

Tea was served and discussion turned to the final wedding preparations. The most pressing concern being one of Dr Hendry's wealthier patients who was due to give birth anytime and who quite expected him to be present no matter his only daughter's marriage.

"I've told them the midwife will be with them throughout and I'll get there as soon as I can. I did try telling her it would be far more convenient if she could wait to have it the day after, just to be on the safe side, but I don't think she has much of a sense of humour given her reply." He laughed heartily at the reflection.

They passed the day before the wedding quietly. Daniel, William and Molly sat and talked about all that had happened in their lives while they were apart and speculated how different things might have been if they had stayed together. Every so often William would get up and pace around and make abstract statements looking for reassurance.

"What if Cecilia doesn't like Dowagiac? Do you think we should move?"

"William, it's you she's marrying, not Dowagiac. You can work out together what suits you best. And, if you're really asking, 'what if she doesn't like you?'" Molly rose and went to her brother's side. "Then how could she not? For you are the finest man she will ever find." She pecked him on the cheek. "Except for my Daniel, of course!"

The First United Methodist Church of Iowa City was an impressive building with its steeple and imposing frontage. It was certainly larger than the church in which he and Molly had married but, by all accounts, there'd be enough people attending to fill the pews. Daniel felt strange wearing a suit. He had worn one on a few occasions, including his own wedding, but whenever he did, he felt as though it was someone else's body and not his own. The collar felt stiff against his neck and he longed to be able to change back into his normal clothes. The pews were filling rapidly as he sat beside William at the front of the chapel. He checked his pockets for the ring but, as he had checked only five minutes previously, he already knew that it was there.

Daniel turned and caught Molly's eye. She was sitting next to Miss Ellie and appeared radiant. They looked so like mother and daughter sitting side by side and whispering to each other conspiratorially. Daniel could only hope that they might have a daughter of their own, so he could watch the next generation by turns.

Daniel was turning his head back to face the front when

movement at the back of the chapel caught his eye. Three men had just entered the church and Daniel froze. Surely, they had not been invited. He looked harder to ensure his eyes were not deceiving him. His mouth went dry and his mind started to churn through what to do. There entering the chapel and finding seats toward the back were Mr Hawksworth with Jed and Rick, the very men who had made his life a misery in childhood and because of whom he'd so nearly lost his liberty. Daniel breathed deeply and calmly. This wasn't his wedding, so why were they here? Surely, if it was for Mrs Hawksworth they could have found her at any time. Then a thought crossed his mind. It had been William, or more to the point his father, who had humiliated them in court.

"Excuse me a moment," he said to William. Then with trembling legs he got up and moved along the row, asking Mr Dixon if he had a moment as he did so. When they were in the aisle as far from the congregation as possible, he whispered to Mr Dixon, "Sir, I think we have a problem."

CHAPTER 20

Breathe, O breathe thy loving Spirit
into ev'ry troubled breast;
let us all in thee inherit,
let us find the promised rest:
take away the love of sinning;
Alpha and Omega be;
End of faith, as its Beginning,
set our hearts at liberty.
Love Divine All Loves Excelling - Charles Wesley - 1747

Until this point the organist had been playing background music as the chapel began to fill. There was a pause then the organist played a fanfare and began a processional, causing the members of the congregation to rise to their feet.

"Don't worry, Daniel. All will be well." Mr Dixon ushered him back to the pews and made to follow.

Daniel began along the row but turned to see that rather than take his seat Mr Dixon had gone to the front of the chapel and was speaking to the minister, their heads bowed together conspiratorially, rather than in prayer. When Mr Dixon moved away the minister nodded. Of whatever nature, clearly an agreement had been reached.

Daniel took a deep breath and looked at William. The groom's head was turned toward the back of the church, straining for a first view of his bride. Daniel felt relieved that William knew nothing of the conversations which had just taken place.

Cecilia looked beautiful as Dr Hendry walked beside her to join William at the front of the church. They stood at the centre of the aisle with the minister before them. Daniel smiled, pleased to find Dr Hendry had not been called away as he'd feared.

When the music came to a close, the minister invited the congregation to be seated and began the ceremony.

"Dearly beloved, we are gathered here to witness the union of William Dixon and Cecilia Hendry in matrimony. This is of course a cause for celebration. I believe we may have present someone who has come without respect for the solemnity of the occasion, although I may of course be mistaken as to his purpose. Sir," he looked out into the congregation toward the back of the church but did not say the name. "If I am mistaken and you are here to support this young couple then I invite you to come to the front to read for us from the Holy Scriptures. If, however, that is not your intent, I would ask you to leave quietly during the singing of our first hymn. This is the House of God and I'm sure you will not mind if our ushers today guide you to the exit in a peaceful manner."

There were murmurs and whispers around the congregation and William looked to Daniel with confusion in his eyes. Daniel smiled reassuringly, although he didn't really feel the smile and hoped that William was convinced.

As the organist began to play and led the congregation into their first hymn, Daniel continued to face the front and could only hope that nothing untoward would occur. As the hymn drew to a close, he felt a draft from the outside as the front doors had been opened and then closed and hoped that it signified good news.

Daniel continued to feel on edge as the service continued. He wished the minister did not need to ask if anyone present knew of a reason the couple should not marry. He knew there was no such reason, but he feared that would be when Hawksworth would make any move. The silence when the question was asked seemed to go on forever and Daniel could feel his heart pounding. The smile on the minister's face looked forced and artificial and in truth he did move forward with the ceremony as soon as was respectful to the law. Daniel sighed. Disaster had been averted. William's wedding would be without incident.

"…I now pronounce you husband and wife."

Daniel wanted to cheer, his relief was so in need of venting. As the happy couple began their walk out of the chapel as newlyweds, Daniel turned to shake Mr Dixon by the hand, before himself being ushered to follow the groom he was standing for. The rest of the congregation were waiting for Daniel and the bridesmaids to follow before themselves joining the procession out of the church. Daniel was only a few seconds behind William and Cecilia, but that was long enough for him to hear the scream ahead of him from just outside the church.

Daniel, together with others in the congregation, broke into a run to the door. As he came out into the daylight the smell greeted him faster than the sight. As he registered the stench of manure, a barely recognisable William thrust a filthy jacket at Daniel and began to run along the road after the departing Hawksworth.

Mrs Hendry and Miss Ellie had reached Cecilia who had muck dripping from her hair and down her dress. They were doing their best to lead her from the bustle while Mrs Hawksworth was wringing her hands and being comforted by Mrs Dixon.

Daniel wondered if he should run after William, though he was uncertain whether he should be joining the action or holding him back. What had surprised Daniel was to see how close to the surface the street fighter still was in his friend. He hoped no harm would come to him, but there was only one of him and Hawksworth had Jed and Rick.

The congregation dispersed rapidly. He assumed many would make their way straight to the reception and wait there for further news. He only hoped that the bride could be comforted and made to look presentable in time.

"Shall I take that?" Mr Dixon was standing at Daniel's shoulder, looking at the jacket. "I don't think he'll be wanting to put that back on today." He laughed, but his face was etched with worry. "Did you see where they went?"

"Not really, sir. When I came out everything was all happening so quickly. They went along Dubuque Street, but I didn't see anything more than that. I should have gone after him." Daniel cast his eyes down.

"No," Mr Dixon said firmly. "You most certainly should not have gone after him. We can't afford you to get into trouble with the courts here again. Let's hope William saw sense as well."

"Daniel, where's William?" Molly was looking around her as she spoke. "He should be comforting Cecilia."

Daniel took a deep breath. "I'm sure he'll be back soon. He…" He looked to Mr Dixon for guidance as to what to say.

Mr Dixon smiled. "I think Molly can probably work it out for herself, you've no need to protect William. He's always had a bit of a hot head." He turned to Molly. "He's gone after Mr Hawksworth."

"Oh, mercy me. I don't think we should tell Cecilia that. She'll be wondering what kind of man she's married. I'll try to keep her distracted and get her into some clean clothes." Molly went off with her usual calm efficiency and left Daniel and Mr Dixon to worry about William.

"We'd be best to go back to the lodgings. He'll have to go back there for some clean clothes before going on to the reception." Mr Dixon hesitated before adding, "If he's run into any difficulties I'm sure he'll send word there rather than direct to the Hendrys'."

Daniel nodded. It was a very strange ending to the first part of the festivities and one they were unlikely to forget. He hoped that William's marriage would improve from this point.

Notes had been sent between the Hendrys' residence where Cecilia was waiting anxiously, the reception, where guests were celebrating regardless, and the lodgings where Daniel and Mr Dixon waited patiently, but there was no news from William. When word did come, to the lodgings as Mr Dixon had suspected, it had not been written by William himself.

George Dixon esq.

Dear sir,
Your attendance is requested at the courthouse immediately, where Mr William Dixon is being held on a charge of assault…

It said little more. Mr Dixon sat down heavily. "Now what do I tell the ladies?"

"Sir, would it help if I were to go to deliver the news to

them in person? I'd rather not come to the courthouse, if it's all the same to you." Daniel shifted uncomfortably at the prospect.

That at least brought a smile to Mr Dixon's face. "Yes, perhaps if you speak with Dr Hendry, he might be best placed to tell his wife and daughter."

"Yes, sir. I will." Daniel got up to go while Mr Dixon gathered the pile of clean clothes that were waiting for William.

"I'll take these with me. It might be best for him to have something clean to wear when he sees the sheriff!"

They parted on the doorstep and Daniel made haste to the Hendrys' residence. What he had not thought was that they might be watching from the window in case someone were to come to the house and it was Cecilia herself who came to the door. Her face was red from crying, although at least now thankfully clean of manure and her hair had been redressed.

"Is there news?"

Daniel was loath to tell Cecilia of the note, but was never comfortable to give anything but an honest answer. "Ma'am there is, but I am tasked with speaking with your father first, if he is at home."

Cecilia looked at Daniel with steely determination. "However bad the news may be, there is nothing you may need to say to my father that you cannot say to me."

Daniel, though taken aback, thought of Molly and realised that what she was saying was true. Then seeing her face realised she may think far worse had occurred. "Oh, Miss Hendry, please let me assure you, as far as I know he is quite well. May I come in and speak with both of you?"

Cecilia looked at least a little relieved and nodded

before leading Daniel through to the library where her father was sitting at a small table writing. "Papa, Daniel is here with news of William, but wishes to speak with both of us."

Dr Hendry rose and almost skipped across the room to join them. "Come in, come in. Now, what do we know?"

Daniel took a deep breath. His hands were shaking. "Sir, ma'am, William is being held at the courthouse on a charge of assault. His father has gone to him at the sheriff's request."

"Well has he now?" Dr Hendry gave a hearty laugh.

Daniel was rather taken aback. "Sir, I…"

"Oh, don't worry about me, Daniel. Come, Cecilia, we'll have this sorted in no time. Fetch my coat and tell your Mama we're going to see the sheriff's wife."

Without further explanation he returned to his desk and began writing another note. Daniel followed Cecilia out of the room and went to join the others in the sitting room to wait for whatever was going to happen next.

"I suspect I might know what's going on," Mrs Hendry said when her husband and daughter had left. "Sometimes being a respected doctor can have its benefits."

The others looked at her eagerly waiting for her to explain, but instead she went in search of tea.

Another hour went by and they received word that the guests had by turns left the reception, giving up waiting for their hosts arriving.

"Well, it can't be helped in the circumstances," was Mrs Hendry's rather matter of fact response. "I don't suppose the young people will feel much like joining strangers now in any case."

It was shortly afterwards when they heard the front door open and close and Dr Hendry and Mr Dixon came in.

"William has gone to wash. He'll be fine," he said to Mrs Dixon who in turn let out a long breath of relief.

Dr Hendry's eyes were positively twinkling. "It seems we fathers have our uses. The patient of mine who expects me at the birth at a moment's notice is the sister-in-law of the sheriff. Thankfully his wife made him see the sense of releasing my newly wedded son-in-law when George and I explained how the situation had come about. I just hope it's an easy birth or we may all be in trouble!" He laughed heartily and everyone joined in.

The laughter stopped shortly afterwards when the door opened and William came in sporting a black eye and walking very carefully with his left arm held close against his body.

"Oh, my poor boy." Mrs Dixon was up and by his side in an instant.

William grinned. "It's all right, Ma, I've my own darling wife to take care of me now and thank God she's forgiven my first act of stupidity." He paused as they once again broke into relieved laughter, then added ruefully, "I have had to promise never to do anything like this again." Then he reached across and took Cecilia's hand in his good right one. "Now, I'm really rather hungry. Is there anything for dinner?"

Mrs Hendry rang the bell and it wasn't long before they were all seated in the dining room.

They had barely had time to make themselves comfortable when a note was brought in to Dr Hendry. He read it and got up from the table. "I'm sorry, ladies, gentlemen, but you're going to have to excuse me, it seems the baby is ready to put in an appearance and I can't very well say that I'm too busy, all things considered. Let's just

hope that it's not a long labour. Goodnight to you all."
Then he left the room and the rather odd party had to
continue without him.

CHAPTER 21

Cecilia smiled at William and he thought he would be happy to simply sit and look at her for the rest of his life.

"Why don't you tell us all exactly what happened from the time you came out of church with me?" Cecilia gently touched his hand to prompt him to begin the story. "And don't leave anything out. There is no point trying to spare the feelings of someone who has had manure thrown at them today."

She laughed heartily and William marvelled at how any girl could take so well such a dreadful end to her wedding day.

Before he began, Mrs Hendry sighed. "I don't think any of us had been looking forward to the reception quite as much as we might have been. That's one of the problems of being one of the town's 'great and good', dear Herbert felt he had to invite so many people that we wouldn't normally spend time with. If I'm really being truthful, a meal with family is much more what I would have liked in the first place."

"And now we have it, Mama," Cecilia said grinning. "Go on, William, tell us everything."

"I don't rightly know where to start." William scratched his head.

"Then begin with the point we came out of church."

He nodded as he began to order his thoughts. "Well, when I realised what they had done to you, my darling, my anger took over. No matter that I was covered in manure. I've known worse in life, but you should never have to know such things and I should be there to protect you from it, not be the cause. I guess I've still got the temper to go with the hair colour." He grinned ruefully.

"I have to say, madam." He turned to Mrs Hawksworth. "Mr Hawksworth can run awfully fast for a man of his years, if you'll pardon me for making a comment on age?"

"Happen he's a deal to be running from," Mrs Hawksworth replied with a resigned look on her face.

"Yes." William smiled. "I dare say he has. As I ran after them, I wasn't really thinking about the fact there were three of them and only one of me. That thought only became apparent after I'd thrown a punch at Hawksworth himself and found my arms being caught afterwards by the other two, Rick and Jed, did you say they're called? Anyway, it was they who laid into me, rather than Hawksworth."

"They're always the ones to do his dirty work, except where Daniel and I were concerned." Mrs Hawksworth cast her eyes down and Miss Ellie reached across and put her hand on that of Mrs Hawksworth.

William moved on, nodding as he did so. "As it turned out, I was rather fortunate that one of the sheriff's men was nearby and stopped the incident before they'd done me any real harm. If you can excuse the black eye and the other bruising." He grimaced. "Unfortunately, all the man had seen was me throwing the first punch, so he was more concerned that I was the aggressor and not at all interested in what might have been the cause. Given I'm not local, the sheriff himself wasn't mightily interested until your father became involved." He squeezed Cecilia's hand.

"Thankfully, while you women might not have the vote, the sheriff, at the very least, is still ready to listen to his wife." He chuckled. "Once she explained my relationship to Dr Hendry and how her sister was in need of his services, everything was resolved remarkably quickly and he even apologised for the inconvenience."

Cecilia kissed his cheek and William felt himself blush.

"I think he was probably glad to get the smell out of the offices if truth be known. It's amazing how manure can permeate an area, but I guess you'd know that with working on a farm." He turned to Molly and Daniel. "And that's it really. I don't think there is much more I can say."

"Do you think that Mr Hawksworth will cause any more trouble?" Cecilia looked anxiously from William to her mother.

"If I know Ned, you won't hear anything more. Not for your parents anyway, and you will be out of town." Mrs Hawksworth shook her head. "I don't think he'd come after me again now either, there'd be too many people looking out for it."

Mr Dixon nodded. "The sheriff, when he heard the whole tale did rather see things in a different light and I think he might be looking out for any opportunity to, shall we say, redress the balance. He says he'll bring Hawksworth in, but without witnesses who'll testify he doesn't suppose he'll get far."

The meal progressed and the conversation became lighter, turning to Cecilia's move to Dowagiac and how she would continue to work with Mrs Dixon there.

After a while William got up. "I know this is the point that the bride and groom would normally retire from the party to begin their life together, but in fact, it's been a very tiring day and, if you will beg our pardon, I rather think I need to get some rest." He was aware of the smiles and looks which passed around the table and each in turn rose and bid them a good night.

As he and Cecilia headed towards the stairs and the pain in his ribs reasserted itself, for the first time that day, William really did wish he hadn't acted in such haste earlier, even if his wife had completely forgiven him.

CHAPTER 22

I was wearing corduroy breeches
Digging ditches, pulling switches
Dodging pitches, as I was
Working on the railway
Paddy Worked on the Railway - Traditional approx. 1850s

The following day Daniel and Molly rose early. They had said their farewells to William and Cecilia the night before and would today begin their travels back to Pierceton, sharing the first part of the journey with Mr and Mrs Dixon, Miss Ellie and Mrs Hawksworth.

"After the events of yesterday, I shouldn't wonder that Mrs Hawksworth wants some time away from this place," Daniel said as he put the last of his things together to be taken to the station. It suddenly struck him as odd to be traveling with so many belongings, though in truth he'd brought precious little with him compared to the others.

"Do you think she'll come back to Pierceton to visit the farm when they're done with their grand tour?" Molly asked, sitting on the bed to tie her boot. "I do hope she does. It would be welcome to have them both around for the birth."

Daniel knelt before her and took over the tying, so she didn't have to bend. The baby was just beginning to get in the way, but Molly would never complain or ask for help. "I don't know which I'm looking forward to seeing the most when we get back, the farm or Junior. It's a shame we didn't bring him to see his sister. Cady is a sweet little thing. She's used to a little more refinement than our Junior."

Molly laughed. "It was funny seeing William's reaction yesterday. His days living rough aren't buried quite as deeply as he'd have everyone believe. I do hope Cecilia will love the whole of him and not just the gentleman he's become."

"Well, she strikes me as a no-nonsense sort of woman, but I guess only time will tell." He held out his hand to Molly to pull her to her feet, then carried their bags down to the waiting carriage.

The journey was Mrs Hawksworth's first long-distance travel and her eager anticipation reminded Daniel of the wonder of it all. As the whistle blew and the smoke billowed back across the engine Mrs Hawksworth clapped her hands like an excited child. They had several days of travel ahead, but those early stages passed quickly.

"I believe Ned was arrested last evening, some while after William came home," Mrs Hawksworth said as they talked about the unusual events of the previous day. "I suppose once William and Cecilia have moved away there'll be no one to speak against him, which seems a shame. I'm guessing no one else was outside to see the... incident."

"Daniel and I were too late to see anything," Mr Dixon said. "Though I'd be more than happy to support William if he chose to go back to testify against the man."

"I don't suppose he will," said Miss Ellie. "If he's got any sense, he'll look to the future rather than the past. He won't want to make the lives of Cecilia's parents any more difficult than they could be."

"No, indeed. They seem delightful people, if a little eccentric now and again." Mrs Dixon smiled at some recollection.

Daniel was thankful to see Iowa City slipping away behind the train and this time could think of no reason why he would ever return to the place. He guessed William would need to go back, on visits to family, but that was something he and Molly need not be part of.

Mr and Mrs Dixon parted company with the rest of the travellers just south of Lake Michigan, while Miss Ellie and Mrs Hawksworth decided to spend a few days with Molly and Daniel in Pierceton before continuing their journey to New York.

When they were alone together in the evening, Molly said, "Do you think we've left everything in order? Will Miss Ellie be happy with the farm?"

"Molly, she gave it to you. If I know your guardian, she'll expect you to make some changes. Besides, James will have kept her informed of what's been going on, I'll be bound."

Ben was waiting at the station with the cart and Junior was bouncing around with sheer abandon. Daniel picked the little fellow up and was licked thoroughly for his trouble. "Where's Duke?" Daniel asked, looking around for the old dog.

Ben sighed heavily. "He's not so good. He had a turn on the night you left and he's not been the same since. If it was my guess, I'd say he's waiting to say his goodbyes."

Daniel stiffened. Duke had carried him through many a bad time on Hawksworth's farm. He owed that dog a great deal. He nodded to Ben but could not find any words.

When they did eventually arrive at the farm, Miss Ellie

had tears in her eyes. "Oh, don't you mind me. I'm just being a silly old woman. It's so long since I've been here, I'd forgotten what it felt like to be at home."

They all met in the kitchen of the farmhouse that evening; Mrs Hawksworth and Ben talking about times back in Iowa City, both clearly a little homesick. Molly, Miss Ellie and James went over the farm's books and talked about the times since Miss Ellie had left for Dowagiac. Daniel and Junior sat on the hearth, either side of Duke who lay almost motionless as Daniel gently cradled his head.

When time for sleeping came, Ben left quietly with James, leaving Duke in Daniel's care. Daniel made a bed up on the floor next to the old dog and fell asleep with his arm curled gently over Duke's chest.

That was how Molly found them at first light, Daniel with tears running down his cheeks and his arm still around Duke's lifeless body.

"He waited for me," was all Daniel could say between his tears. "He waited for me."

Once Daniel was washed and dressed, he went to find Ben to select the best place to dig a grave for Duke. Junior was at his heels, but shared their quiet and sombre mood. He did not dance around Daniel's feet or chase any birds which passed by. Once Duke was buried, close by Ben's cabin, Daniel returned to the farmhouse for breakfast.

Normally, it would have been a pleasure to show Miss Ellie and Mrs Hawksworth around the farm but, that day, nothing felt right to Daniel and he could think only of Duke. By the afternoon he was pleased that the women went into town and he was able to throw himself wholeheartedly into working. He wanted to lose himself in tiredness and labour as he had done in his darkest days with Hawksworth. By nightfall, Daniel was ready to sleep and whilst Junior would normally sleep downstairs in the kitchen, Daniel made no complaint when the little dog quietly followed him and curled up as close to his master as he could be.

The following day brought a short note from William, together with a cutting from the Iowa City Republican reporting the strange events of his wedding day and indicating that no charges were to be brought. William finished his note by concluding,

...Cecilia is now quite recovered, although she says she will need to revise her plans for using her dress on any future occasion, unless she turns her hand to farm work.

We will be returning to Dowagiac in the next few days and will be moving to live in a small house neighbouring Ma and Pa. It is their wedding gift to us and we look forward to making it our home.

Your ever-loving brother

William

It was a further couple of days before Miss Ellie and Mrs Hawksworth continued their journey to New York.

"We need to get on before any snow starts," Miss Ellie said as she got the last of her things together. "I don't suppose those trains are all that warm in winter." She raised a blanket that she'd kept separate. "I'm prepared for almost anything."

Mrs Hawksworth was similarly prepared and their bags were loaded into the cart.

"Now don't you go worrying about me, my girl. We're staying with a respectable family in New York and will be well away from the areas that Daniel has warned us about.

We'll watch out for any rogues and pickpockets. We've a good idea what goes on, you've all made sure of that." Miss Ellie took Mrs Hawksworth's arm. "Now come on, Liza, we've a train to catch and an adventure to go on."

Daniel felt a twinge of sadness that they too could not go to visit New York again, now that their circumstances were so different. He wrapped his arms around his wife and held her to him as they waved goodbye to the adventurers.

"Do you think they'll make it back in time for the baby?" Molly asked anxiously, wiping away a tear.

"I think that probably depends on whether the baby waits its time. I can't see them being back very soon if they still plan to travel on to Washington." He brushed Molly's hair away from her face. "You'll be fine. I know it would be good to have Miss Ellie here, but I'm sure Mrs Spencer and Sarah will take care of you if she's not. Besides, I've helped the cow when she was in calf and it can't be very different." He grinned and Molly broke into a broad smile.

"Daniel Flynn, you always were an old romantic," and she knocked him playfully on the arm.

Over the next few weeks Daniel and Molly settled into a routine on the farm. In the quiet moments Daniel would often spend an hour or two down at Ben's cabin with Junior contentedly at his feet. He also spent time at Duke's grave, remembering what the dog had meant to him. The wildflowers he occasionally left were as much for his parents, who had no graves, as for the little dog himself.

"I'm surprised we've heard no more of the Reese boys," Daniel said to Ben one afternoon.

"Happen they'll be back sooner or later. James heard they'd had a good year, so maybe they ain't so bitter as they were. I like to think me coming made a difference, but I suspect it was more this little fellow than me." Ben scratched behind Junior's ear. "He'd nip their ankles the minute he knew they were about, if they came up here when he was around."

Daniel nodded. He wanted to think the problems were in the past, but he'd lived around bullies too long to expect them to change. At best they'd be laying in to someone else, and at worst they'd be back. Molly always looked for the good in folks and had relaxed more than he was willing to do.

"What's the news from the travellers?" Ben was always keen to hear what they were doing, as much for his affection for Mrs Hawksworth as for any other.

"Nothing new, since last week. They've a rally to attend and then they're moving on to Washington. I think they hope to be there for the Christmas time."

Ben nodded sagely. "I'd be looking for somewhere warmer if I had the chance to travel at this time of year. Mind, I'm probably happier here than I would have been in the south of our country. Life might have been hard, but at least I've been free."

By Christmas Molly was needing to slow down a little and rest. There were still a few weeks until the baby was due, but by the end of a day she was ready to put her feet up. Miss Ellie and Liza Hawksworth had moved on to Washington and were enjoying the sights as much as they had done in New York, whilst at the same time attending meetings of the women's movement and getting involved where they could.

Christmas on the farm was quiet with no need for casual labourers in addition to their normal farmhands. Despite that, for Daniel it was one of the happiest he could remember. They had put up a few decorations which brightened the house during these darker days.

"Now close your eyes, Daniel Flynn." Molly was grinning broadly after breakfast on Christmas morning.

"And why would I want to do that when I need to be going outside to fetch something in?" Daniel was longing to see Molly's reaction to the present he had for her.

"Because I'm going first, so I am."

Molly's look of determination made Daniel smile and he did as she had bid him.

"Now hold out your hands."

He followed her instruction and felt something very soft placed into them. When he opened his eyes resting across his arms was a jumper which Molly had knitted in secret, in the softest wool that Daniel had ever owned. On top of the folded jumper was a much smaller one which matched it perfectly, but was the right shape and size for Junior. Daniel broke into a broad smile. "It's wonderful, but shouldn't you be giving this to the little fellow?"

Daniel went over to where Junior was lying and held it up against him. "I do believe he'd say it was just his colour." He went over and kissed Molly. "Now it's my turn."

Whilst Molly stood waiting in the kitchen he went out of the door and across to the barn. Carefully, he removed the sacking he'd laid over the top of the gift, so she wouldn't see it even if she had gone in there and carried Molly's present back to the house.

"Right, you can look now," he said putting his handiwork down in front of her.

"Oh, Daniel, it's beautiful." Molly ran her hands over the crib.

Daniel had made the bed out of an old tree. He'd spent

many hours making every edge smooth and bringing out the beauty of the wood.

"When did you have time to do all this?" Molly asked him.

"Probably at the same time you were knitting these." He put his arms through the sleeves of the jumper and pulled it on. "It fits perfectly. Thank you."

On many of the evenings James and Ben sat with them in the farmhouse, a quiet and contemplative group, each happy with his own thoughts, but enjoying the companionship the others afforded.

"Sing for us, Daniel," Molly said one such evening. "It's been a long time since we listened to you sing. Sing songs of the old country, though it's long faded in my mind."

Daniel wished that his Uncle Patrick was there to play the fiddle and for a moment wondered if there were any way to contact his family back in Ireland. He knew nothing of post to such far off places and wondered if it were even possible. He took up the words of an old favourite song and in his head, he heard his father's voice once again as he sang.

I've been a wild rover for many's the year,
And I spent all me money on whiskey and beer.
And now I'm returning with gold in great store,
And I never will play the wild rover no more.

It was funny hearing Ben and James joining in the chorus sounding almost Irish as they did so and, as odd as the group was, it felt like a family to Daniel.

CHAPTER 23

Daughters of freedom arise in your might!
March to the watchwords Justice and Right!
Why will ye slumber? wake, O wake!
Lo! on your legions light doth break!
Daughters of Freedom, Ballot be Yours - Edwin Christie - 1871

"Do you think this is wise?" Molly asked, passing the latest letter from Miss Ellie to Daniel.

Daniel took it and read through from the beginning to the end before looking up at her in surprise. "Surely, Miss Ellie won't get involved in that, will she? Being part of the American Equal Rights Association is one thing, but protesting at the White House…"

"I've known her long enough not to be surprised by what she does, but if you are going to demonstrate for any length of time, surely it would be better to wait for the warmer weather. I suppose it's not happening for another couple of weeks so maybe it won't be so bad." Molly was clearly worried about her guardian. "Do you think she's doing the right thing?"

Molly looked out of the window and Daniel joined her, watching the snow falling.

"Maybe the weather is better in Washington, but even so." He read the letter through again and shook his head. "She hasn't said if she plans to be back for the baby."

"No," Molly said, looking sad. "There are only another

four weeks to go if baby's on time, but I don't suppose it will be." She rested her hand on her bulging clothes. "In his or her own time."

The weather was still cold three weeks later. Molly was now more than ready for the baby to make an appearance, but they needed to be patient. Daniel had been with the chickens when Molly came into the yard shouting.

"Daniel! Daniel!"

He dropped the meal and ran, surely the baby must be coming. When he got to Molly, she was red-faced and waving something towards him.

"Have your waters broken? Shouldn't you be inside? Shall I send for Mrs Spencer?" He began trying to bustle her towards the house.

"Daniel," Molly said very firmly. "It's not the baby."

He took a few moments to register what she'd said. His heart was pounding and his mind was busily running through all that needed to be done. He stopped suddenly. "What did you say?"

"I said, it's not the baby. It's Miss Ellie."

He could tell by the look on Molly's face it was something serious and, as his breathing slowly began to return to normal, he took the piece of paper from her hand. It was not in Miss Ellie's handwriting which confused him and his first thought was that she must be ill. He turned to the back and found it had been written by Liza Hawksworth, then nodded and turned the page back over and began to read.

It is with regret I must write to tell you things have not gone well for us since we have been here in Washington. There has been an unfortunate incident when Ellie, together with some of the local ladies, were protesting outside the White House. I was unwell and could not be with them that day. I don't know now whether things might have been different had I been there, or whether I would be in the same difficulties.

Anyway, there was a misunderstanding over the actions they were taking and where they were at the time. They are now awaiting trial and are being confined without bail. I have written to Mr Dixon, but I do not think he will be able to attend on this occasion. The Association does have its own representation locally and I am trusting they will take care of Ellie's best interests as well as their own local members. It is a worrying time for us all and I cannot do anything but stay here in Washington whilst I await what is to happen.

I will send you news as soon as I have some.
Your humble servant

Liza Hawksworth.

"This can't be," Daniel sat heavily leaning against a water barrel. "Whatever are we to do?"

"I don't suppose there's anything much we can do. I can write to Mr Dixon for his advice, but we can only trust that she's in good hands. Oh, what was she thinking?" Molly burst into sudden tears and Daniel quickly got up and went to her.

"Are you thinking of the baby coming and her not being here?" he asked as he encircled her with his arms.

"I don't rightly know what I'm thinking," Molly replied, gulping back the tears. "I'm frightened for her. She's so far from family and oh, what if anything were to happen to her?"

Ben came out of the dairy as they were heading back to the house. "And what's the cause of all this?" He asked as Junior tried to jump up and lick wherever he could reach on Molly.

"Miss Ellie's been arrested for protesting at the White House. Why couldn't she just have stayed at home?" Molly's tears began again.

Ben stopped and took hold of her arms in a most uncharacteristic manner. "Now just you look at me one minute, girl."

Molly's sobbing stopped abruptly and both she and Daniel looked at Ben in surprise.

Once he had their attention he continued, "She didn't stop at home because she believes that the likes of you and me should be fairly treated. You don't want a lifetime of being bossed by people like them Reese boys. She don't want a world where you don't get a say because you're a woman and I don't get a say because I'm black."

Daniel had never seen Ben so passionate about anything.

"She ain't doing it because she's selfish. She's doing it because she's brave and angry and she's doing it for you and me. I knows you understand that. You gave me a home and a retirement because you believe in everyone being equal, so don't you go complaining because she's not home with us." He let go of Molly's arms and looked embarrassed. "I'm sorry, I spoke out of turn, but..."

Molly looked at Ben and laughed. "No. No you didn't speak out of turn. You spoke what needed saying and you're right. I'm sorry. It's just..." She waved in the general direction of her enlarged waistline. "Now," she said with her more normal resolution, "what can we be doing to help her?"

Both Molly and Ben turned to Daniel and he felt himself blushing. "I guess that look is because I'm the one who knows how it feels to be in prison."

Molly nodded.

"Well, the two things that meant most to me were the food that people sent down to me and…" he paused remembering and then in an unsteady voice said, "the rosary that belonged to your mother. It told me that you were there for me and I hadn't been forgotten."

Before Daniel was able to say another word, Molly had marched to the farmhouse and by the time he and Ben could get through the door she was already reaching up above the fireplace to take the rough-hewn wooden rosary down from the wall.

"Molly, we've no way to get it to her. It's too big for a letter." Daniel went to support his wife, so she didn't fall back from where she was reaching somewhat off-balance.

"Then I'll take it. I brought it to you and I'll take it to Miss Ellie."

The determination in her voice alarmed Daniel. "But you could give birth at any time. You're in no position to go anywhere." However important this was to Molly, Daniel couldn't see an answer. He certainly didn't want to be away from her when her time came.

Ben was hovering in the doorway. "Missie, if you'll let me, I'll go for you. Miss Ellie's doing this for me as much as she is for you."

Molly turned, a spark of determination in her eyes as she got down from the hearth and marched across to the tin on the shelf the other side of the room. She took some money from it and thrust it toward Ben. "Please do. Take as much as you can carry from the general store for her to go with it."

"Are you sure, Ben? It won't be an easy journey and the weather is not good." Daniel was worried for his friend and wondered if the risks were worth it.

Ben smiled his gap-toothed grin. "I was a little envious of the ladies having all the adventures. Happen it's my turn to go a little way."

"Maybe James could go with you?" Daniel said, thinking it best that Ben didn't travel alone. Besides, Miss Ellie was James's kin and it may need that to get anything to her in the jail in Washington.

Ben nodded. "I'd best be on my way." He wrapped his hand tight around the rosary and looked toward Molly. "We'll be safe with this to protect us. Don't you be worrying."

There'd be more work for Daniel to do with both Ben and James away, even though the pair of them were supposed to be retired. He just hoped that the baby was late in coming, although he realised that Molly's discomfort meant she hoped the reverse.

Daniel went with Ben and James into town to put together the parcel they would take to Miss Ellie and to see them off on the train. Their first stop was the store where Mrs Spencer and Joseph were both bustling around restocking shelves.

"Why the need for all of this?" Mrs Spencer asked as they rang the odd assortment through the till.

Daniel prepared to give a bland reply but Ben in his excitement beat him to it.

"I'll be taking them to Miss Ellie in Washington. She's been arrested fighting for what's right."

"What?" Mrs Spencer was evidently shocked.

As far as Daniel knew, Molly had never made her friend aware of Miss Ellie's earlier arrest in Dowagiac and thought it best to keep it that way. He saw Joseph move closer so he could hear Ben.

"They were protesting outside the White House.

Standing up for equal rights for the likes of you and me," Ben said to Mrs Spencer.

"Oh, Lord have mercy, whatever was she doing that for?" Mrs Spencer was clearly shocked by the very idea.

Ben's face took on a steely resolution. "Because it's the right thing to do and she's brave enough to do it." He said nothing further, but picked up the bundle of goods, nodded to Mrs Spencer and made his way to the door.

Daniel followed behind, without a word.

"They wouldn't know what was right if it jumped out and bit them," Ben grumbled as they set off for the station.

CHAPTER 24

"Shoo." Molly ushered Daniel out of her way. "I'm fine, I am quite capable of working in here for a while. Junior will keep an eye on me. Besides, I like the dairy work. There's something very calming about it. You've enough to do with Ben and James away without fussing over me. Really, I feel on top of the world." She thought that might be a bit of an exaggeration, given the baby was now a little late and was getting in the way of everything she tried to do, but there were errands to run in town and Daniel needed to go to do them. Besides, she was only another animal doing what came naturally, or so she tried to tell herself.

A week or so had gone by and they'd received word by letter that James and Ben had reached Washington. However, they were as yet unable to deliver their package to Miss Ellie. Molly was certainly anxious for further news, but would have to wait for Mrs Hawksworth to write again.

Molly was just cleaning up after butter making when she felt the early contractions starting. From all she'd been told there would be plenty of time yet until baby appeared. She took a few deep breaths until the contraction passed and continued with her work. By the time all was done in the dairy the intervals between the contractions were already starting to reduce and Molly had to hold herself up against the bench as a wave of pain swept over her.

'Back to the house for you, my girl.' She smiled,

realising that the voice in her head was that of Miss Ellie. She might not be able to be there in person, but years of living with her common sense had had a great impact on Molly.

As she crossed the yard her waters broke and she stopped and took a breath or two as she thought about what needed to be done. Daniel wasn't back yet and there was no way for her to get help. She tried calling out to the bunkhouse in the hope that one of the regular workers might be around, but received no reply. She decided to get herself inside and make what preparations she could, hoping above all else that Daniel would soon be back.

She ran through in her head all the things that she had been aware of when Michael had been born. She shuddered at the recollection and wished the rosary were with her now for the comfort it might give. She crossed herself as she went into the kitchen.

Moving about the kitchen was hard work. The contractions were coming more often and all she really wanted to do was curl up with the pain. Each time she took a few deep breaths and then tried to focus on what she needed to do. She managed to get two large pans of water onto the stove and found the pile of towels that she had left neatly ready. She was just considering trying to carry things upstairs when a contraction came that was so strong she could do nothing by lie down on the kitchen floor exactly where she was.

By now her face was beading with sweat and the contractions were much closer together. There was no time for further preparations, this baby was coming into the world now and it was doing so right here in the kitchen. As the next contraction overwhelmed her body Molly let out an involuntary scream. No one was near enough to the farmhouse to hear it and, as the pain rolled away, she wondered how difficult it would be to do this on her own. Her heart was racing and blood was pounding in her ears as she tried to take slow, steady and deep breaths. She thought she heard horses' hooves, but couldn't be sure it wasn't just her own pulse in her ears again. She continued breathing steadily until another wave of contractions overwhelmed her.

This time as she screamed she could have sworn she heard an answering shout of, "Molly!" And prayed she might be right. She tried to steady her breathing once again as the sweat dripped from her face. Her hair, released as it was from her bonnet, clung around her.

The kitchen door flew open and crashed against the cabinet behind it at the same time as the next contraction came and Molly screamed once again. This time she knew the voice was real, Daniel was by her side and clutching her hand.

"Molly, I'm here."

He looked alert and ready to deal with anything and Molly thanked God for his presence.

"I need to get help, stay calm. I'll send one of the hands. The horse is already out, they can go straight away." He squeezed her hand gently.

"Don't go," Molly almost shouted as another contraction came.

"I've never done this before, Molly, at least not for a human. If something goes wrong we're going to need help. I'm only running to the bunkhouse." He squeezed her hand again and ran out of the kitchen before she had the chance to protest further.

"Daniel don't g… AARGGHHH!" The frequency of the contractions meant that Molly knew the baby wasn't going to be waiting much longer. She lay panting on the kitchen floor, thinking hard about when the cows last calved. She could do this. Daniel could do this. They'd be fine. She tried to steady her breathing and at the same time felt the overwhelming urge to push. Then she lay back and waited for whatever would happen next.

In what seemed like both moments and hours at the same time, Daniel was back by her side. As she lay panting he put down the pails of water and placed a cushion beneath her head. When she screamed he was at her side holding her hand and she gripped tightly as she pushed. Then lay back to try to keep her breathing deep and even.

Daniel mopped her face with a cloth and spoke gentle words of encouragement to her. She was so glad to have him close.

This time the contraction was overwhelming and she pushed as hard as she could.

"It's coming, I can see the head. Thank God it's the right way around. We can do this Molly."

The waves of contractions continued and Molly pushed for all she was worth, then miraculously, she heard a tiny cry and felt the overwhelming relief of knowing her baby was in the world.

Daniel was muttering to himself under his breath as he tied off the cord with some string then cut the cord separating baby from mother for the first time. Molly watched feeling both exhausted and elated at once.

"Is it a boy or a girl?" She asked quietly.

"I've no idea." Daniel laughed. "I've been so busy trying to get everything right and make sure all was well, I haven't even looked." He finished what he was doing, wrapped the infant gently in a towel and passed the baby to Molly. "Molly Flynn, I'd like you to meet our daughter."

Molly held the infant to her chest and felt tears flowing gently from her eyes. Daniel wiped them away, but then one of his own tears splashed down on her.

Daniel fetched some more cushions to prop Molly up more comfortably and a blanket to cover both her and their daughter.

"Mary," Molly said softly as the infant began to suckle for the first time and Molly felt an overwhelming rush of emotions of happiness and determination, protection and most of all love. She bent down to kiss her daughter's forehead. "Mary Flynn, welcome to the world."

She heard hooves coming into the yard and this time she knew the sound was real. She reached across with her free arm and laid it on Daniel's. "I'm glad we did this together, just you and me."

"You're amazing, Molly. You're absolutely amazing." Daniel was smiling down at her with such softness that she wanted to capture his look in her mind forever.

Again, the door flew open and Mrs Spencer and Sarah came rushing in.

"Where is she?" Mrs Spencer gasped out of breath.

Calmly, Molly looked up at her and said, "I'd like you to meet Mary. Mary, this is Mrs Spencer and Sarah."

"Oh, my Lord, whatever are you doing down there." Mrs Spencer looked pale with shock and Sarah came to her friend's side.

"Everything happened so quickly. I didn't have time to go anywhere else. Daniel helped deliver our daughter."

"You can't have men in at a birth." Mrs Spencer sounded horrified. "Whatever next? Now," she said, "I'm taking over here. Daniel, you need to leave us to it."

Molly laughed. "Daniel has been wonderful. He's been the perfect midwife."

Daniel grinned and quietly shook his head. "You need some rest and I could do with some fresh air. I won't be far away."

Molly realised he didn't want to go upsetting Mrs Spencer now she was here, and he was right, Molly did need to rest.

As Sarah and Mrs Spencer began to clean up around Molly she simply gazed down at Mary as she lay against her chest.

Molly would be stiff if she stayed here on the kitchen floor for too long, but right now she couldn't imagine getting herself up the stairs to their bedroom. She lost herself in watching Mary breathing in and out. Every breath bringing new wonder that she and Daniel had created this living being, their daughter. Molly was oblivious to all else, except Mary.

Eventually, Molly looked around her. An hour had passed. She could see the hands on the wall clock had moved around. Sarah was sitting by her side silently watching them both.

"How are you feeling?" Sarah asked.

"Surprisingly well," Molly said trying to move to be sitting up a little more.

Sarah bent down to help her and propped the cushions more tightly behind her. Then Mrs Spencer came over to join them.

"When you're ready we'll get you and the little one upstairs so you can rest properly."

Molly couldn't help but be surprised at how much clearing up Mrs Spencer had achieved while she had done no more than watch Mary. You would never know what had taken place only a short time ago. Molly looked at her baby daughter now sleeping in her arms and smiled. She didn't know such love was possible. It felt as though there was a powerful rope from her own heart to that of her daughter's, the link was so deep and so strong.

"Where's Daniel?" she asked Sarah.

"Mother will let him back in when you're changed and in bed upstairs. Until then he's been told to go about his work." Sarah grinned at her.

"But…"

"I know, but there's no arguing with Joseph's mother when she's got an idea in her head. I know when to keep quiet in this family."

A momentary look of pain seemed to pass over Sarah's face and Molly wondered whether there were things her friend didn't tell her about. She nodded, knowing not to make Sarah's life difficult.

Mrs Spencer came and took Mary from Molly and carried her upstairs ahead of them. Sarah then helped Molly to stand and followed behind as she went up to the bedroom. By the time Molly got there, Mrs Spencer had already laid Mary in her crib and was plumping up the pillows for Molly.

Sarah helped Molly to find clean clothes and change before she got into bed. Mrs Spencer meanwhile was fussing around the room, tidying things and Molly frowned.

"It's better that it's me here to help you and not Miss Cochrane. The longer she stays away the better."

Molly bristled and turned from where she was getting into bed. "I'm sorry, what did you just say?"

"You don't need her grand ideas at a time like this. What you need is someone who's had children themselves and knows how things really work."

Mrs Spencer was still moving things in the room that in

Molly's mind were not her business. Molly could feel herself becoming angry and as calmly as she could said, "I think I need to sleep now, perhaps you could leave me. I'm sure Daniel will be able to manage things if you want to go home."

Sarah looked at her and nodded. She could clearly see Molly's annoyance and began to shepherd her mother-in-law toward the door.

"I was just saying," Mrs Spencer continued, but Sarah cut in.

"Let's go and make some tea and then perhaps we should get back to the store for a while." Sarah turned to Molly looking anxious.

Molly could feel her nostrils flaring and wanted nothing more than to tell them to get out, but she bit her lip and hoped that Sarah would be successful in getting Mrs Spencer away before Molly gave her a piece of her mind. There was nothing in the world that Molly would have liked more right now than to have had Miss Ellie by her side, except perhaps still to have had her own dear Mammy.

When Molly next woke it was to hear the sound of Mary crying and to see Daniel trying to rock her gently in his arms. For a moment, Molly looked at them in wonder, before reaching her arms out to take Mary so she could feed.

Daniel came and sat next to her.

"Has that woman gone?" Molly asked.

Daniel grinned. "I presume you mean the delightful Mrs Spencer. Yes, with some persuasion from Sarah she eventually left."

"I could have…" Molly paused. "Oh, I don't know what I could have done, but I won't have her insulting

Miss Ellie in her own home, or anywhere else come to that. And how dare she send you out of the way?"

"I know my place," Daniel said grinning at her.

"But that's the point. You do know your place and your place is right here beside me and Mary." She looked down at their daughter and all her annoyance melted away. "She's just perfect, isn't she?"

"She's as beautiful as her mother is." Daniel bestowed a kiss first on his daughter and then one on Molly.

CHAPTER 25

Molly was up and working within days of Mary being born. She fashioned a sling from some cotton material and bound Mary to her chest so that her hands were free as she moved about the farm. She found herself singing the songs that Daniel so often sang, quietly and gently to soothe Mary so she slept while her mother worked. At other times when she was in the farmhouse, Mary would spend time in her crib in the kitchen with Junior stationed beneath it, ready to alert Molly at a moment's notice if Mary needed anything.

Mary was already two weeks old when they received a letter telling them that Ben and James would be back on Thursday and asking for Daniel to meet the train. The letter was short and contained no news of Miss Ellie. Molly could only wonder about her guardian and pray that she could be home soon to see her new granddaughter. She was eager for the news the two men might bring and waited anxiously for Daniel to return with them.

It was early evening when they arrived and a rare occasion on which Junior left his post. The little dog scratched madly at the door as soon as he heard the cart. Molly wondered how he could possibly know that Ben had returned, but he certainly seemed to. She opened the door and the little dog flew into the yard to greet him.

"Mary's sleeping, but there's food prepared for all of us, we could eat before she wakes," Molly said by way of greeting as the party trooped into the kitchen.

"There's something more important than food, missy." Ben grinned at her as he came in.

"A letter!" Molly gasped.

"Well, not exactly a letter as such."

Molly felt suddenly tired and disappointed.

Ben stepped aside saying, "I do hope you've prepared a lot of food."

From behind him, Miss Ellie stepped forward and Mrs Hawksworth stood in the doorway.

"Oh, Miss Ellie!" Molly rushed over and flung her arms around her guardian. "Am I ever happy to see you."

"Come now, child, you'll have me in tears if you get all emotional. I must say I'm rather pleased to be here too."

Molly could wait no longer. She took Miss Ellie's hand and led her to the crib. Gently she lifted Mary up and presented her to Miss Ellie. "I'd like you to meet your granddaughter. Mary, this is Grandma Ellie."

She turned to look at Miss Ellie who, for perhaps the only time that Molly had ever seen, had tears rolling down her cheeks as she took the baby in her arms and cradled her. Molly smiled to see Mary staring in Miss Ellie's direction and gurgling in response.

"I should have been here."

"You're here now, that's all that matters and so is Grandpa Ben." She stepped across the room and ushered Ben forward to where Miss Ellie was holding Mary and looking at her with almost as much love as Molly felt.

"I never rightly thought I'd be a granddaddy to any child when I lost Esme and Flora. I will be very happy to be granddaddy to this dear girl." He turned to look at Molly and his eyes were glistening too.

The evening passed in recounting the stories of what

had happened while they had all been away and what the women had got up to in Washington and New York. Ben and James recounted their journey with a thorough delight in having travelled to such a great city.

Once the meal was over, Daniel took the rosary and returned it to its position on the wall.

"When the guard brought that in to me, I will admit to being homesick, but grateful that you were all there for me. I don't know how poor Liza coped with all the worry and trying to get us all released." Miss Ellie thankfully seemed little affected by her own part in the ordeal.

Molly thought she might be slightly thinner, but not unduly so.

"I didn't do it all on my own." Mrs Hawksworth blushed as she spoke. "The women of the Washington association played their part."

"And Mr Taylor from what I can gather." Miss Ellie exchanged a meaningful look with Mrs Hawksworth and Molly could only guess that there might have been rather more to it, from the shade of pink on Mrs Hawksworth's face.

"And what exactly was it you were arrested for this time?" Molly asked Miss Ellie with mock exasperation.

Miss Ellie tried to look solemn, but the twinkle in her eye showed no remorse. "I might have refused to move from where I was sitting, quietly minding my own business. I wasn't alone you understand. Most of the other women took more notice of what was asked of them. I simply pretended I hadn't heard and stayed resolutely where I was. Which might have been just a little closer to the White House than they were happy with."

"You mean the steps of the house!" Mrs Hawksworth shook her head. "How she had the courage to be there, I'll never know."

"I think it was more a question of audacity than courage," said Miss Ellie breaking into a wide smile.

Spring was always a time Molly enjoyed on the farm and, with Mary growing day by day and Miss Ellie home, this one was proving a very pleasant time. She went about her work happy in the knowledge that whether Mary was with her or being looked after by her grandmother she was getting the very best of care. She looked forward to the regular breaks from her labours to feed Mary and as she walked back to the house her heart would miss a beat in the expectation of seeing her little girl.

There were even times when Daniel carried Mary around, although with his taking on the heavier work that was more difficult.

As Mary grew, Molly started to find it easier to carry the baby on her back, but Mary was still happy with the arrangement.

It was a fine afternoon and Miss Ellie and Mrs Hawksworth had walked into town leaving Molly working in the dairy. Molly was singing as she worked and couldn't imagine feeling happier. She came out and crossed the yard just as the older women were returning.

"That woman should learn to mind her own business." Miss Ellie was marching across toward the farmhouse.

"Whatever has happened now?" Molly laughed at the fury on Miss Ellie's face as she followed them, presuming some minor incident had occurred.

"How dare she? That's what I say. How dare she?"

Molly's smile faded. "Miss Ellie, who? What?"

Mrs Hawksworth shook her head to Molly, indicating she should probably leave things, but Molly now felt she needed to know.

Molly unstrapped Mary and began to feed her as Miss Ellie sat stiffly in a high-backed chair.

In clear precise words Miss Ellie began. "That Mrs Spencer. That woman. How dare she comment on my granddaughter?"

"What exactly did she say?" Molly asked as she gently cradled Mary.

"She said that you are no better than those girls in the Indian settlements who carry their babies in cradleboards as they go about their work."

Molly felt a sense of relief that it was nothing worse that had been said, but Miss Ellie wasn't finished.

"First of all, who does she think she is commenting on how you are bringing up your daughter. Secondly, what does she know about any of the Indian settlements? She isn't interested in anything outside her own backyard and she's far too interested in those things. She said… she said…"

Molly realised from the anger that whatever Miss Ellie was about to say next was probably the real heart of the problem.

"She said that you should know your place and shouldn't be running a farm and that I was no use in advising you because I'd never even been married, never mind had children."

Molly's heart sank. It was clear that Mrs Spencer had really gone too far. "Miss Ellie, there is no better counsel than you have been to me. I wouldn't choose another even if I could. Now please, take no notice of her. I'm only glad it was Daniel I married and not her older son." As she said the words, Molly realised just how true that thought was. She loved Daniel dearly and she could never have imagined being happy with Henry in the way that she and Daniel were.

Miss Ellie looked at her and in a moment of unusual emotion held her arms wide for Molly to come to her. Molly laid Mary in her crib and went to her guardian. The embrace was warm and honest, and Molly realised how much Miss Ellie had missed out on throughout her life. When Miss Ellie's arms relaxed, Molly stood back and took the older woman's hands. "Please, Miss Ellie, Mrs Spencer isn't half the woman you are. I'm very proud of all you have done and all you do now. More importantly, I could not love you more for the mother you have been to me and for all you've done for Daniel. You have become as much my mother as Mammy was and I love you just as dearly."

Miss Ellie couldn't speak, but held tight to Molly's hands and nodded.

After a length of time had passed, Miss Ellie cleared her throat. "Liza and I were thinking of going back to Dowagiac for a while. There's a rally there to organise." She grinned at Molly. "If I promise not to get arrested this time, would you mind if we were away for a few weeks? I'm loath to miss all the changes in Mary but it's her future as much as anything that we're working for."

Molly smiled at her. "Of course you must go. I'm quite sure that Mary will understand when I explain it all to her. She'll be attending rallies herself before you know it." She pecked Miss Ellie on the cheek and went to retrieve Mary from her crib.

Molly and Daniel were sad when Miss Ellie and Mrs Hawksworth moved on in their travels. "It's going to be very quiet around here without them," Molly said.

"I think you'll miss them being able to take care of Mary most, with all the farm work getting busier." Daniel

189

looked over her shoulder as she wrote up the farm's ledgers.

Molly smiled. "Grandpa Ben has asked to take over some of those duties. I don't think I've ever seen him looking so happy. He loves sitting rocking her cradle with Junior by their side."

"We really do have the luck of the Irish, with all the family we've found along the way." Daniel said and began to sing to Mary.

As I was a walking one morning in May,
I saw a sweet couple together at play…
O, the one was a fair maid so sweet and so fair,
And the other was a soldier and a brave grenadier…

"I don't want her finding any brave grenadier just yet. We've her Christening to prepare for before that."

Daniel laughed. "I'm definitely leaving that one to you. I have no idea how these things work."

"Well, I was thinking of asking Miss Ellie, Sarah and Ben to all be godparents for her. If anything ever happened to us, I know they'd take care of her."

"Well it sounds to me as though it's all worked out, which is good news. When will it be?"

"Well," said Molly, "I spoke to the minister and he says it should be a couple of months from now, in the summer. As long as you're happy then I'll go to speak to Sarah about it and then arrange the date. I'll need to write to Miss Ellie too. Will you ask Ben?"

"I'd love to ask him. He's going to be thrilled." Daniel went out of the kitchen whistling the tune of The Nightingale as he did so.

Molly took up a pen and began to make some notes on the back of an envelope. She hoped that the inclusion of

Sarah might make Mrs Spencer a little more positive about things.

CHAPTER 26

As the day was fine and warm, Molly decided to walk to see Sarah. She strapped Mary to her back and smiled as she did so, thinking of the disapproval that might bring about in Mrs Spencer. She sang quietly to Mary as she walked. By the time they arrived at the general store, Molly was starting to wish that she had brought the cart rather than walking. Mary was getting heavier all the time and Molly was more tired than she was used to being, or than she had allowed for.

The bell rang as she went into the store and Joseph came out to the counter. Molly took the opportunity to discuss the shop's order for cheese and butter before going through to the back to see her friend.

Henry Jnr was growing up fast and came running to greet Molly. He took her hand and led her through to where Sarah was sewing.

"Well look who's here!" Sarah put down her needlework and came across to welcome Molly.

As Molly unstrapped Mary, Sarah began to coo over the baby.

"Well isn't she growing into being a pretty little thing. What do you think, Henry?"

The boy ran over to view the infant. "Can she come and play outside?"

Molly laughed. "Not yet, but I'm sure she'd love to when she's a little older."

Henry seemed disappointed and soon lost interest, going out to find mischief elsewhere.

"Oh, Molly," Sarah said, her face bright with excitement. "I have such news for you. Henry is going to have a little brother or sister. What do you think?"

"That's wonderful news. He'll have a playmate of his own before we know it." Molly was glad to find her friend in such good spirits. She knew that she and Joseph had been hoping for another child for some time. "I have news for you too, though of a different kind. Daniel and I were wondering if you'd stand to be one of Mary's godparents? It's the more important to both of us for having no family of our own. "We'll ask Miss Ellie and Ben too, but you are my oldest and dearest friend and I would be honoured if you would say yes."

"Yes, yes. Why, of course I will. It will be my pleasure to do that for you. If it hadn't been for you, I wouldn't be here today and I shall always be grateful." Sarah took her handkerchief from her pocket and dabbed her eyes. "Don't mind me. Everything is setting me off at the moment."

"Oh dear, is my wife at it again. I'm guessing she's told you our news." Joseph had come through to the back from the shop.

"That's not why I'm crying." Sarah started crying again as she spoke. "Molly's asked me to be one of Mary's godparents."

Joseph frowned. "One of? Who are the others?"

"Naturally she's going to ask our guardian and then for Daniel she's asking Ben." Sarah patted the tears away once again and smiled.

"She expects you to share the role with a coon and a jailbird? I don't think so. No wife of mine will be shown up in that way. I forbid it." With that Joseph marched out of the room.

This time, Sarah's tears were not ones of joy, but were racking sobs which totally overwhelmed her.

Furious as Molly was, something in her friend's reaction prompted pity and she went to Sarah's side. She started to wonder just what Sarah's married life might be like and how much her friend wasn't telling her about. "Shhh now, it'll all be fine. You'll see." In her heart Molly didn't think for a minute that it was going to be fine, but she could think of nothing else to say to her distressed friend.

"I think you'd better leave," Sarah sobbed through her tears. "Please go. Don't say anymore."

Molly opened her mouth to reply, but closed it again. She wrapped Mary up in her shawl and carried her from the store. A flash of thought went through her mind and she thought of Mrs Hawksworth and wondered just how bad Sarah's life might be.

When Molly and Daniel wrote to Miss Ellie asking her to be godmother, they received a letter by return in reply. Molly was delighted with what it said, 'Nothing will keep me away from being there. I will return in plenty of time so that you have no need to worry that I won't be there.'

Molly had chosen not to tell Miss Ellie about Joseph's reaction and the effect it had had on Sarah. Miss Ellie was her guardian too and, although they had never been as close, she knew how much it would pain Miss Ellie to know.

Ben had of course been overjoyed to be asked and a day didn't go by when they didn't find him by Mary's side for some of the time.

It was early July when Miss Ellie returned and there

were still three weeks to go to the Christening. Mrs Hawksworth accompanied her once again and they planned to travel on to a rally in Pittsburgh shortly after that.

Molly had sent out an invite to Sarah and the whole of her family on her husband's side, but had received no reply and had had no opportunity to speak privately with her friend. She only hoped that when the christening day came Sarah and the Spencers would be present, whether or not Sarah felt able to stand as godmother.

Mary was to be christened in a beautiful lace gown, which Miss Ellie had brought out of a draw in her room. "It was the one I was christened in," she said simply to Molly. "It would be a pleasure to see it used again after all this time."

"Oh, but it's beautiful." Molly marvelled at the intricate lacework and supposed it must have been very expensive and hard to come by when Miss Ellie was a child. "Should we try it on her now?"

"I wouldn't, child. There's only so long that Mary keeps anything clean and it would be a shame for her not to look her best on the day. It is loose fitting, I'm sure it will be fine."

William had written a letter to Molly and Daniel explaining he would not be able to travel for the Christening as Cecilia was herself pregnant and he didn't want to be away from her for the length of time it would take. Molly smiled as she read it. How lovely that Mary would have a little cousin close in age. She wondered if there would be many times they would meet. She supposed there was blood family somewhere back in Ireland, but Mammy had never spoken of her own family so it would be almost impossible to find any on her side.

ROSEMARY J. KIND

Maybe Daniel's side would be easier to find, but after the passing of fifteen years she suspected that would be difficult as well.

There were a good number in the church and Molly looked around eagerly for the Spencer family. They weren't there. Daniel saw her disappointment and gently squeezed her hand. She was grateful that he understood. She still hoped they would arrive before the service started.

"She looks a picture, doesn't she?" Ben said looking down at Mary in the lace gown.

"She certainly does." Molly couldn't help but smile.

"My ma and pa would be so proud if they could see you both now," Miss Ellie said as she took her place.

As the service began, there was still no sign of Sarah and for all the joy, Molly felt a twinge of pain thinking about her friend. She hoped Sarah was well and was surprised that Miss Ellie had made no comment.

Mary was the model child throughout and positively beamed as the ceremony was completed. It was afterwards as they were all walking home that Miss Ellie said, "They're a good enough family, but some of their ideas are misguided. Tell me, child, was it because of me or Ben?"

"I hoped you might not notice." Molly didn't want to answer the question.

"Not notice?" Miss Ellie let out a deep laugh. "Sarah is just as much my ward as you are. Of course I'm going to notice. I wasn't made welcome when I tried to visit her and young Henry last week. Joseph told me they were out, but I was quite certain I could hear the voice of a child in the background."

"It was both." Molly decided honesty was the best approach. "And yes, it was Joseph who put a stop to it. It wasn't Sarah." She felt anxious to defend her friend and looked intently at Miss Ellie.

Miss Ellie nodded. "Men are much the same the world over, thinking they can control everything around them." Then they fell into silence for a while.

When they were all back at the farm, Ben asked them to walk down to his cabin with him. Although James was grinning, Molly had not the faintest idea what was going on. When they got there a sheet was blocking their view, hanging over a line between the trees. Molly was intrigued.

Ben moved in front of everyone. "James and I have been working on a little something for Mary as she grows. She's not big enough for all of it yet, but she will be in time. I hope it's all right." Then he removed the sheet to show a small swing with an enclosed seat so she wouldn't fall out and a little wooden house nearby. There was also a platform at low level in the tree and a little ladder leading up to it.

"But it's wonderful," Daniel said moving closer to look at the swing. "She really is going to have the happiest childhood of any child."

"How did you do all this without us knowing?" Molly opened the little door to the house to look inside.

"We built it all further along behind the old barn, so it was out of sight and then put it all in place in the last few days." James climbed up onto the tree platform. "It's really very safe, as long as she doesn't fall off, of course."

"Miss Ellie ordered in the things we needed which we couldn't find around the farm. We've all worked together on it. I do hope she likes it." Ben looked anxious.

"Like it? I'm sure she'll do rather more than like it. We'll never be able to get her back to the house with all this to enjoy down near the cabins." Molly went and kissed first Ben and then James on the cheeks. "Thank you both. It's wonderful. You might just find me hiding down here too. I sometimes wish I had somewhere quiet to sit and read." Molly sighed.

"I built something similar for my Flora. She loved it before she passed." Ben looked very sad as he spoke.

"Then all the more, I hope that you will enjoy every minute of watching Mary grow. She's got the best granddaddy a girl could have." It was Miss Ellie who spoke. "In fact," she continued looking at James. "I rather think she's got the best two granddaddies."

James smiled and for the first time Molly realised how much he saw them all as family now too.

CHAPTER 27

On the shore, dimly seen through the mists of the deep,
Where the foe's haughty host in dread silence reposes,
What is that which the breeze, o'er the towering steep,
As it fitfully blows, half conceals, half discloses?
The Star-Spangled Banner - Francis Scott Key - 1814

Daniel looked down from the ladder to see James with a deep frown on his face. He went down to ground level and stretched. "What's the matter?"

"I was just weighing up whether to say anything or not. It may be nothing, but I was talking to some of the men earlier." He shifted to his other foot as he spoke.

Daniel put down the basket that he was still holding. "Whatever it is, by the sounds of it we need to know."

"The Reese brothers! Ed and some of the others were in Marsh's bar last night. The Reese brothers were there."

"I'm guessing that's not the news, given they're always there." Daniel wanted James to get to the point, but he knew better than to try to rush the story.

"Ed heard them talking."

It was clear that recounting the events was making James very uneasy and Daniel wondered what was coming next.

"He heard them talking about Cochrane's Farm and saying it was time they finished the job." James looked down as he spoke. "It doesn't sound good."

"No, it doesn't. I need to talk to Molly about this. I guess crop picking can wait a while." He had been bringing in some of the peaches for jam making.

"I'll take over here." James seemed relieved to be able to help.

"Thank you. I'll be back when I've spoken to her." Daniel set off up the orchard leaving James taking the basket back up the ladder to the tree Daniel had begun picking the fruit from.

Molly was in the dairy finishing the butter making when he arrived. She was singing a lullaby as she worked.

Daniel smiled. "You do know you haven't got Mary in there, don't you?"

"I know," Molly said laughing. "She's down with Ben. I was just singing to myself. I know someone else who used to do quite a lot of that." She kissed him. "And to what do I owe a visit from my wonderful husband, when he's supposed to be gathering peaches for me?"

"We may have a problem. Apparently, the Reese brothers were heard to say it was time to finish the job. We're only just bringing the hay in, should we do anything differently? We can't afford to lose it all again."

"Are you sure they're talking about the hay? They burnt all there was to burn of that two years ago. Would they really just do the same again?" Molly cleaned her hands on her apron and went out into the sunshine as they talked. She stood looking down toward the fields and barns, surveying the farm.

"I don't know. We don't keep the corn here longer than we have to when it's picked, save what we're keeping for ourselves. Do you think they plan to destroy the crops as well? Daniel was trying to think through the possibilities.

"I don't know, but I don't like it. I'm going for a walk

to take a good look at things. Are you coming?"

Daniel nodded and they set off around the farm. Molly was silent for a while and Daniel chose not to disturb her thoughts. At intervals she stopped and turned to take in all that was around her. She did so first at the chicken coop, then behind the barns. She then walked to where the cornfields began and across the orchard to the stream and on to the cabins. It was only when they came in sight of Ben gently rocking Mary's crib that a smile broke out on her face and she began to speak.

She went to sit in the shade opposite where Ben was sitting and Daniel went to sit on the bench near his friend.

"And to what do I owe this visit in the middle of a working day? Or have you come to see Mary?" Ben looked down at Mary's sleeping form.

"It's you I've come to see while we were passing. We've been walking around the farm thinking," Molly said.

"Is this about those Reese boys?" Ben sucked on his teeth in apparent contemplation.

"James told you?" Daniel asked.

"I was there when Ed told him what went on." Ben nodded to them both.

"And what can we do?" Daniel looked first to Ben and then to Molly.

Ben grinned. "When I was a young man, I'd have said we take the fight to them, but I can't see us getting far with that one." He paused then added, "I never got very far with it when I was young neither!"

They all laughed.

"Other than having a round the clock guard I don't know what we can do," Molly said. "They could come at the farm from several directions. We've no way of knowing when or where it would be. We can stack the hay further apart, but if the wind is in the wrong direction and strong enough, that will be no barrier."

"It might just be worth setting a guard while we're storing the corn before it goes. If we lost all of that it would be a high cost to the business." Daniel wondered how easy a guard would be. Once harvest was over many of the farm hands would move on. They could perhaps pay some of them to stay on just to guard it, but the cost of that would be one they weren't expecting either.

"Junior and I could sleep down there for a week or two." Ben reached down and scratched the little dog's ears. "Couldn't we, boy?"

Junior gave a comical single bark in apparent agreement.

"I can't ask you to do that. For one thing it could be dangerous." Molly sighed loudly.

"Junior will be up and fighting at the slightest thing. I'll be fine, missy, and it won't be for long."

Molly got up and went over to the crib. "I may as well feed Mary while I'm here, then I need to get back to work. I'll think about it all some more, but it's very kind of you and I think you're right about Junior."

The little dog was sitting up ready for whatever action was required of him and Daniel couldn't help but be glad they'd got him.

Daniel headed back to the peach trees to find that James had made good progress in his absence.

"I'll take these up to the house while you get some more down," James said wiping the sweat from his brow. "Did you reach any conclusions."

"Thank you. Yes, I think so. Molly's concerned about protecting the crops until we can get them away. Ben and Junior have offered to sleep down with the corn while we're waiting to send it off to market. Well, Ben offered, I dare say that Junior would have done if he could talk."

"I'll join him. It won't be for long and I'll be as sheltered there as in the cabin." James passed an empty basket to Daniel who was now on the second rung of the ladder.

"That's mighty kind of you. Perhaps I should be down there too."

"No," James said firmly. "You need to stay close to Molly and the little one. They need as much care as any crop does."

Daniel sighed. "There's got to be something more that we could do."

James shook his head. "You've not lived here long enough for the sheriff to back you against those boys and there's still too many around who've known their family a long time. I don't rightly know what you can do, except hope they get bored pretty soon."

Daniel wished they could all just get on with running their lives and not bother about the Reese brothers. This wasn't good for any of them.

By the time he went up to the farmhouse later in the day, the smell of jam making drifted out into the yard long before he reached the door. It brought a much needed smile to his face. Molly was busy at the stove stirring the contents of a large pan.

"You know," Daniel put the basket of fruit he was carrying onto the table. "It's coming home to things like this that makes me realise it really is all worth it and we shouldn't just pack our bags and head out West to take our chances with the others who are trying it."

"We can't be travellers all our lives. I like living here and if I'm not very much mistaken, so do you. We aren't going to let them beat us. If I gave in that easily what would it say about all that Miss Ellie is fighting for on my behalf?"

Daniel loved to see the fire in Molly's eyes when she was determined, but he couldn't help worrying about what lay ahead.

The following weeks were hard ones. From dawn to dusk they worked gathering in the crops and ensuring everything was stored as safely as possible. Ben took care of Mary by day and slept with the corn by night. Although Daniel thought they were asking a lot of the old man, he had never seemed happier and whistled to himself as he went about the farm.

With the extra labour they had to help with harvesting, the bunkhouse was full and Daniel found it hard to see how much could be done by the Reese boys without someone hearing. He reminded himself of the hay fire a couple of years previous as a way to ensure he didn't become complacent. Everywhere he went he kept watch for anything unusual. He saw nothing. None of the workers had heard anything more in town and Daniel began to wonder if they were worrying about nothing.

September was soon upon them and he stood with Molly looking out across the farm.

"That's the corn gone and the hay is as safe as it can be. It looks like it was just a threat. It's been a good year and we've a little put by. Let's hope it's the start of better times." Molly rested her head on Daniel's shoulder as she held Mary in her arms.

"Here, let me take her." Daniel reached and lifted Mary gently to his chest with her head nestled into his neck. "It won't be many years before she's helping around the farm as you used to do."

"I've been thinking about that." Molly seemed to

hesitate. "There are still lots of orphans needing homes. We could give that opportunity to someone else. We'd already understand some of what they'd been through and how hard it can be."

Daniel nodded slowly. "Maybe we should wait to make sure those Reese boys have really given up before we do. I'd worry there'd be a risk of that being enough to make them more determined." He paused and looked across the farm. "Would you want to bring a boy or a girl into the family?"

Molly smiled. "A brother and sister would be good if it were possible."

"You've already got this all worked out, haven't you?" Daniel laughed. "You're still the Molly I first saw with that jug of grog back in New York."

"And you still sing like an angel. Sing for us now, Daniel."

He stood and looked across the fields and began.

… Now it catches the gleam of the morning's first beam,
In full glory reflected now shines in the stream:
'Tis the star-spangled banner, O long may it wave
O'er the land of the free and the home of the brave…

CHAPTER 28

I sat within a valley green,
I sat there with my true love,
My sad heart strove the two between,
The old love and the new love,
The Wind that Shakes the Barley - Robert Dwyer Joyce - 1861

"What does she say about us renting this place out and moving?" Daniel was anxious to hear how Miss Ellie might have reacted to their suggestion.

Molly smiled at him. "You can read it for yourself, but basically she is not going to object if we do it."

"That's great news." Daniel picked his wife up and swung her around.

"Don't be too eager. I think you need to read everything she writes first." Molly passed the letter to him.

Daniel was surprised by the fact that there seemed to be several pages. "Do I need to read all of it?"

"Well you can skip the parts that tell you about how they got on in Pittsburgh and the page that tells you about the birth of your new nephew."

He could tell Molly was teasing him. She knew he'd read it all, though by the look of it that would take some time. He made a drink and went to sit by the window to get enough light to make it easier.

Miss Ellie's letters were always interesting to read. She wrote well and her letters conveyed her character. "What do you make of that?" He asked Molly who was sitting playing with Mary. "Thomas Hendry Reilly Dixon!" Then under his breath remembering "Thomas H. Reilly, how William first introduced himself to me in New York and before he changed his name." Then more directly to Molly he said, "It's clever isn't it? Doesn't it show you just how much he's changed these last couple of years."

"And so the name of Reilly will continue after all. I think it's a lovely idea." As Molly tickled Mary's toes their daughter laughed.

Daniel went back to reading about Miss Ellie's travels with Mrs Hawksworth and how, thankfully, on this occasion there had been no difficulties. Then he got to the important part about the farm.

They had heard about another farm some distance away that was available to rent. Daniel thought that he and Molly could take the opportunity to expand activities, by moving there and paying a manager to run Cochrane's Farm. He saw the main benefit as being that they would no longer live on the doorstep of the Reese boys. It would be a big step, but after much discussion Molly had at least agreed to ask Miss Ellie for permission to consider it.

He reread part of the letter.

It would indeed be very odd to see a stranger managing the farm, although I dare say I understand the reasons for your considering it. I still look at it as home, although I've spent precious little time there in the last couple of years. I guess I would be happy with a room in whatever place you're calling home when I come to visit.

Daniel nodded to himself and was grateful for how reasonable Miss Ellie was being.

He read on.

I do wonder what thought you've given to James and Ben. Whilst James might not be quite so needful of your company, Ben moved across the country to be with you and I can't rightly see him happy with someone else running the farm he's living on. Both of them would miss Mary dreadfully. Then of course there's the matter of which home Junior would live in. There are more things to think about than the farm itself.

Daniel sat up and stared out of the window in the direction of where the cabins were. He hadn't really thought about those things and, written down by Miss Ellie, he now felt a little selfish for not having done so.

"What are you thinking about, looking so far away?" Molly came over to him carrying Mary on her hip.

"Ben mostly. Miss Ellie's right. This isn't just about the farm."

Molly didn't say anything but simply put a hand on his shoulder.

"We could ask him to come with us." Daniel said after a while. "He is part of the family."

"Why don't we see what we think when we look at the place? None of this might come to anything."

Daniel smiled. As ever Molly was as much the voice of reason as Miss Ellie. "Yes, you're right." Then he read what there was left of the letter before putting it on the table and going out into the evening for a walk.

The available farm was just past Huntington, about thirty miles from their current place. The plan was to leave early and have time to look around the land when they arrived. They had then been invited to stay overnight before returning the following day. It was too far for a single day's journey, however they undertook it, so the offer had been appreciated. Daniel wanted to go as soon as possible, before the nights started to draw in.

When he came in from his walk he sat down and put his head in his hands.

Molly's voice was gentle as she said, "There's no good our being secretive. We're going to have to ask Ben and James to look after things while we're gone. Besides, if we are really thinking of doing this, we're going to have to talk to them sooner or later. We can't just go." Molly's knitting needles continued clicking as she spoke.

Daniel knew that she was right, but that didn't make the whole thing any easier. "When do you think we should go to see it?"

"Well there's nothing to stop us leaving here next Tuesday. If I get the dairy orders delivered Monday, then the next two days will be quieter."

"I suppose that gives us time to write to say we're coming so they're expecting us. We'd better talk to James and Ben tomorrow then. I'll come down with you when you take Mary in the morning. If we do move, we will find it hard looking after Mary if we don't have Ben to help us. I'm starting to think this whole idea isn't such a good one after all. I just wanted to find a way to protect my family." He sighed. "I'm going to bed."

It had been a long day, but still Daniel didn't sleep. He couldn't get out of his mind how settled they were at Cochrane's Farm and the injustice of feeling they needed to be away from the Reese brothers.

On the Friday morning, once the cows had been milked and Daniel had been back to the farmhouse for breakfast, he and Molly walked down to the cabins to see Ben and James. Daniel was happy to let Molly do the talking, as he had not the least idea how to explain this in the right way. He was carrying Mary as they walked down, she was seven months old now and getting much bigger. She'd be running around the farm before they knew it.

"To what do I owe this honour?" Ben was outside with Junior as they approached. Junior came rushing over to Daniel, but by the look of him, it was Mary he really wanted to check on.

"Well," said Molly, sitting on the bench seat. "We've been thinking about the problems with the Reese boys. We're still worried about something happening, especially around Mary." She paused and took a deep breath. "Anyway, there's a farm for rent over near Huntington and we were wondering whether it might be an idea for us to move there for a while." She paused again, seeming to want to go slowly both as she chose her own words and for Ben and James to understand what she was saying. "We were thinking, that maybe we could put a manager in to run this place for a year or two while things settle down. If we went ahead…" Molly got up from the bench and walked around. "…You could either move with us or stay here as you prefer."

She turned to look at the two men, both of whom Daniel could tell were taken aback by the proposal. He thought he should perhaps try to help a little. "We haven't decided for certain yet. We're going over to look at the farm next Tuesday. We'll be away overnight and hoped you might look after things here while we're gone."

Ben sucked on his teeth as he was wont to do when deep in thought. "I don't rightly know what I think. I can't say I'd be all that happy. I've grown to like it here." He looked across at James who simply nodded.

"Would you at least look after things for us next week

so we can go to visit?" Molly looked anxious.

"You know we will, missy," Ben said sadly. "You know we will."

Daniel gave Mary to Molly and then headed off to his work. He felt less optimistic than he had done and doubted now that the idea was quite as good as it had seemed. Miss Ellie had been right, but then, she usually was. He thought they would have been better to have discussed it fully with Miss Ellie before having got this far with the idea.

The weekend was quiet and neither he nor Molly were very talkative. The more he thought about moving, the more Daniel realised it may not be the answer. They were both fairly subdued on Monday when they sat down to make the final plans for their journey and pack what they would need to take.

"If we leave at six then we'll get a good start on the day," Daniel said when they had finished talking it through.

"Mary will probably sleep for much of the journey so it shouldn't be too bad for her. As long as she doesn't try crawling around the cart, we'll be fine." Molly gave a weak laugh.

"I'm starting to think that if Ben won't come with us then I don't really want to move." Daniel shrugged as he spoke and suddenly remembered how his own father used to do the same.

"I know. It really is hard to know what to do for the best. We might be an odd little family, but James and Ben have become part of it, and I've grown very fond of them. I'd best put Mary to bed if we're going to be off early." Molly got up and lifted Mary, then turned to Daniel. "Are you coming now?"

He looked at her but stayed sitting where he was. "In a

while. I want to do some more thinking first."

CHAPTER 29

Molly had only been asleep about an hour when Mary started crying. She roused herself and went over to her daughter who was thrashing around in her crib, pushing away the covers. Molly leaned down and touched her daughter's forehead. It didn't feel too warm, but Mary was clearly unhappy about something.

Molly lifted her daughter up and rocked her in her arms, but still the child grizzled. She was dry and had not long been fed so it was not likely to be either of those things. She put Mary over her shoulder and walked a little around the room, trying not to make too much noise as she did so. Daniel could not have been long in following them to bed and she didn't want to disturb him. There was enough moonlight to see all Molly needed without a candle, so she drew the curtains back, then continued to move about trying to settle Mary.

Daniel was letting out gentle snores behind her and she was glad to hear that at least one of them was sleeping.

Molly continued to walk around the room. She could feel her own eyelids closing and just hoped Mary would go back to sleep soon. Instead the child began to cough. In the end, Molly decided to take her into another bedroom so her coughing and crying wouldn't wake Daniel. She began to wonder how they would fare the following day if Mary was starting with some illness. She rocked Mary as she looked out of the window at the stars, but Mary began crying again. Molly was beginning to feel frustrated and decided to take her downstairs to see what remedies she could find on the shelf in the kitchen. Miss Ellie kept many things available, together with a little hand-written log of what might work for which ailment. Right now, Molly hoped that she would find an easy solution to Mary's gripes. She was generally a well child and this was out of character.

The ticking of the kitchen clock was the only comfort Molly could find as she dozed fitfully in the chair between Mary's bouts of coughing and crying. She wondered at the timing and began to think it best that she stayed at the farm with Mary while Daniel went to Huntington. He was as well placed to consider if they could make the farm pay as she was, though he didn't always believe in his own ability.

By the time Daniel came downstairs all Molly wanted to do was sleep. She would have liked to pass Mary over to him and go straight to bed, but that wouldn't work if he was to get away early. The best she could hope for was some help from Ben or James later in the morning.

"You're up even before me," Daniel said. Then he paused and looked at them more closely. "Is everything all right?"

Molly shook her head. "Mary's not well. I don't think it's anything serious, but we've been up most of the night. I don't think it would be fair to take her to Huntington. You should go for us and I'll stay here."

"But you know more about farm management than I do. You should be the one to go." Daniel ran his hand through his still untidy hair.

Molly smiled. "Thank you, but I've had no sleep either. I wouldn't know one end of a cow from the other this morning and that won't get us very far. You can do this, Daniel. You really can."

"How can I decide if it's the right place for us to call home?" The concern was clearly etched on his face.

"I think you'll know. We trust you to choose well for us." She kissed his cheek.

Daniel marched the length of the kitchen and back. "If I must, I'll take the horse but not the cart. It will be much quicker if I ride. I can't ask her to bring me back in the day, but I can be back much the sooner tomorrow that way and I needn't leave so soon this morning. I could take Mary for an hour so you can rest before I go."

Molly could have cried at the considerate nature of this man she loved so much. She nodded and got up from the chair. "I'll do that. I really need some rest. Wake me an hour from now and I'll be fine." Without further comment, she passed Mary over into Daniel's arms and went upstairs to get back into the still warm bed.

It was eight o'clock when Daniel finally went to saddle the mare and make ready to leave. Mary had finally settled and Molly was wondering if they could all have gone, but the decision was made now and both she and Mary would be better for a day at home. Once Daniel was away she would go down to see if Ben would mind Mary for an hour or two now that she was quiet.

James was already away to town on errands when she took Mary down to Ben. She could have done some of them herself later in the day. She felt a little guilty for putting him out, but she could use the time productively to catch up around the house.

James was back when she went to collect Mary at lunchtime.

"Well, I was only telling Mrs Spencer that I was a poor

215

substitute as you and Daniel were away the night and here you are." James puffed on his pipe as he relaxed outside the cabins.

"I don't know about a poor substitute, but it will set tongues wagging if they think we're off gallivanting." Molly grinned. "Did you tell her where we were going?"

"Why no, I don't think that's business of theirs."

"Good," said Molly. "It's far better if she's left to wonder. Now, how has my daughter been behaving herself?"

Mary was crawling along the porch as though the previous night hadn't happened.

"As good as gold for her Grandpa Ben." The old man put out his leg to stop Mary getting as far as the steps. She laughed and turned right around to crawl back the way she'd come.

"The least I can do is cook supper for you both, if you'd like to join us?" Molly reached her arms down to help Mary to stand up.

"Well I don't suppose we'd say no to an offer like that." James looked across to Ben who nodded.

"We'll see you later then." Molly lifted Mary into her arms and used her own hand to hold the girl's wrist to wave goodbye. Both the old men laughed and waved back. All Molly could think was that it would be impossible for them to move if it meant separating either of those wonderful people from her daughter.

Supper with Ben and James was pleasant enough, but the empty place at the end of the table felt very strange to Molly. She wondered how Daniel was getting on and what he thought of the farm. Looking at the old men at the table, in her heart she knew that leaving all this behind was not the answer, but she didn't know what was. She wondered how many generations of their family would need to live here before they were accepted in the way the Reese family was. It was ironic really as the town itself had only been here for a generation or two so no one was truly local in the sense of having lived there for hundreds of years. Mind you, they would be even newer to Huntington if they did move.

"Well that was a welcome change to my own meagre cooking." Ben sat back comfortably in his chair and rested his hands on his stomach. "And how's little Mary now?"

"She seems fine, thank goodness. I think we were right to stay here, though."

"Yes." James moved his chair away from the table. "You can never be too careful."

Molly realised that even though she'd lived with Miss Ellie since childhood she had no idea how James came to be on his own. For a moment she wondered if he'd ever had a family of his own, but thought she might be better to ask Miss Ellie than to risk upsetting James.

It was dark when Ben and James set off with their lanterns back to the cabins. The nights were drawing in again and Molly sighed thinking about the winter ahead and wondering if it would be kind to them.

Mary had been asleep for much of the day and, as Molly scooped her up, she hoped that wouldn't mean another restless night lay ahead. It had certainly seemed that the herbal remedy she'd found on the kitchen shelf had been effective. She thought about giving Mary another dose now, but decided it might be better to wait to see if it were needed.

She prepared Mary for the night ahead and laid her in her crib on the other side of the room, near the window. Despite her long hours awake the previous night, Molly didn't feel ready to sleep. She wondered where Daniel was and if he was thinking of her. She blew out the candle and opened the curtains, looking out into the night across the farm. It was a still night and there was nothing moving, almost as though the scene were frozen in time. She tried to work out which direction Huntington was in from there, but concluded she'd need to be looking out from the other side of the house.

Eventually, Molly drew the curtains back across the window to stop any early light from disturbing Mary. Then she picked her way carefully across the room and, leaving the bedroom door ajar, she went along the landing to a room on the other side of the house which looked out in the direction of Huntington. For a few minutes she looked out of the window and watched the nothingness beyond. Then she pulled the old rocking chair to the window and sat and gently rocked herself to sleep.

CHAPTER 30

So goodbye, Muirsheen Durkin, I'm sick and tired of
working,
No more I'll dig the praties, no longer I'll be fool.
For as sure as me name is Carney
I'll be off to California, where instead of diggin' praties
I'll be diggin' lumps of gold.
Muirsheen Durkin chorus 1840s

Daniel pulled back on the reins and slowed the horse to a
gentle walk after they passed through the town of
Huntington itself. The ride had not been too bad. The
roads were good and he was now a proficient enough rider
not to incur undue discomfort. He looked around trying to
take in the surrounding countryside. He smiled. In reality
it was little different to the area he already knew around
Pierceton and he wondered quite what he might have been
expecting.

He was not due at the farm until late in the afternoon,
which, now he'd got his bearings, gave him the time he
wanted to go back and look around the main town. If they
were going to call this place home, he needed to get some
sort of measure of what it was like. It wasn't a large place,
that much he knew before he came, but it seemed to have
much the same things as they found in Pierceton and he
was satisfied that life here would present no new hardship.
He tied the mare up and spent a little time wandering

around the streets in search of the general store. He knew well enough that he could gauge a lot from the welcome or otherwise that he received there. He smiled wondering if they already knew he might be around from the Huntington gossip trail.

The bell rang as he tentatively opened the store door. He sighed, wishing he could be one of those people who strode into a room, but he wasn't and there was no good thinking about it too much. He supposed he should be grateful he had the confidence to go in at all.

"Good day to you, sir."

The young fresh-faced woman behind the counter was smiling widely and Daniel thought she seemed genuine enough. He relaxed a little and smiled in return. "Good day to you too, ma'am."

"And how can I help you this fine day?"

Daniel selected a small loaf of bread and some cheese that would help to quell the hunger from his journey and which gave him time to have a little look around the store. If the young woman realised that he was new to the area she certainly didn't say so and he was pleasantly surprised not to find himself questioned about his visit. He didn't doubt there'd be some talk about the stranger, He couldn't imagine there were many who passed through the town without belonging, but perhaps it would only be of passing interest.

Once he'd left the store, he led the horse out to the edge of town and sat to eat his purchases. He was interested in the flavour and texture of the cheese, as, if they moved here, they would need to sell their own produce. He nodded. Theirs would compare favourably. It occurred to him that they, being outsiders, might have more difficulty getting the store to stock their goods. Not for the first time that day, he thought that starting in a new place might just bring a whole different set of problems. Perhaps every town had its Reese brothers or at least their equivalent.

The horse nuzzled her interest in the food and he shared a little with her as he was always wont to do. He stroked her nose when they'd finished and she nibbled back affectionately. Daniel smiled. He did enjoy the times he could be close to the animals.

He remounted and turned the horse away from town once again and toward the farm. The instructions he'd been given were clear enough and it wasn't long before he found the right track off the road, clearly marked as Dawson's Farm. He pulled the horse up and took a deep breath. He wished dearly that Molly were here with him, but travelling without the cart had certainly made the journey easier.

They walked on until the farmhouse came into view and from there Daniel dismounted and led the horse the rest of the way, taking in as much as he could as they went. An old man was waiting in the yard as he approached and Daniel raised his hat in greeting.

"Good day, sir." He stopped just short of where the man was standing.

"Flynn?"

It was clear the old man was used to saying little other than the necessaries. "Yes, sir, I am."

"Tie the nag there." The man pointed to a post by a water trough, then turned and started to walk across the yard, clearly expecting Daniel to follow.

Daniel hastened to tie the mare with enough room so she could stretch down to the water. He whispered to her as he did so, "I don't think you're a nag." Then he hurried on behind the old fellow. A fit and tanned man about ten years older than Daniel came out of the farmhouse into the yard to join them. He stretched out his hand to shake Daniel's hand.

"Sorry about Pa, he's a man of few words. He's been tucked away here far too long. That's why I'm getting out. I don't want to end up like him holed up here for the rest of his days. He might be too old for adventure, but I'm not. I'm having me some fun before I forget how to live. I'm Zak. Zak Dawson."

"Daniel Flynn," Daniel replied wondering if the old man came with the farm or whether he was planning on moving out. "So where are you headed?"

"I'm off out West, grab me some of the action before everyone gets there first."

Daniel nodded but said nothing.

Zak was as talkative as his father was silent, which suited Daniel as he was always happier to listen, if silence weren't an option.

"You're not the only one interested in the farm."

Daniel nodded, that didn't surprise him, but he'd been led to believe that he and Molly had first refusal.

"In fact, I showed another man around this morning. He'll be letting me know by sundown tomorrow."

Daniel frowned. "Excuse me, I thought you were waiting on our decision before offering it elsewhere."

"Well I know that's what we said, but I ain't got time to be messing around if you says no, have I?"

Zak Dawson said it as though going back on his word was the most natural thing in the world and Daniel bridled.

"Come now, you wouldn't expect anything different, would you?" Zak simply continued as though it were nothing. "Now, this here is the barn…"

Zak's voice became suddenly nothing more than a drone to Daniel. He couldn't do business with a man who wasn't straight with him. He'd be paying rent to this man and even without the question of where the old man fitted into the scene Daniel was feeling very uncomfortable. He wondered for a moment what Molly would do. Then he knew. She would tell him to trust his instincts and his instincts were telling him that things just weren't right. What else would be different than he'd been led to believe if this was Zak Dawson's attitude? They'd barely got to the other side of the yard before Daniel's mind was made up. He had no intention of spending a night under the roof of this man and had no desire to rent his farm.

Being assertive wasn't something that Daniel found easy. Zak was a confident man, that much was evident. Daniel took a deep breath and pulled himself up to his full height. "I've seen all I need to."

"And you'll take it?"

For a moment Daniel stopped in his tracks, wondering if he had heard right. He was astounded that any man could think he'd take the farm after so little time looking.

"No, I'll not take it. I won't deal with a man who's not straight with me." Then he raised his hat once again. "Good day to you and your father." Then he spun on his heel and headed back to where the mare was patiently waiting. "Well, my girl, you weren't expecting to be on the road again so soon and I can only apologise. But I'm guessing you're as happy to leave this place as I am. We'll find a stop on the way back, but if it's all the same to you, I'd like to get some distance between us and Dawson's farm before we do."

The horse whinnied and Daniel would have sworn she'd understood. Maybe the water in the trough didn't taste too fresh either.

As Daniel rode, he guessed there were people around Pierceton who probably weren't so different from the Dawsons. Come to that, much of what he could say might well apply to those Reese boys. What a shame they'd not got into their heads the idea that they could get rich quick by going West. For a moment he wondered if there were any way to encourage them to do just that. Given their reluctance to leave the bar, they would probably think it all too much effort to even think about.

Once they'd passed Huntington it was a good while before they came to another settlement. "Sorry, girl. I should have paid more attention on the way out. I didn't realise it was going to be this far."

The mare didn't reply and Daniel put his hand gently on her neck. "I wish we could make it all the way home, but that's not an option tonight. We'll rest up here, but don't you go thinking I'm going soft on you. We'll be off again first light tomorrow."

The lodging he'd found wasn't much, but it would serve all the purpose he needed and he'd spent much of his life in far worse, so he would not complain. The stables were adequate and the horse would be well rested by the following day.

He had some supper and as he ate realised just how hungry he was. Then he went to his room and as he did so he thought of Molly and Mary and looked out of the room's tiny window into the dark beyond and wondered if it were the right direction to see them. He looked up at the moon and the stars and smiled to think they were the self-same ones that Molly could see. He wished more than anything that he was home now and had never had this crazy idea to consider taking on Dawson's Farm. Maybe there was a different way to think about the problem with the Reese brothers, but just for the moment, Daniel couldn't see what it was.

CHAPTER 31

Ben had had a lovely day looking after Mary and then having supper at the farmhouse. He sighed as he sat on the porch when he got back. He was happy here. If Daniel and Molly moved to Huntington he didn't rightly know what he'd choose to do. He liked the companionship of living alongside James and being able to do work around the farm if he chose to. Most of all he liked looking after Mary and dreaming the dreams he thought he'd lost all those years ago. He looked across to the little house he'd built for Mary and thought back to the one he'd built in Iowa which had hardly been used either.

As he thought of Esme and Flora a tear rolled down his cheek. Mary was his second chance and watching her grow was his salvation. Wherever she went, he would go too and if he had to build another little house, then he'd do that as well.

Junior came and sat close to Ben's leg. The little fellow always seemed to be able to sense when his presence was needed. It was a relatively mild night and Ben began to doze in his chair with the silence of the fields surrounding him and the vague sound of the stream continuing its unceasing journey to places it had never been.

Ben was deep in a world of dreams when he awoke suddenly with the sound of Junior barking. The little dog was jumping at his leg and barking repeatedly.

"Hush, boy, you'll wake the neighbours!"

Junior took no notice of his reprimand. He grabbed the leg of Ben's trousers and tugged. None of this was like Junior and a note of alarm ran through Ben. As he began to get up from his chair Junior started running up the lane barking madly then back toward Ben. Ben went inside to find his lamp and get it lit, by which time the little dog was frantic.

"What's going on out there?" James shouted across from his cabin.

"I don't know but I'm about to go and find out." Ben took up the torch and started to follow Junior who kept circling back to make sure he was still there.

"Sweet Jesus!" Ben exclaimed as he rounded the corner and the farmhouse came into view. He didn't need the light from his torch to see what the problem was, the far end of the house was ablaze. "Dear God. Molly and Mary." He started to move as fast as he was able toward the house. "Molly!" He shouted as loudly as he could in case she was already out of the building. "Molly!"

The fire was definitely taking hold and there was no time to think about the options. He pulled his shirt off. Damping the shirt in a pail of water in the yard he put it to his mouth and ran to the back door. As always it was unlocked and whilst the kitchen was a little smoky it was clear the fire had not started in there. He opened the door which led to the stairs and as quickly as he could made his way up. The smoke was thicker here and it was hard to see what he was doing. Junior barked and Ben listened for where the dog was directing him. Junior had darted into the room on the left at the top of the stairs. Ben wasn't familiar with the layout of the upstairs of the house, so had no clear picture of which room he should be looking for. He went across the room following Junior's barks and found Molly overcome by the smoke on the floor of the bedroom.

With one hand keeping the cloth to his nose and mouth, he lifted her as best he could and dragged her back toward the stairs. Half carrying her and half dragging her he got her down to the kitchen and out of the back door.

By this time James had made his way to the house as well.

"Take Molly away from the fire. I'm going back for Mary." Ben coughed a couple of times, re-wetted his shirt and headed back into the house.

Junior was ahead of him. Ben could only hope that with the dog moving in the air at a lower level it might prevent Junior himself being overcome by the smoke. Ben cursed his own arthritic knees for preventing him from moving at floor level too. He was struggling enough to breathe, he could do nothing to help the little dog.

Ben's first thought was that Mary would be in the room where he'd found Molly, but Junior was heading further along the landing. He could feel the temperature increasing and not just from his own exertions. There were flames starting to lick at the house's rafters. Ben didn't have the luxury of time for a thorough search. Logic told him Mary would have been with Molly, but Junior was adamant. Ben had to trust the dog.

The smoke was thicker now and Ben's eyes were stinging. Even with the damp cloth he was coughing at intervals and could feel the effect of the smoke like a vice gripping his chest. He hoped and prayed that Mary was in some way protected from the worst of the smoke and completely away from the fire itself. He could hear the flames crackling from somewhere not far away. It was taking hold of more of the building. Ben struggled along the landing trying to see where Junior had gone. Junior's own barks were distorted and Ben wondered how long the dog could hold out. Relief swept over Ben as he found Junior standing at the foot of a baby's crib. It had to be Mary. Ben held his breath as he moved to see if she was all right. As he did so there was a crash from somewhere further along the farmhouse. Time was short.

The quickest and safest way to get Mary out would be through the window. He went to open it. He needed James to come around to that side of the house, but he had no idea where James was and Ben's throat was so affected by the smoke that there was little hope of him shouting. His first thought was to fashion a sling out of the sheet and try to lower Mary to the ground, but they were too high and it would take more than two baby sheets, quite apart from the risk of her falling out. He opened the window and a gust of night air came in to him. The air served to fuel the fire, but he couldn't avoid that. His eyes were smarting and he could see very little, but there was nothing to even get hold of directly by the window. He could see no way of climbing down.

He turned away from the window. He had to think.

CHAPTER 32

Molly coughed and felt a searing pain run through her chest. Slowly, she opened her eyes and felt confused. What was happening? She coughed again and had no choice but to spit out the contents of her mouth. Her throat, nose and eyes burned, and she felt weak. An instinctive thought came to her and she was suddenly far more alert. "Mary!" She tried to get up, but James put a hand on her to deter her movement. "But I've got to get to Mary."

"Ben's gone back in. You stay there. You're in no state to do anything. We'll find her."

She coughed and wretched again and realised she didn't have the strength to get up. "She's..." Molly coughed. "... round that side of the house. Her cot's near the window." She pointed toward the right from where James had laid her. She went to get up again but was shaking too much to have control of her arms or legs.

He nodded. "I'm going around to see if I can help. How far along?"

Molly closed her eyes for a moment trying to think how many windows each room had. "Fourth window along." Then she lay back and coughed again.

She felt another surge of energy as something deep within spurred her to save her daughter. She climbed unsteadily to her feet and started unsteadily to follow James to the side of the house. "I can't lose another," she said, under her breath to no one in particular. Then tried to shout the same words. "I can't lose another! I can't lose Mary!" But all that came out was a croak.

The smoke was not blowing in this direction and although her eyes were still smarting, Molly could see more clearly. James was beneath the window trying to find anything he could use to climb up. There was nothing. Besides that, he was an old man. He was in no state to be scaling a wall. Molly wished that Daniel was here. He might at least have stood some chance, but without anything to hold on to the task would be nearly impossible. She thought of her daughter and suddenly she was sick. She wretched into the grasses behind her and then wiped her mouth with her apron. The smell of smoke from the material almost made her gag again.

She started to hunt for anything to pile up to give some height. Somehow, she had to reach the window. She began to drag a barrel across the yard, but had to pause after each heave. She felt a rush of pain through her chest with every effort. She focused on Mary and tried again with a strength which was beyond anything she'd felt before, but even so it was going to take too long. She wondered why James wasn't helping then turned to see where he was.

James was shouting up to the window. She presumed he was hoping that his voice might help direct Ben toward the right room.

Molly wished she could be clutching the rosary right now, but she tried to focus on its shape and her lips moved as she said the words of the Hail Mary quietly to herself and continued to heave the barrel. She was reciting it for the third time when she realised that the window nearest to Mary's crib was already open. James was trying to let Ben know he was there, but where was Ben? He must have been there to open the window, but where was he now?

A moment later, Ben appeared with Mary in his arms. Molly suddenly realised, by their gesturing, that Ben planned to throw Mary down for James to catch. Molly gasped. She left the barrel and started to stagger across to them. What if he missed? Could Mary survive a fall from that height? She tried to reassure herself that James was strong from farm work. He might be old, but he was strong. They threw bales of hay and sacks of feed and she could never remember either a bad aim or a missed catch. Let this one not be the first! She repeated the Hail Mary again. Her eyes were open and fixed on the bundle that was Mary.

James was standing close to the wall of the house, his arms stretched upward. Ben was leaning out of the window holding Mary by her arms and dangling her down. The distance between the two of them was not too far as long as James didn't miss catching her. Molly prayed that Mary wouldn't choose that moment to wriggle or kick. She began to tear off her skirts. They could use them to catch Mary in. As she did so she could already hear Ben count down so that James knew when to expect to catch her. Her skirt was going to be too late. They were dropping her right then.

"Three, two, one, now!"

Molly took a deep breath in and screwed her eyes tight.

CHAPTER 33

Ben had been mightily relieved to see James coming to the window of Mary's room. He gulped in lungfuls of the fresher air and steadied his nerves.

Mary was sleepy and he hoped that if he took her by her arms she would only associate it with the games they played in a morning, when she'd laugh and chuckle as he held her dangling high above the ground. The distance from him to James was still a good few feet, but he trusted James's ability to catch her and he could see no alternative. Now wasn't the time to remember his brother falling from the rock face when they were children. He needed to focus solely on Mary and banish Jeremiah's face from his thoughts. More importantly, he needed to banish the image of Jeremiah's body lying broken beneath him. He took a deep breath.

He counted down, his heart racing. He could barely watch but he knew that now was not a time to close his eyes. He had to keep Mary steady so that she fell straight into James's waiting arms.

"Three, two, one …"

When Ben let go of Mary's tiny wrists he prayed more fervently than he'd ever prayed. He stood rigid watching for what seemed like minutes, rather than the very short time it really was, as the baby dropped through the air.

Ben heard James call 'Yes!' and thanked God that if nothing else Mary would be all right. She'd seemed well enough that he thought she'd recover quickly from the effects of the smoke.

He turned from the window. "Run, Junior. Run, boy. Find Mary. Get out while you can." The little dog didn't need telling twice. He ran down the landing away from Ben and toward the stairs. Ben turned to see flames licking at the doorway of the room and searched for the cloth he'd used to cover his face. He couldn't find it, but there was no time to lose. If he didn't go now he'd be trapped and he'd already realised there was no way he could make himself jump from the window.

He started to move across to the door, but it was hard to see the way.

The fire meant that it didn't seem dark, but the smoke was thick and the way uncertain. Ben's foot caught on the corner of something and he tripped, reaching out his hands to find anything to steady himself with and finding the open door. It moved as he grabbed it, but he managed to stay upright. He felt something tug at his trousers and realised that Junior had come back for him. He tried to use the toe of his boot to encourage the little dog to save himself.

Ben then worked his way to the doorway and out onto the landing. He could feel the intense heat but was in no position to move quickly. Moving carefully was his only hope. His heart was beating fast as he inched his way along the landing. He could feel pin-pricks to his arms as sparks danced in the air. He could neither see nor feel where Junior was now, but he could hear the fire crackling in the timbers somewhere close by and could see flames licking at a door further along the landing behind him. He hoped the main stairs were intact. There was another staircase at the other end of the house, he knew that, but that was the end he could see the flames so there was little point in heading that way.

As he felt his way along the corridor, he found another doorway to his left. He must be nearly back to the room where he'd found Molly. There couldn't be much further until he reached the stairs. Every breath sent searing pain through Ben's chest. He wasn't going to be able to cope with this much longer if he didn't get out.

The last thing he heard was an almighty cracking from somewhere above him and he could only think that it must be a burning rafter breaking free.

CHAPTER 34

"Yes!" It was James shouting.

Molly opened her eyes to see him gathering Mary to his chest and her knees gave way beneath her.

"Now get out. As fast as you can. Get out," James was shouting up to Ben.

Molly moved back, presuming that he would come out of the window. That was surely the safest way out now, but Ben had already moved away, out of view.

James came over to Molly. "I think she's all right. She's breathing anyway. I guess Ben was too scared to jump. I'll get around to the kitchen to see if I can help clear the way."

Molly could feel the tears rolling down her cheeks as she took Mary from him. Mary coughed and her eyelids flickered but closed again. Molly held her daughter to her and cried. Now they just needed Ben and Junior to get out of the house and join them.

Suddenly Molly realised how thirsty she was. There was no possibility of going to the kitchen and pouring water from the pitcher. She'd have to go and draw some fresh from the well. She looked across at the house and saw flames licking the roof. Where was Ben? He must be out soon. There was nothing to be done for the house, that much was certain. The fire would have to do what it chose with that. Molly felt too numb to think about it. She walked unsteadily toward the yard holding Mary tightly. Every so often the baby would cough and then seem to be instantly asleep again. It was hard to tell how much the coughing was from the fire and how much whatever already ailed her. Molly wanted to help with Ben, but there was nowhere to safely lay Mary and in truth, she didn't want to let go of the child.

Just then Junior limped out into the yard. Patches of his fur showed blackened marks and he was struggling to put down one of his paws. He went straight to the trough in the yard and drank. Molly thought he'd got the right idea. She was relieved to see the little dog and was sure if he was there, then Ben would not be far behind. She went as close to the house as seemed safe, hoping to be of some use to Ben as he came out.

James came across the yard to her. "There's no going back in there." He nodded toward the house. "I can't do anything to help." His voice carried an overwhelming sadness.

She nodded, but said nothing.

James walked away to the well and came back carrying a pitcher of water. Gratefully Molly passed Mary to James then cupped her hands into the water and scooped out some to drink. She drank a second draught and then scooped more to splash onto her face. She felt better for it. She'd wait a little longer before she tried to get Mary to take anything. For now, it seemed better that her daughter was sleeping. She took Mary back into her arms and moved to where she could see the door to the house waiting for Ben to appear.

Molly held Mary tightly to her, as much for the comfort as anything. Feeling her daughter's heart beating against her own was helping to calm Molly's rising sense of panic. There was still no sign of Ben. Junior was hobbling to and fro looking as anxious as she felt.

James bent down to examine Junior's paws. "He's lost a fair amount of skin from one paw and it's raw with burns. Poor chap." James took Junior over to the water and put his paws in deep. The dog yapped but didn't struggle.

"I'll make up a poultice to put on the worst of it, once I can get to anything that will help." Molly's thoughts drifted to the shelf in the kitchen and then she stopped. She couldn't get to the shelf. For all she knew the shelf was no longer there. "You'll have to wait until morning, little fellow. Maybe Ben has some in the cabin." Then she looked back across to the house straining to see if there were any sight of Ben joining them. She bit back the tears fearing she knew the answer. If it had been too dangerous for James to go back in to look for him, there was little chance of Ben getting out safely. Yet, Junior had made it, so maybe there was hope.

As she watched, there was an almighty sound and the roof collapsed into the upstairs of the house. Molly screamed and started to move toward the house. "Ben! Ben!"

James rested his hand on her arm and shook his head. "There's nothing we can do."

"But he only went in to save me and Mary. He shouldn't suffer."

"He did what he had to do. He did what I would have done if he hadn't got there first." James was choking on his words. "We love you both. You're our family."

"There must be something we can do." Molly made to go closer to the burning farmhouse.

James shook his head and tightened his grip on her arm. "Trust me, there's nothing." As he spoke the first arrivals from the town came running across the yard.

238

"Was there anyone in there?"

Molly simply wailed, "Ben. Ben was still in there. He rescued us."

James took charge of the new arrivals and started to form a chain to carry water to the house. They began with the area around the back door, to create a path to get to Ben, if it were possible.

Molly knew it was far too late for the house itself. With the roof already gone, there'd be little of the building to save and, without a miracle, no possibility of Ben coming out alive now. She sat nearby rocking Mary back and forth, stunned and senseless, wondering what Daniel was going to say when he returned. The tears flowed as she sat there, as though everything she'd never let herself grieve for had come together in a single rush.

Molly's tears ran down into Mary's smoky blanket. As they did so Molly could hear Mammy's voice in her head. It made her start. She thought she'd forgotten what her own dear mother sounded like, but there it was. 'You can be strong, so you can. You've a child to take care of yourself now.'

"Mammy." Molly stood up and looked around her, almost expecting to see the woman who brought her into the world.

She took a deep breath. Sitting here crying was going to help nobody. She could see little to be gained by joining the water chain. The house was clearly a ruin and Ben presumably part of it. She could at least check on the animals and make sure they hadn't been spooked by what was happening. Molly used Mary's blanket to fashion a sling and strapped Mary tightly to her. It was much harder to do with the size Mary was now, but she'd manage like that for a while. By the time she had been around the chickens, the cows and the other horse and done what she could to reassure them, the fire was starting to die down.

The chain of men carrying water looked tired and ragged from their exertions over the last couple of hours and she'd dearly like to have brewed them a drink and cooked some breakfast, but she had absolutely no means of doing so.

"Thank you," she said to each of them as she went along the line. It seemed wholly inadequate, but it was all she could say. "Thank you."

"Have you thought about how it took hold so fast?" James asked when she got to him.

"What do you mean?" She began to untie Mary as she spoke to him.

"I mean that while a hay stack might go up that quickly, a house usually takes a little longer. What had you got burning at that time?"

Molly felt as though someone had slapped her. "I had nothing alight. It didn't start in the kitchen or in the rooms we were in. It started at the far end of the house. We don't use some of those rooms from one week to the next. It's a big house." She looked over to what remained. "At least it was."

"Then I'm guessing it didn't start on its own." James shook his head. "If I'm not very much mistaken there's a murder gone on tonight and there could have been more."

Molly gasped. She reached across to the wall of the dairy to steady herself. She was grateful that building was still standing, though anything inside would likely be flavoured with smoke.

"You think this was started deliberately?"

James nodded.

"You don't think…" she didn't need to finish the

sentence as the truth dawned on her. "You mean…"

"Well I can't say for certain, but I think there's people out there who know more than they ought to."

"Isn't there anything more we can do to try to get to Ben?" Molly felt numb and couldn't believe there was really any possibility that Ben was lost to them. It was just unbearable.

James sighed. "Come now, there's nothing more that can be done tonight. You've a few hours to rest before Daniel comes home. Why don't you go down to Ben's cabin? I think he'd want you to do that. I'll milk the cows and then try to get some sleep myself. There's going to be a long day ahead tomorrow you need to rest first."

Molly knew he was right, although she could not imagine sleeping. It would at least be good to have somewhere to put Mary down for an hour or two. If Molly herself did sleep, she guessed she'd be awake in time before Daniel returned. She wanted to meet him on the road so he could at least know his wife and daughter were safe, before he heard the news of Ben and saw what little remained of their home.

Going into Ben's cabin felt completely wrong. Molly shivered. She felt as though she were trespassing and he might be there and be surprised by her presence. She hadn't been in the cabin all that often in recent months, in the better weather the two men were more likely to be sitting out in each other's company rather than tucked away, each in their own world. It occurred to her how much Ben had grown to mean to James and how much James might now miss his friend.

She put Mary down gently onto the bed and turned to realise Junior had limped in behind her. After how brave the little dog had been, she had to tend to his needs before her own. She went to look around the kitchen area for anything which might be used to act as salve to his burns. She found some honey and a strip of cotton to use as bandaging. Gently she set about washing Junior's paws in cool water before applying the strips of honey-soaked bandage. He'd probably lick most of the honey off, but maybe that would do him good too.

The little dog sat completely still as she worked and then lay down at the side of the bed as she climbed in next to Mary. As Molly closed her eyes, all she could see were the image of flames engulfing the house. Sleep was unlikely to come.

Molly had no idea how much time had passed when Mary woke, hungry as usual. Struggling to open her eyes, Molly drew Mary in towards her own body and cuddled her, even her cries were a pleasure to hear this morning. They were enough to tell Molly that Mary was all right and relatively unharmed by the experience. Junior woofed, but seemed to carry on sleeping until Molly finally swung her legs out of bed to look for food in Ben's kitchen.

The old man had lived frugally and there was little around, but thankfully there was cereal, and some buttermilk from the previous day. At eight months, Mary was not fully weaned but where possible Molly was encouraging her to eat some solids. What Mary didn't want Molly would finish.

She looked across at Junior, the little dog still looked dishevelled and would benefit from a full bath, but that could wait until later. Molly presumed she probably looked and smelled much the same, but she had no time to address that and no other clothes to wear. For now, the priority was to meet Daniel before he was left to fear for their safety.

Once they were finished eating and Junior had been outside, she tied the little dog carefully to the porch of the cabin so that he wouldn't follow them as they walked. His feet needed to rest and the rough ground wouldn't help them heal. Had it not been for needing to carry Mary she would have carried Junior. For a moment she wondered about taking the cart, but decided that she'd rather walk. Though her lungs still hurt, she longed to be in the fresh air and feel the peacefulness of walking. She left Junior some water and knew that, whilst he'd be frustrated to be left behind, he would at least not be in pain. James would be around the cabins, so nothing was likely to happen to the little dog here in daylight. Then strapping Mary to her back, Molly set off along the road to meet Daniel, before he got too close to Pierceton.

CHAPTER 35

Swift to its close ebbs out life's little day;
Earth's joys grow dim; its glories pass away;
Change and decay in all around I see;
O Thou who changest not, abide with me.
Abide with Me - Henry Francis Lyte - 1847

Daniel had planned to leave the guest house early but had underestimated his exhaustion. He slept deeply and by the time he awoke the sun was already well up into the sky. He got dressed as quickly as he could and went to see if he was too late for any breakfast. He was glad to find there was still the chance to eat and did so before going out to saddle the horse.

It seemed the mare was as well rested as he was and the two of them began a companionable journey along the road toward Pierceton.

He only had a mile or so left to go when he saw a figure at the side of the road walking in his direction. From a distance the figure looked awfully like Molly, but he wondered why she would be there and not waiting for him at home. After all, she had no way of knowing what time he would arrive.

As the gap closed, he realised that the person walking toward him, with her shoulders slumped and black patches on her clothing was indeed Molly. He pulled the horse up and dismounted.

"Molly. What's happened? What's wrong?"

Mary was strapped to Molly's back and as Molly fell against his chest, he wrapped his arms around them both. Daniel's heart was beating fast as Molly wept on his shoulder. He had so many questions, but it was clear she wasn't ready to talk. He comforted himself that both wife and daughter seemed all right and that whatever had occurred they were in one piece. As Molly nestled against him, he breathed through his nose and smelled smoke. He stiffened. Had they lost the hay again? But Molly would surely just have told him that. Daniel's heart beat faster as he waited for her to speak.

A few minutes passed before Molly released herself from his embrace. She took his hand and turned to walk toward the farm. Daniel still waited patiently for her to speak. With his other hand he led the mare.

"I needed to see you before you saw the farm," Molly began slowly in a husky voice.

Daniel felt himself tensing, wondering what was going to come next.

Then Molly swung around to face him again. "Oh Daniel, there's been another fire. Ben…" Molly let out a howl of anguish.

He stopped suddenly. "Where? What happened?"

"The house… the house is gone."

Whatever Daniel thought it might have been, it was not that. "You weren't in it were you? No one was hurt?"

Molly nodded. She seemed to be having difficulty forming any words. Daniel bided his time but his heart raced. He was desperate for her to continue.

"Ben…"

He wanted to shout, 'What about Ben?' but bit down on the words. He'd known Molly a long time and it was clear how much she was hurting.

"Ben died saving Mary and me." Her eyes were cast down as she spoke.

Daniel ran over the words again in his head before he understood what she meant. Then he drew her to him in a tight embrace and held her. He stood numbly in the middle of the road, holding his wife and daughter and not being able to fully comprehend the import of what she'd said. Ben, who meant so much to all of them. Ben, who they'd brought to live with them for his retirement. Their Ben was dead. It simply couldn't be.

Daniel was far away but realised Molly was talking again.

"We've lost the dearest friend and we've lost the farmhouse. We've got nowhere to live."

Daniel started to feel anger flooding into him. The anger wasn't about the farmhouse. He'd lived in a bunkhouse long enough not to mind privations. His anger was for the gentle man who meant so much to him, to all of them.

"How did it happen?"

"I don't know. It started at the other end of the house."

"The Reese boys!" He clenched his fists.

"We don't know that. Surely they wouldn't deliberately set out to kill someone?" Molly looked into his face as she spoke.

He watched her a while as he thought. Then he said, "The wheel on the cart could have killed you. We lost Michael because of the hay fire. Do you really think they wouldn't kill someone deliberately?"

Molly nodded, a deep sadness etched across her face.

He kissed her. "They didn't think you'd be there. We were supposed to be away."

Molly put her hand to her mouth. "And James told Mrs Spencer we were away! It would have been all over town. Holy Mother, when James suggested it, I couldn't believe it could really be the Reese brothers. What do we do?"

"That's a hard one to answer. I guess we need to talk to the sheriff, but I don't rightly know as he'll listen. We need to telegraph to Miss Ellie too. She has to know as soon as possible."

They were now at the turning to Cochrane's Farm and Daniel looked along the lane. He could see smoke still rising gently in the distance and knew that was where the house was. He felt numb. How could anyone do this to them? And what about Ben? He'd been Daniel's hero when he was young and he still saw the old man as the father figure he'd missed out on.

As he walked into the yard and saw what remained of the house, he felt sick. They weren't going to need to call in the sheriff. He was already there in person and James was deep in conversation with him. Daniel's legs were shaking as he took the mare to the stable, unsaddled her and gave her food and water, then returned to the yard.

The sheriff came over to them. "It's a nasty business. I sure am sorry for you folks."

James joined them. "Sheriff's pretty sure it was started deliberately. There's oil over by the old cellar door. There's not much chance of going in. Fire's out but it's still smouldering in there."

"Is there any sign of Ben? Can we send a search party in?" It was obvious there could be no real hope of finding Ben alive, but Daniel couldn't bear the thought of just giving up.

The sheriff looked him straight in the eye. "I'm real sorry, Mr Flynn, but there ain't no way anyone left in there would be alive."

Daniel felt his shoulders slump and nodded. "Can we try to get in to this end of the house to see if we can save anything?" Daniel could see that the kitchen was not as badly damaged as some of the rest of the house and anything they could salvage would be useful.

The sheriff sighed. "Well you can, but it's a mighty big risk you'd be taking. I guess I'd probably do the same if it was my house."

"I'd like to see if we can find Ben and give him a proper burial," James said quietly. "Perhaps we can find one or two of the men to help us. I've sent word to Ellie. She'll be coming as soon as she can." He paused. "She can stay in my place, there's room enough for another if I tidy up a bit. I got some food in while I was in town. I've laid it out in Ben's cabin. Junior's safely tied up, it should still be there." He gave a weak smile.

Daniel nodded. "Come, Molly." He put an arm about her shoulder. "Let's go and sit down while we work out where to start. James, Sheriff, will you join us?"

"No, sir, though it's kind of you to ask. It looks like I've got me some work to be doing. No one goes killing an innocent man on my patch and doesn't hear from me about it." He raised his hat to them and went to untether his horse to ride back to Pierceton.

James went with them down to the cabins.

"I'm not sure it feels right being here without Ben," Daniel said as the cabin came into view.

James turned to him. "Painful as it is, you're going to have to get used to it. You've no other place to live and Ben wouldn't want you homeless." Then with a little less warmth he asked, "So how did it go in Huntington."

Daniel sighed. "Molly, how would you feel if I said

we're staying here and seeing this through?" He was surprised to see a smile break across her face.

"Last night for a time I might have thought otherwise, but the truth is I'd say I was mighty relieved to hear it. This is my home, right here."

"I'll second that." James sounded far happier again. "What happened?"

"It wasn't just what happened. I was thinking on the journey about how settled we are here and how running away never got anyone anywhere. Then, when I got there, I didn't take to the folks we'd be renting from and I knew you'd be unhappy if I signed us up to it. I didn't even stay under their roof. We'd have been leaving one problem and walking into another."

James clapped him on the back. "Well it looks like we need a plan to get this here farm rebuilt and you can count on my support in doing it."

Daniel smiled for the first time since meeting Molly that morning. "Molly, is that all right with you?"

"It's better than all right. It's the best news I've had for a while. I guess Ben is going to have to forgive us for making his cabin our home."

"He'll be close by and it's nothing he wouldn't have wanted you to do. Now let's get ourselves some food and work out what needs to be done."

Much as Daniel tried to eat, he had no desire for food. He fed most of what he'd taken to Junior, who was sitting on the end of the bench with his head on his master's leg. Years ago, it had been Duke, the little dog's father, who helped Daniel through the darkest days. This time it was Junior who had saved his family, but at the cost of Ben's life. If only Daniel hadn't gone to Huntington. Daniel was finding it hard to shake off the feeling that all this was his fault.

He felt Molly's hand on his. "There would have been nothing you could have done."

"If I had been here, Ben wouldn't have needed to go into the house." He brought his fist crashing down on the table making the crockery jump and settle back in place. He then lifted Junior up and carried him out of the cabin. More than anything, he needed to be alone with the dog in the fresh air. He carried Junior down to the edge of the stream and held the little dog close while he wept for his friend.

CHAPTER 36

Molly moved further away from the table when Daniel left the cabin.

"Give him time," James said. "We started our grieving some hours ago, it's new to Daniel."

Molly sighed. She had seen the pain and guilt etched on Daniel's face and she knew him well enough to know he'd find the latter hard to shake off. They sat in silence for a while, the food sitting in front of them on the table. She put a cloth over everything while they waited.

She was grateful that Ben had kept the cabin so neatly. His belongings were sparse, but there was enough to get them started. She could only hope they'd be able to salvage some of the things from the house. She hunted around for paper and something with which to write.

"What is it you're after? If you're looking for paper, I don't reckon Ben did a whole lot of writing," James said. "While we're waiting, I'll go across to my cabin to see if I can find something."

"Thank you." Molly relaxed a little. It was good that James was there to help. They were lucky he didn't want to spend his retirement with his feet up, smoking a pipe in the shade.

While he was gone, she tended to Mary's needs and then let her play on the floor. She heard the door open and presumed it was James returning, but Junior hobbled over to Mary and sat close to his charge.

Molly turned to see Daniel framed by the doorway. She held her arms out to him and he came forward and held her close. They were still standing like that when James returned.

"I'm sorry," he said as he came through the door.

Molly and Daniel broke apart.

"It's fine," Molly said, wiping a tear from her cheek. Shall we have something to eat?" She turned back to Daniel, "We waited for you." She went across to the table to remove the covers and they all sat silently and began to eat the bread and cheese which James had bought earlier.

After a while, Molly said, "I'm guessing I'll have lost all the farm ledgers. I don't rightly know what's what without them." She sighed.

"Let's wait until we've had chance to find what's left." Daniel put his hand over hers. "We're going to have to visit the bank to find out what we can do."

Molly nodded. "I'm going to start by cleaning out the dairy. At least if that's up and running we can be earning some money to keep us going."

"It's the quieter months on the farm. I can help." Daniel squeezed her hand.

Little by little they worked out what they would need to do to get started and determined that they'd spend the day with Daniel trying to salvage anything possible, while Molly first sorted out the dairy and then if time allowed began doing what was needed to the cabin.

They still had a couple of labourers about, who could be pressed into service where needed, and they'd help Daniel with the house first.

"I should go into town as soon as I can," Molly said.

"A day won't change much."

She knew Daniel was right, but her head was spinning

and she felt as though she needed to do everything at once.

They set about the day's tasks. James was to care for Mary so that Molly and Daniel could concentrate. Molly would go down to the cabin to see them at intervals. Molly really wanted to be going into the house with Daniel to make sure he brought the most useful things, but she had to trust him and could only ask him to look for the things she had most need of.

Thankfully it was a fine day, so putting their belongings out in the yard would not bring them to further harm. As Molly worked in the dairy, she had to resist going to see what if anything the men had brought out. However, the sound of a cart trundling into the yard did bring her out as, to her recollection, they were not expecting any deliveries.

"Sarah! Joe!" Molly was sincerely surprised to see her friend.

Sarah got down and embraced Molly. "Oh, my poor dear. How are you?"

"We're fine." Molly was fighting to hold back the tears.

"Ma sent us to bring these to you. People in the town thought you might find some of it useful." Joseph smiled at her. "Is Daniel around to help me unload?"

"For us? Oh, how kind." Now Molly couldn't stop the tears and they cascaded down her cheeks. "Daniel's gone into the house to see what can be saved. I'll help to unload. Perhaps we can take the cart down to the cabin so we don't have so far to carry things."

Joseph nodded and got the horses moving slowly again down the track to the cabins.

As they unloaded the cart, and put what it contained onto the porch, James came out to help with Mary in his arms. "Looks like folks have been mighty generous."

"Yes," Molly said quietly. "I don't know how we'll ever thank everyone."

"Well." James lifted down a sack of flour. "If you ask me, this looks like an olive branch and no mistake. I'm guessing there's folks out there that don't feel all that easy in theirselves. They may not have treated you so well and this is by way of an apology."

"There are even fresh clothes for Mary. I really am grateful for those. What she's got on still smells of the fire and I'd nothing else to change her into." Molly lifted a cardigan which looked brand new and about the right size for her daughter.

"I'll get her sorted once we're done with this," said James indulgently tickling the little girl under her chin and making her giggle. "We'll get you right, Mary."

"Oh, James, look at this." Molly held up a small jar of ointment that would help the burns on Junior's paws.

"I'll see to Junior too. I'm guessing he'll be mighty grateful for that." James smiled at the little dog who was still limping very badly and trying to avoid putting down all of his paws at once.

"Well that's everything. I wish I could stay to help." Sarah shot a look at Joe. "But Joe says we need to get back." She took both of Molly's hands but said no more.

Molly felt the warmth of love from her friend, but could see the conflict in her eyes. She nodded and kissed Sarah's cheek. "Thank you. We'll try to find a way to thank those who've helped too."

The cart disappeared along the track and Molly decided to sort just one or two things before going back to work.

Molly had not been in the dairy long when she heard Daniel shout from the yard. She wiped her hands on her apron and went out to him. She realised she'd not yet told him about the gifts they'd received but she could tell by the happy look on his face that he'd got something for her first.

Daniel was covered from head to toe in patches of soot and dirt from his activities.

"Close your eyes and put your hands out," he said as she approached him.

Molly laughed and did as he had asked. She was expecting to feel the weight of a large book in her hands, presuming he had found the ledger. Instead what he put there was relatively light, but she knew instantly from the texture of the wood and the attached chain exactly what she was feeling. She opened her eyes and drew the wooden rosary to her. "Oh, Daniel, I never thought I'd see this again. My one link to Mammy. If only it could have saved Ben too."

Daniel's face fell. "We found him at the top of the stairs. A beam had fallen on him. I think that's probably what killed him. He didn't seem to have been trapped by it. I think it had killed him outright. I couldn't bear to think he was burned alive. He's not a pretty sight, but we do have something to bury. The men have found a box to bring him out in and told me to leave them to it."

Molly nodded, clutching the rosary tightly and praying for Ben's soul as Daniel spoke.

After they had stood in silence together for a few moments, Molly told Daniel about the general store's cart bringing out gifts from well-wishers. Then Daniel led her over to the pile of things they'd brought out from the house. Most of them were at least partly charred, but the kitchen pots and pans were unscathed.

"The ledger?" Molly looked eagerly at Daniel.

He shook his head and started looking through the pile until he came to a charred hard front, which had once been followed by the precious pages of their accounts for the farm.

Molly straightened her shoulders and pulled herself up. "Then I'll just have to sit down tonight and try to remember what I can. Then when I go to see the bank tomorrow…" In reality she had absolutely no idea what she would say to the bank. They'd recovered from losing the hay and their finances were not bad, but to rebuild the farmhouse was a massive cost. They had insurance for the farm, of course they had, but until the cause of the fire was proved it was unlikely that would be paying out. She hoped the matter would be settled quickly.

"James has spoken to Pastor Wilmott. They're sorting out a proper funeral and burial for Ben."

Daniel looked strained as she spoke and Molly realised just how much her husband was grieving for his friend. "Are you all right with me making changes in the cabin?"

He looked up at her. "I know we have to. There was only one of Ben and there are three of us to find room for. I just don't want to feel as though we've forgotten him."

Molly put her hand into his. "We won't ever do that. He's been an important part of our family and we'll always bring Mary up to know about her Grandpa Ben." She hesitated and then a thought struck her. "We should write to his family. They need to know. We can do that this evening as well as the books." She tried to smile, but it was hard to manage.

CHAPTER 37

Michael row the boat ashore, Hallelujah!
Michael row the boat ashore, Hallelujah!
Jordan's river is deep and wide, hallelujah.
Meet my mother on the other side, hallelujah.
Michael Row the Boat Ashore - African American Spiritual
1860s

It was strange waking up in the cabin the following day. Daniel felt disorientated as he got up from his makeshift mattress on the floor. There was only a single bed in the cabin and Molly and Mary had shared that. That was one of the things they needed to sort, but there was little useful that could be rescued from the upstairs of the house.

Not that he'd slept well. He had spent much of the night alternating between anger and guilt. If only he hadn't decided to go to Huntington. He knew recriminations weren't going to change things, but he couldn't help the thoughts churning through his mind.

The only way he had ever been able to deal with his problems was to throw himself into work and he was determined to make the best of the day. He and Molly wanted to make good progress with the farm chores so they could go into town to start on all that was necessary.

Daniel was amazed by the amount they'd managed to achieve the previous day. Molly had completely cleaned the dairy and it was now airing, almost ready for production to begin again. He had not rescued much from the house, but the kitchen table and chairs were still usable as were all the pots and pans. The stove would take some moving, but it was used to fire and had not suffered unduly as a result. They'd store it in one of the outbuildings until there was a new kitchen for it to move into.

Despite his grief, Daniel's hope was founded on one thing, he believed this must truly be the end of the Reese brothers working against them. After this, no one would stand by and let it continue, or so he hoped.

Ben had loved Daniel's singing and so, as he worked, he sang to his friend. He sang sad ballads which told of loss and hymns which gave him hope his friend was at least now in a better place. A place without inequality, without injustice and without bullying.

Whilst Molly went to see the bank, Daniel went to see Pastor Wilmott. Although James had already seen him the day before there were still arrangements which needed to be made. The Pastor asked him what he knew of Ben's life and Daniel told the precious little the old man had shared. He realised he didn't even know what had led to the deaths of the man's wife and child as he'd never felt comfortable to ask.

"The only family he's still got is a distance away in Iowa. We've written to them to tell them what's happened, but they're old now too and unlikely to make the journey."

The pastor nodded.

This wasn't the church that Daniel and Molly had married in, but it was the one that Ben would have chosen, so it was the one where his funeral would be. There was little need to delay and the service was arranged for two days following.

Daniel shook the pastor's hand and went on his next errand to the sheriff.

"It was them all right. Those Reese boys have death on their hands and no mistake. Of course, there'll be a proper inquest and all that, but it most certainly was them as done it."

Daniel felt relief wash over him. If the sheriff was certain of the cause, then hopefully that would address their worries with insurance. "How do you know, sir?"

"I'd like to say my boys worked it all out from what they found up at your place." His rotund body wobbled as he guffawed. "Of course, I'd like to say that, seeing it's the only real excitement we've had around here in a while. But truth is Reuben Reese got the jitters and confessed. Jacob's none too happy about it. He's still saying they was in Marsh's same as always. They may be Marsh's best customers, if you take no account of them never paying, but Marsh ain't having any of it this time. I reckon he doesn't want blood on his hands without due cause. It's not like there was a proper fight or nothing. I've got the pair of them locked up. They ain't getting no bail from me, no, siree. I guess they'll need a trail, but it sure don't look good for them."

"Thank you, sir. That's mighty comforting to hear. Would you excuse me so I can pass the news on to the bank? Molly's meeting with them now."

"Sure thing. You tell them the sheriff will be sending his report in real soon."

Daniel thanked him again and made his way back along the main road to the bank.

The teller was busy when Daniel walked in and he felt frustrated having to wait in line. He couldn't just go barging into the manager's office however important the news seemed to be. Eventually Daniel was taken through to where Molly was earnestly talking through the figures with their manager.

"Good day, sir." Daniel shook the man by the hand. "Don't look so alarmed, Molly, I've come with good news."

Molly raised her eyebrows in anticipation and Daniel took the seat next to her as indicated by the manager. "I've been talking to the sheriff, and it seems one of those Reese boys has confessed to them starting the fire."

Molly's face relaxed.

The manager nodded. "Well that is indeed good news, but it may not speed the insurance company's payment overly much. They'll want to do their own investigation to be satisfied."

"But won't the sheriff's report tell them all they need to know?"

The older man shook his head. "What if the farm were, shall we say, in difficulties and you had colluded in the starting of the fire?"

Daniel clenched his fists. "Surely anyone who knows us would see that was ridiculous. How could they…?"

"Please sit down, Mr Flynn. I'm just telling you how the insurance company will look at it before they're happy. I'm just working with your wife to put together the information they will ask for to prove that isn't the case. Your account with us is in good shape. I shall be retiring shortly but I'm hoping that we can sort this before I go. You've been good customers of the bank and Miss Cochrane before you. I'll do my best, Mr Flynn."

Daniel sank down into his chair and moved his hat around in his hands. "I'm sorry. It's just going to be hard for us for a while. We really need to get the house rebuilt as soon as we can."

Molly rested her hand on his arm. "We'll get there. Don't worry. I shall be a little while longer yet. If you want to get back to the farm, I can walk back later."

Daniel felt useless. "The walk will do me good. I'll leave the cart for you and I'll head back on foot. Good day, sir." He bowed his head and left the room heading back to the lobby of the bank and out into the brightness of the day. He kicked at a stone. It wasn't Molly's fault, but he felt frustrated to be on the outside of things. He needed to go and chop wood, or do some other repetitive task outdoors, to relieve his frustration.

Daniel worked hard on the farm that evening and the following day. Even if they did have to wait for a visit from the insurance company there were still preparations he could be making for when they rebuilt the house. Whilst he worked he could block out thinking about Ben. He was sorry that they couldn't wait to hear from Miss Ellie or Ben's own family before burying him, but that was how it was. It made him think back to the night in New York when they'd wheeled Mammy's body to the Potter's Field and he wondered if Molly was thinking the same.

Daniel had hung the rosary up in the cabin as one of the first things they'd done, but he'd noticed that Molly had taken it down and was carrying it in her pocket. He could understand her need of it and almost wished he had it too. They were both dealing with their grief by working rather than talking about it and by their embraces when neither of them wanted to let go of the other. It must be harder still for James, but he seemed to be bearing it.

When they went into town for Ben's funeral, Daniel expected it to be a quiet affair. He was surprised by the number of people who seemed to be milling around. "It's busy in town today. Is there something happening that we don't know about?"

Molly wiped her eyes. "I don't think so. I think they might be here for Ben. I guess there are a few people who feel guilty for not stepping in to stop what was going on."

The church was full and Daniel wept openly, wishing his friend could see it. He imagined the bemusement with which Ben would have greeted the event and thought how ironic life could be. Daniel neither knew nor could have taken in all the faces, but he saw the sheriff as well as Franklin Marsh from the bar, the latter coming as something of a surprise to him. He didn't see the Spencers and he hoped, for Molly's sake, that was just because he hadn't noticed them and not because they had stayed away.

By the day's end, they were a sombre party returning to the farm. Ben's body was in the ground and they'd lost the truest friend anyone could have. Junior limped towards them as they returned. His paws were healing slowly, but even he seemed to realise life would not be the same again.

Daniel sang quietly to himself as he worked over the next few days. Thankfully Mary was the one thing brightening all their lives and she was starting to make rapid progress moving about, which kept them all watching out. James was enjoying caring for her during the day, which freed Molly to work harder than she was able while tending to the child.

Friday's post brought a letter from Iowa.

My dear Daniel and Molly,
    I arranged for the letter to Ben's family to be taken to them

and read out to them as you requested. They were visibly distressed by the contents and asked that I should write to you to thank you for ensuring they knew. They did say that they wished he'd never left them, but the reality was that he was happy with you. You must move on from this tragedy and honour his name by the things you do.
Your humble servant

Herbert Hendry (Doctor)

"You know," Molly said as she laid the letter aside, "he's right."

"What about?" Daniel was lost in his own train of thought.

"Honouring Ben. Do you remember how passionate he was when he made me understand Miss Ellie being away when I thought I needed her more?"

"Yes, I do." From the fire in Molly's eye Daniel knew there was more to come.

"Do you remember what he said?"

"Not exactly." Daniel was betting he was about to find out that Molly did remember.

"I remember his exact words. 'She ain't doing it because she's selfish. She's doing it because she's brave and angry and she's doing it for you and me.' Then he said, 'You gave me a home and a retirement because you believe in everyone being equal.' We've lost Ben because those Reese boys didn't see us all as being equal. We need to fight back, for Ben as much as for us."

Molly looked more determined than Daniel had seen her in a long time. He took her hands. "Don't you think there's been enough harm done?"

"Oh, don't get me wrong. I'm not planning to fight back in the ways those boys have. That wouldn't honour Ben's memory at all. If you'll support me, I want to get involved in fighting for equality. I don't know how exactly, but I can't leave it all to Miss Ellie. I've another idea too, but I need to think that one through a little before I explain."

Daniel smiled to see his wife so determined. He saw the child who had kept them all alive on the New York streets and the woman he'd grown to love so much over the years. He wrapped his arms around her. "Of course I'll support you. I'll be proud to do that."

CHAPTER 38

"Daniel! Daniel!" Molly ran from where she'd been seated outside the dairy, with the letter still in her hand. She thought Daniel had said he'd be repairing the chicken coop that morning, but he was nowhere to be seen. She headed down to the barn and found him trying to renovate some of the furniture that had come out of the house.

"There you are. They're coming today." She was out of breath as she told him.

He looked at her blankly, unable to speak for the nails he was holding in his mouth.

She shook her head and realised she hadn't explained herself very well. "Miss Ellie, William, Cecilia and baby Thomas, they're all arriving by train this very afternoon. Miss Ellie is hoping to stay with James and the others will stay in a guest house in town."

Daniel put down his hammer and took the nails from his mouth. "I guess I'd better leave this for now so we're ready to go and get them. What's still to be done?"

Thankfully they were on top of most of the work, but Molly listed the remaining chores and then leaving Daniel to move on to those, she went down to the cabins to see James.

They all went to the station to meet the train. Although the circumstances of the visit were not ideal, Molly knew it would lift all their spirits. Daniel was holding Mary and as soon as Miss Ellie stepped down onto the platform

Molly rushed to greet her.

"Now stop that, child. Anyone would think it was a while since you'd seen me."

Despite the admonition Miss Ellie was smiling broadly as she stood back and took both of Molly's hands. "You've had a tough time. If it's all the same to you, I plan to stay a while until you're back on your feet."

Molly could feel the tears of relief rolling down her face. "Yes, please, yes." Then before she had time to say anything further William had embraced her and she felt the strength of familial support and thanked God it was so.

Once William let her go, she went over to Cecilia almost shyly. "It's been a long journey for you." She looked down at the sleeping Thomas. "I'm very grateful that you have come."

"How could we do otherwise?" Cecilia asked earnestly, kissing her cheek.

They took William and family to the guest house before heading back to the farm. "I need to talk to all of you tomorrow," Molly said, "but I'm guessing Miss Ellie wants to see what has happened to her home right now."

William and Cecilia bid them a good evening and arranged to go out to the farm after church the following day.

"Oh, mercy, me!" Miss Ellie proclaimed as the charred remains of the farmhouse came into view. "Whatever would my poor daddy have to say about that?"

She was trembling when she got down from the cart and Molly took her arm to walk around with her.

"I'm sorry," Molly said quietly.

"Oh, child, you have nothing to apologise for. Those Reese boys are the only ones to blame and make no mistake. They might even have done it if I'd stayed on here." Ellie Cochrane dabbed at her eyes with her handkerchief. "It's still a shock seeing it though. I grew up here and have some very happy memories."

"We'll rebuild it exactly as it was."

Miss Ellie turned to face Molly and took hold of her arms. "Now, you listen up, girl. You'll do no such thing. You'll build it exactly as you would like it to be. I might have been attached to the place, but I'm not so daft as not to have known it needed some improvements doing. If it hadn't been for losing Ben, I could have said they'd done us a favour. We can talk to someone together about how it should be when it's rebuilt."

Molly hugged her guardian. She was so grateful to have this tower of strength by her side once again.

It was raining the following day and Molly was conscious that there was nowhere back at the farm where they could all sit round and talk. They could have asked the Spencers if they might go back to their house and Molly was quite sure that her friend's in-laws would have agreed. However, she didn't want what she was about to discuss to be all around the town before nightfall. If she was going to make a success of the idea then the fewer people who knew, the better.

They went instead to the guest house where the Dixons were staying and with the agreement of the landlady, who would be out visiting her sister, they took over the parlour.

Molly laid out the food she had prepared for them to eat. "I'm sorry, it's not much, but I couldn't think what else to do."

"It's perfect, child. Now you sit down and let me take care of you for a while." Miss Ellie laid a hand on Molly's shoulder and Molly felt herself relax, grateful not to have to carry the burden of the day.

As everyone took bread and cheese Molly waited, thinking about how to raise the subject she wanted to discuss. She hadn't even talked to Daniel about it and wondered if he would mind that they all discuss it together without time to consider it first.

"Daniel, I hope you'll forgive me for this being the first you hear of the idea as well."

Daniel grinned. "We're amongst family, there's nobody better to share it with."

His reply gave her confidence to go on. "Well, now that the Reese brothers have been charged with arson and the sheriff says it's a pretty clear case, I've heard in the general store that the bank are going to foreclose on the loan on Reese's Farm." Molly paused while that much of her story sank in.

"It's not as though those boys are going to be free to do any farming any time soon." Miss Ellie raised an eyebrow as she spoke and they all laughed.

"Anyway," Molly continued, "it set me to thinking, what if we were to buy what's left of their farm?" She saw Daniel blink rapidly and wondered if he would find her plan too frightening. She continued. "Their land does border ours, along the strip you bought when their daddy was struggling a while ago." She turned to Miss Ellie for confirmation and the older lady nodded, clearly listening attentively to what Molly was saying. "We could simply extend Cochrane's farm and bring the rest of their land into it too. We'd need to take on more hands to help us work it, but I reckon we can manage that. It would also give us chance to employ people who mightn't find work otherwise and do just a little bit to start to change this country of ours. We'd need to raise the money for the land…" She looked across to William.

"And that's where I come in?" He asked with a broad smile on his face. "You'll be needing a lawyer?"

Molly nodded.

"Where would we live?" Daniel had concern in his eyes.

Molly put her hand on his. "We could still live in Ben's cabin until our farmhouse is rebuilt. I didn't think you'd want to live in the Reese family home."

His face relaxed and she knew she'd been right. He nodded.

"I guess I'd like to know what you all think and whether you just think I'm crazy."

To Molly's surprise it was James who spoke up first. "Don't you think it might stir up more trouble if you do? Them boys'll quieten down now if you leave things alone. This might just get them started again."

Miss Ellie turned to her cousin. "Now come, James. When we were children you weren't one to walk away from a challenge. If it weren't for you, I'd not have done half the things I got into trouble for."

"Well that's as maybe, but I'm older now, even if not wiser and I just lost a dear friend through what those boys can do."

They all fell silent for a while.

"You know," Daniel said, "I think Ben would have supported Molly's idea. He didn't think Miss Ellie should give up her fight for what's right and wasn't afraid to tell Molly so when she wished Miss Ellie could be here. I don't think he'd want us to give up now either. It will be a whole lot of work, but if there's a way to make it happen, I'm right here with you."

Daniel broke into a wide smile and Molly felt her heart

flutter. With Daniel's support she knew she could do anything.

James was nodding slowly. "I guess you're all right. I'm just a bit tired of all the trouble."

"You don't need to play a part in it if you don't want to," Molly said in an attempt to reassure him.

James gave a wry smile. "What, and miss out on all the fun?" They all laughed.

Molly looked across at William, waiting for him to speak.

Just as he opened his mouth, Thomas let out a loud wail. Cecilia apologised and excused herself to attend to him. "Well," William said grinning, "it certainly sounds as though my son has a view. If only he could express it more coherently." They all laughed. "I'd really like the opportunity to talk to my father before we take this very far, if there's enough time for me to contact him. I've half an idea that we could share the investment with you and that way you'd need to borrow less from the bank. I've a notion to become a gentleman farmer, don't you know."

They all laughed again, then began discussing what would need to be done to bring about the deal.

Miss Ellie took Molly to one side when she had the opportunity. "I'm so very proud of you, girl. My own dear daddy would be proud of you too."

Molly felt her cheeks glow. She knew that was praise indeed.

CHAPTER 39

I wonder how often these men must be told
When a woman a notion once seizes,
However they ridicule, lecture or scold,
She'll do, after all, as she pleases,
The Bloomer's Complaint - C Schuessele - 1851

Once the decision to buy the farm had been reached, Daniel was keen for everything to progress. He was frustrated that paperwork could take so long and was only glad that it was Molly dealing with all of that side of things and not himself.

William and Cecilia had stayed for most of the week, but then had to return to their life in Dowagiac. Daniel wondered whether, if they had a part share in a farm in Pierceton, they might spend more time there, but thought it unlikely. They had a very good standard of living with the Dixon family and somehow he didn't think farm muck would be a good substitute.

It was the middle of November before the insurance assessor had finished his work and they received confirmation that they could rebuild the farmhouse. When Molly showed him the letter, he whooped with joy causing Mary to try to copy him, which made them all laugh.

They worked with Miss Ellie to agree what the new farmhouse should look like while demolition of the old farmhouse began. Then, little by little over the winter

271

months, whilst the weather held good, work on the new house started. In the meantime, they made Ben's cabin cosy enough and Mary enjoyed splitting her time between her parents and her honorary grandparents.

Junior's paw was slow to recover and although he was left with a limp, they thought it was more because he'd forgotten he could walk normally again, than because it still hurt. He wore it as a badge of honour for his bravery.

Finally, when February came, the bank announced the sale of the Reese family farm and Molly was first at the bank when they opened the next day. Miss Ellie had gone with her when she made her proposal and Daniel had waited back at the farm, looking up from his work at every noise in case it signified their return.

In the late afternoon when they did get back, Molly's face looked thunderous. She got down from the cart and strode over to where he was.

"He wants to see you and William. Apparently, the new bank manager thinks that as women we may not be sufficiently competent to execute such a large transaction. Given his predecessor was happy enough with our own farm's affairs, I don't know how he can have the effrontery to treat us like this. How can it be a different matter to borrow money from the bank, when we have proved we can manage our own money well enough?" She marched past him down to the cabin, pulling her bonnet from her head as she did so.

"Don't fret. She'll calm down later. Let's just say the new bank manager here is a little old-fashioned in his ways and may need some assistance in understanding your wife." Miss Ellie gave Daniel a meaningful look and then went after her charge.

Daniel looked across to the farmhouse. There had been

little progress over the last few weeks and he couldn't help feeling frustrated. Tonight was a night to sit in comfort around a family table together, but it was too cold to sit out and there was no possibility of all of them squeezing in to either cabin. He sighed. Molly was right to be annoyed, of course. She was the business brain behind all they did. He was far happier working out here than poring over ledgers.

He cleaned up in the pail by the barn and went down to the cabin.

Mary was on the seat by the window as he approached and he heard her joyful voice announce his arrival. It made him smile. He went in and swung her into a big hug then ventured to approach Molly.

"It's all right. I've stopped biting." She looked at him sheepishly and he kissed her nose.

"You are right to be annoyed. I can't bear the thought that you face such prejudice and I certainly don't want Mary to have to be confronted by it as she grows up. So what do we need to do?"

"Well, I've already sent a message to William. That's one of the things that took us so long, finding the fastest way we could contact him. I guess you could do with a suit. Your wedding one didn't make it through the fire." Molly brushed a piece of straw from his overalls.

"You're telling me these aren't smart enough?" He pulled a face at Mary and she giggled. She might not have understood the conversation, but her response was right on cue.

"We don't have much time to waste. Even though we've offered the full price, the bank says they'll take another buyer if one comes along before they see us all together."

"But that's not fair." Daniel began to understand why Molly was so annoyed when she came back. "How long do you think it will be before William comes?"

"We've asked him to get Mr Dixon to send word immediately to the bank and come as soon as he can." Molly looked anxious.

"Then I'd better get myself into town tomorrow to find something to wear, unless James has got something I can borrow."

"Daniel Flynn, how much taller than James are you? Where exactly do you think his trousers would come to on you." Molly's laughter came as a welcome relief and once she'd started, she didn't seem able to stop. She wiped her eyes. "Oh dear, I needed that. I guess it's worth asking but I don't suppose it's much use. We could have asked William to bring something for you."

"I'll be more comfortable in something of my own choosing and I may have other occasions to wear it in a few years. Mind you, once we've got a proper kitchen again, I'm rather hoping you might spoil me with some of your home cooking." He looked at her plaintively.

"You're not exactly starving," she said patting his stomach. "Besides, you'd better finish our kitchen first. There'll be no baking until you do."

The following day Daniel made himself look as presentable as possible and set off into town. Buying a suit was the last thing he felt like doing and seemed to him like money which could be better used on something practical. He reminded himself what was at stake and went in search of the men's outfitters in the town. Most of his clothing came from the farm supplies store and suited the purpose, what wasn't from there was made at home. He knew nothing of collars and jackets and didn't really know what to ask.

Though his welcome seemed less cordial than that of other customers entering the store, he soon explained what he needed as well as the limitations of his budget and was found a suit and shirt, which, with little alteration, would serve his needs. Molly would be able to collect his purchases when she did the rounds with the cart the following afternoon.

Going back out into the late winter day, Daniel felt relieved to be outdoors with the ordeal of suit buying behind him.

Irrespective of hearing nothing from William, Molly had arranged for them to go to see the bank together at the end of that week. When the time came, Daniel discarded his overalls and put on his suit, feeling awkward and uncomfortable as he did so.

"My, don't you look smart?" Miss Ellie said when he came out of the cabin.

"I told him that too, but he won't believe me." Molly laughed and smoothed the lapel of the jacket.

Daniel sighed. "Let's get this over with."

Waiting outside the manager's office, Daniel wondered what, if anything, he could possibly add to what Molly had said. Yes, he was male, but what did that count for in reality? The Reese brothers could claim the same but hadn't paid their bills. When they were shown in, Daniel felt uncomfortable and suspected he must look so as well.

"And where is the other gentleman?"

The manager had not even bothered with pleasantries or introductions, making Daniel feel even worse. However, as the man behind the desk was looking straight at him, he felt compelled to be the one to answer. "We're still waiting to hear when he will come. We thought…"

Daniel didn't even finish what he was saying before the manager cut across him. "I'm sorry, we do have other people interested in buying the farm and I am very busy. There's no point you coming until you're all present. Good day."

Molly's anger was palpable, while Daniel was dumbfounded by the response and got up to leave. He ushered Molly towards the door before she could give in to her inevitable explosion of frustration. When they were out into the road, he could hold her back no more.

"Did you ever see such rudeness? How dare he treat us as though we were less than nothing. I've a good mind to move our account to another bank, but that would mean going out of town."

Whilst Daniel wanted to reason with her and calm her down, he couldn't help but think Molly may well be right.

The days passed with Daniel helping with the work on the farmhouse when he was free of his normal routine. Once the roof was on, he could really help to make a difference, but that was a few weeks away yet. They were worried that no word had come back from William and there was no sign of his arrival.

"They said there are other people interested. The bank's not going to wait for us forever," Molly said sadly. "All because they won't deal with women, we could miss out on this opportunity."

"Is there nothing else we can do?" Miss Ellie asked.

Molly shook her head. "I guess I could go back to try to see the manager again, but I'm not sure it will help. I'm going in to town tomorrow, I'll try."

"Do you want me to come?" Daniel felt he should be by Molly's side, but really didn't want to put that suit on again if he didn't have to.

Molly shook her head. "I'm as well to go on my own. He's made clear he wants William there too before it will make any difference."

"Perhaps he'll be here soon." In his heart Daniel was starting to doubt if William planned to come at all but was cross with himself for having so little faith in his friend. William's days of denying them were behind him, weren't they? He certainly hoped they were.

In the end it was Miss Ellie who insisted on accompanying Molly and the two set off to deliver the orders before Molly tried to see the bank.

CHAPTER 40

Molly was in a much better mood when she and Miss Ellie set off into town. That morning they had received news that the roof would be going onto the farmhouse the following week, which should mean there'd be no further delays due to the weather.

"At last we can start to plan for getting curtains made and furniture sorted. It will be good to have more space now Mary's growing so much. She's going to be walking before we know it and then the cabin will be hard work."

"There's far bigger families than yours live in cabins like that," Miss Ellie chided her.

"Oh, I know, and Daniel and I have lived in far worse." Molly shuddered as she remembered the shack in New York where they'd lived with Mammy. "I guess a girl can get used to better times." She grinned. "That reminds me. What would you say if Daniel and I were to take an orphan into our family?"

Miss Ellie smiled broadly. "I'd say there'd be no one better to understand what the child was going through, but you've a good deal on your plate already and you can't expect it to be easy just because you were an orphan yourself. There's some as has problems too deeply rooted to dig out easily."

Molly thought Miss Ellie's words were wise ones. She remembered back to life on the streets and the number of children involved with the gangs. It made her wonder if they were too young to think of taking someone in, but she still felt she wanted to go ahead if they could.

Once the rounds were complete, they headed for the bank. She was waiting patiently to ask the teller if the manager were free to talk to them, when the man walked through the bank to go into his office. She moved out of the line and as she did so looked across to Miss Ellie who was sitting patiently near the door.

"Sir, can you spare a moment?"

He turned and squinted at her as though he was only vaguely aware who she was. Miss Ellie had got up and come across to join her. He looked at Miss Ellie and recognition dawned. "I'm sorry."

Molly took a deep breath. "We can wait a while, if you will have time shortly."

He looked at her with his brow furrowed in confusion and Molly was taken aback.

"No," he said slowly and firmly, "I'm sorry, but the farm is sold."

Molly gasped and put her hand to her mouth. "But, sir you said we should present ourselves to you. I thought…"

"And you haven't presented yourselves, have you? I asked for the men folk to be present and that hasn't happened. It's been bought by someone out of state." Then he waved his hand in general dismissal and turned away.

Molly stood rooted to the spot. She was aware of the silence around her and that others were staring in their direction. Miss Ellie took her arm and gently steered her out of the bank.

"And that, child, is exactly why I'm prepared to get arrested if I have to in order to make a very important point."

"Then I think it's about time you counted me as one of

your number." Molly's initial feeling of being stunned had been replaced by indignation and anger. "We need to change this town. Where do we start?"

"It's not just this town," Miss Ellie said. "It's the whole country that needs to change. Mr Lincoln would be mighty disappointed even to see the way the change he brought about is being undone. There's work to do and no mistake."

"How can men get away with treating women like this? I'm as good in business as many men in this town." Molly wanted to march into the manager's office and tell him exactly what she thought.

"I dare say you're better than most." Miss Ellie shook her head. "Even so there's precious little we can do here."

"Well there should be." Molly stamped her foot in frustration. Then stomped toward the waiting cart.

Over the next couple of days both Molly and Daniel threw themselves into work on the farm. In the late afternoons, if there was still light, Daniel worked on the farmhouse while Molly spent time with Mary and Miss Ellie, the latter telling her all that was happening in the American Equal Rights Association.

They were into March and the days were lengthening. Now that winter was past, work on the farm was becoming busier and Molly tried not to think of what might have been. She had finished her work in the dairy for the day and walked up the lane to the post box to see if anything had been delivered to them. She was feeling disheartened and more than a little worried that they had still heard nothing from Dowagiac. When she opened the box there was a letter and her heart missed a beat.

The handwriting was Will's and she rushed to open it. There was a single sheet of paper which simply read:

Arriving Thursday 4pm.

Molly ran across the yard in search of Daniel waving the letter. "That's this afternoon. They're going to be so disappointed when they find they've had a wasted journey. I've got deliveries to do. I could meet William when I'm done."

"We'll all go. There's nothing that can't wait another day. I wonder if James or Miss Ellie want to join us."

"I'm going down to rescue them from Mary, I'll ask." Molly kissed her husband feeling happier to have at least heard from William, even though his journey would be fruitless.

They were all fairly quiet as they went to the station later that day. Molly presumed that William planned to stay at the guest house once again. She only wished the farmhouse was ready so that she could have offered him accommodation.

As the train pulled in, Molly saw William holding Thomas up to the window to see them all.

The train door opened and Miss Ellie said, "Why, they're all here!" And she went forward to greet Mr and Mrs Dixon.

Molly shook her head and looked across to Daniel. "What on earth are they going to say when they find they got here too late?"

"I know," he said and shrugged.

Mr Dixon called a porter over and asked him to unload their luggage. Molly frowned when she saw just how much there was. "They really are going to be very unhappy when they hear the news," she said quietly to Daniel.

William's opening words, once they'd all said hello

were, "Well I guess we had better start celebrating."

"Oh, brother of mine, we've really nothing to celebrate, except of course it is indeed wonderful to see you all. Oh dear, I'm not sure how to tell you this." Molly paused and then decided to come straight out with it. "We didn't get the farm." She sighed. "The bank manager had other people interested and he's sold it to someone from out of state." As she said it she could feel a tear forming and sniffed hard.

"And that, dear sister, is where you are wrong." William was grinning as broadly as she'd ever seen him.

Molly shook her head and looked up at William to see his expression had not changed. She stopped. "What's going on, William?" She put her hands on her hips and stood in front of him.

"You look just like you used to when we were children. Now don't be angry with me." His look was one of mock remorse.

"William, what have you done?"

Mr Dixon came up beside her. "I think it might help if I were to take over. Can we get all these things to the guest house and I'll explain everything to you? In the meantime, please be patient."

Molly's heart was racing. How could she be patient? This was the single biggest thing she'd ever tried to do. If they could have added the Reese Farm to their land it would made an enormous difference to what they could achieve over the next few years. For one thing they could provide regular employment to more people and Molly had some ideas that they could use the opportunity to help some who were passed over elsewhere or whose working conditions were not as they should be.

She walked with Daniel, clasping his arm tightly. She

was silent, unable to find words to ask about the journey or general matters as she was so focused on knowing what they meant about the farm. She could hear Miss Ellie enquiring about little Thomas, but it was all just noise to her as she walked.

After what felt an interminable amount of time to Molly, they were seated in the guest house parlour once again. William was still grinning but said nothing.

Molly could contain herself no longer and turned to Mr Dixon. "Will someone please tell me what is going on?"

CHAPTER 41

As Molly looked at Mr Dixon intently, he seemed to blush.

"Forgive me, Molly, Daniel, everything has had to move very quickly. If I had taken the time to consult you on my actions the land would have been lost to us." Mr Dixon shifted in his seat looking uneasy.

Molly had so many questions, but for the time being managed to keep them in check.

"When William received your letter, I sent a telegraph direct to the bank manager to enquire about the situation. I did not in that communication outline my connection to you. From the fact he would not deal with you directly, it was clear to me that he had his prejudices and I feared that he might be finding excuses not to do business with you."

Molly felt her anger rising, but Daniel put his hand on her arm to still her.

"In any event, rightly or wrongly," Mr Dixon hesitated, "I introduced myself as a separate buyer. For one thing, I've come across men like him before and if they don't support you at the outset, they can be too hasty to foreclose if the opportunity arises at a later date. The manager has accepted my offer and I'm due to sign the deal tomorrow."

Molly was confused. "But then you'll be the owner of the farm." She felt disappointment wash over her. She did not want to be a tenant on the land. She wanted to build for the long term.

Mr Dixon smiled and shook his head. "Only in a

manner of speaking and for a very short time." He looked across to William who Molly realised was almost bouncing in his seat.

"Didn't you get my letter explaining everything?" William asked.

Molly shook her head. "The first I heard was the one telling me you were arriving today."

"That explains your reaction." William grinned. "What Pa is going to do is split the title to the land into two parts. Cecilia and I will buy the house from him, and you, as long as you still want to, will buy the land. Our loans won't be with the bank, they will be with Pa. What do you think? Oh, do say we've done the right thing."

Molly had so many thoughts whirling around in her head that she simply didn't know where to start. It was Miss Ellie who took charge of trying to unpick all the tangled ends.

"Now, if I have understood correctly, are you saying that you and Cecilia are moving to Pierceton?"

"Yes, ma'am we most certainly are." William's grin was infectious.

Mr Dixon continued, "When we received your note asking for help in buying the farm, William came to see me to talk it through. As we talked, it became clear to me that with the worry of the fire and all that's gone on, William would quite like to bring up his and Cecilia's family close to your own, so I sat down with Ma to do some thinking."

Molly looked at her brother, surprised and warmed by the thought that he wanted to be closer to them.

"As you know, William has been apprenticed to me in the law office for some while now and he's ready to start undertaking work for himself. I know he's expressed an interest in politics, but we don't really have the connections where we are that would get him very far along that path. Dowagiac is hardly the centre of the world." Mr Dixon laughed and everyone joined in.

"Well, I still enjoy what I do. I'm not ready to be giving it all up just yet. There might be enough to keep the two of us happy, but he'd be right in thinking I'd be keeping the best work for myself." Mr Dixon looked sheepish at his own display of selfish honesty.

"Sorry," he said. "I'm rambling. In short, William is going to be opening a law office here in Pierceton. We're just ironing out the last of the details needed for him to do so under my patronage. It's more complicated with it being another state, but we're nearly sorted."

Molly's face lit up. "You really mean you're moving here?" She turned to William and Cecilia.

William nodded and looked to his father who clearly indicated he should take up the story. "Well obviously if we're living here, we will need somewhere to live, other than a guest house." They all laughed again. "Cecilia and I love the idea of Thomas growing up in the countryside rather than in the town. If we were close enough to get into town easily, but far enough out for there to be fields then it would be perfect. Reese's Farm does just that. We don't need the land and you don't need the house."

Molly looked at her brother through narrowed eyes. Was he saying what she thought he was?

William grinned at her again and carried on. "You will need to repay Pa rather than the bank, but his rates are favourable and I'm happy to act as your lawyer."

"You are the out of state buyer," Miss Ellie looked at Mr Dixon shaking her head. "And we thought it was lost to someone we didn't know."

"Ma'am," Mr Dixon said, "I hope you can forgive me.

It is of course scandalous that he wouldn't sell to Molly direct in the first place. I've seen the figures and it's clear she's a good businesswoman."

Molly felt her cheeks glowing and looked shyly up at Daniel who was beaming with pride.

"And the reason you've got so many trunks is because you're moving here now," Molly started to put all the pieces of the story together.

"What's more," William said. "It means you have at least one ally in the town. I'm still going to try getting involved in politics, but I'll have to stand on my own two feet to do it."

Molly was thrilled to think Mary would grow up with a little cousin nearby. She'd hoped her daughter might find that in Sarah's children, but it was clear that Joseph would stand in the way of that idea. "What about your family?" Molly asked Cecilia. "And Mr and Mrs Dixon come to that!" She looked at William's adoptive family.

"My family are no further from here than they were from Dowagiac," Cecilia said, bouncing Thomas on her knee.

"And we, my dear, shall be visiting regularly," Mrs Dixon said with some degree of determination.

"We sign the final papers tomorrow and then the real work begins." Mr Dixon looked remarkably pleased with himself now the story was told.

"The farmhouse needs a lot of work," Cecilia said earnestly.

"Maybe we can work on both of the farmhouses together." Molly thought it might be fun to spend some evenings with Cecilia while the children played together. It would still be a little while before Thomas would be doing much playing, but that time would pass quickly.

The rest of the evening became a celebration as they talked to and fro about what needed to be done and what plans they had. There would be a lot of work to turn Reese's Farm around and bring it up to the same level that Cochrane's Farm was already achieving, but Daniel and Molly had been drawing up plans for that when they thought they could buy from the bank, so they were ready to put them into place.

"Do you think," said Miss Ellie, "that when you move back into the house, I might keep Ben's cabin as a place I can retreat to when needs be?"

"Why, of course, but we rather thought you'd be in the house with us." Molly was concerned in case Miss Ellie felt she was being pushed out.

"If it gets too cold for these old bones I may well do that, but I reckon James might like a bit of company of an evening and you young folks need some space of your own. But don't you worry, I'll still be happy to look after Mary, and Thomas come to that." She looked across to Cecilia. "And I'm sure James will be happy to help."

"Indeed I will. I take being a grandfather very seriously, even if just being an honorary one." He winked at Molly.

"I don't think there can be a better kind than that," Mr Dixon said looking at his own grandchild.

Over the next few weeks Molly and Daniel were constantly busy with the farmhouse and the farm, trying to make the improvements necessary to Reese's Farm in the hope of getting the best out of that year's harvest. There would be other changes to make, but they would need to wait until the following winter when there was more time. In the meantime, while William set about establishing the

Dixon's law office, Cecilia began to make improvements to their own farmhouse with Miss Ellie helping where she could.

The style of each house was completely different. Molly and Daniel were establishing a practical place where meals could be provided to workers and the business of the farm could be conducted. William and Cecilia were creating their own country house, as different in purpose as any could be. What had been the yard became a garden surrounding the farmhouse, without a chicken or cow in the immediate area. They looked on to the new boundary fences of the extended Cochrane's Farm, but that was the extent of their farm experience.

It was only Cady who saw things a little differently, trotting over to play with her brother at every opportunity and rolling in the mud when she did so. Molly washed the little dog off regularly in the yard before sending her home. She didn't mind, she was just so happy they were all nearby that she would have done nothing to put obstacles in the way.

Molly hoped Mary would grow up to be happy in either place and not think one better than the other. Molly was well aware that prejudice came from those around you and felt confident that Mary would find none within her own family, but knew all too well about the problems of the wider world.

CHAPTER 42

"The timing is not great, but I do have to go." Miss Ellie closed the trunk and nodded to James that it was ready to take out to the cart.

"We're going to miss you, aren't we, Mary?" Molly bounced her daughter up and down in her arms. She'd got rather used to Miss Ellie being around again and even though this would be a short separation she felt it more keenly.

"The conference is only for three days and I do promise I won't get myself in any trouble while I'm there."

The two women laughed.

"Besides," Miss Ellie continued, "I'm rather looking forward to seeing the others there. And yes, before you ask, we are all planning on coming back here afterwards, so just you and Cecilia make sure the spare rooms are ready."

Molly grinned. It would be good to see Mrs Hawksworth, Mrs Dixon and Cecilia's mother, Mrs Hendry, all here in Pierceton. It would be quite a gathering.

"Now," said Miss Ellie, "I must be away, I need to meet the other Pierceton women who are going and not miss the train." She kissed both Molly and Mary on the cheeks and then went out to where James was waiting to take her to the station.

Now that Molly, Daniel and Mary had moved back into

the farmhouse, the plan was to clean out Ben's cabin ready for Miss Ellie on her return.

Molly had set up a small pen just outside the dairy that Mary could play in while she worked. Junior always sat beside it keeping watch over his charge. It wasn't ideal for any length of time, but Mary was happy enough and it meant that Molly could work more easily when there was no one else to take care of their daughter.

She was singing quietly as she worked and, as she did, became conscious of a voice outside. It seemed odd that Junior hadn't barked. She wiped her hands and went out into the yard. Molly smiled to see Cecilia with Thomas in a wheeled chair talking to Mary who had crawled to the side of the pen to see them.

"Oh, Molly, I didn't mean to disturb you." Cecilia looked embarrassed to have been overheard.

"Nonsense, it's time I had a break. Come over to the house for a drink."

Relief swept over Cecilia's face. "Oh, may I really. That's most kind. Some days seem so very long and I don't quite know what to do with myself."

It had not occurred to Molly that Cecilia would be feeling lonely or bored up at the house. She'd been so busy working that it simply hadn't been in her mind. "You're welcome to come down to the farm anytime. Although you might like to borrow some overalls if you do and not risk spoiling your clothes."

"This old thing?" Cecilia looked surprised at what she was wearing.

Molly couldn't help but think that if that was an old thing, she hoped Cecilia never came to the farm in a newer garment.

"You're very kind," Cecilia said, taking the drink that

Molly offered and sitting down in a chair in the kitchen. "William is so busy setting up the office and I know I've got the house to sort out, but I can't do that all day with no one to talk to. There are no meetings to go to either while the other women are away at the American Equal Rights Association anniversary. I do wish I could have gone. If I'm honest, the more time I'm spending on my own the less confidence in myself I have. I really wish there were some work or other I could do which would keep me occupied and feeling useful."

Molly was struck by how sad Cecilia looked and had a thought. "Look, I know that your real passion is politics and the law and that you've never done anything like this before, but would you like to learn some of the work in the dairy with me? I could even pay you a little if you'd like and make it a real job? I had been thinking about getting some help in now Ben isn't around to work with me." Molly sighed thinking how much they all missed Ben.

Cecilia's face transformed into a wide smile. "I would love to do that. Would you really teach me? I'm not quite sure what William would say."

"You leave my brother to me. Besides, if he hopes to win work from people within the equal rights movement, he needs to take note of it himself." They both laughed.

Molly found she enjoyed showing Cecilia how to make butter and cheese. Cecilia was bright and learned fast and the two of them were able to get through the work quickly. Molly had other farm work to do and during those times Cecilia worked on sorting out the cabin for Miss Ellie or went back to ensure the work on their own house was progressing. Reese's Farm had been renamed The Red House, now that it was a normal family home. In town, however, it would take years for people to refer to it as anything other than Reese's.

On the afternoon that Miss Ellie was to return from New York, Cecilia went with Molly to do the deliveries, while James looked after both of the children.

"The journey's not as speedy with our old cart as with your lovely trap." Molly took the reins and the horse plodded up the track away from the farm.

Cecilia looked pleased with the compliment. "You wouldn't get everything in if we used that. It's no good when there's a load to carry."

Their last stop before going to the station was the general store and Molly was pleased to find Sarah in the shop. She'd seen very little of her friend in recent times and missed her. They unloaded the order for the store and picked up the provisions they needed while Sarah and Cecilia got to know each other a little. Joseph was stacking new stock onto the shelves and Molly was aware that he was keeping an ear on the conversation.

"Will you stay for some tea?" Sarah asked. "I'm sure Joe wouldn't mind if I stop for ten minutes and Henry would love to see his Aunt Molly."

"We still have some time before Miss Ellie's train comes in, that would be a lovely idea." Molly looked to Cecilia for confirmation and she nodded.

"Why of course, she's been with a number of the others from the town in New York hasn't she? No wonder it's been quieter in here than normal."

Joseph came over and pointedly butted into the conversation. "Sarah, mother needs you to take these out to the Murray's. They need them this afternoon."

Sarah looked confused and flustered. "Can't I do that after we've had some tea?"

"No, I think you had best go now." Joe spoke with an

abrupt firmness that left Molly rather taken aback and Sarah looking cowed.

"I'm sorry," Sarah said. "Perhaps we can have tea another time." Her eyes seemed to plead with Molly as she spoke.

"It would be lovely to have you and Henry out to the farmhouse sometime. You've not seen it since we finished the work." Molly thought getting out of the store might do her friend good. "I'm sure Miss Ellie would love to see you too."

"I'd like that." Sarah spoke wistfully.

"Sarah knows her place, here in the store." Joe was standing in front of Molly looking very stern. "She won't have time to come out to the farm. It won't be appropriate. Thank you, ladies and good day to you."

Molly could see Cecilia's anger rising and put her hand on Cecilia's arm lest she made the already difficult situation worse. Cecilia nodded to show she had understood and saying polite goodbyes to Sarah they both left the store.

Once they were outside, Cecilia could clearly hold her views in no longer. "This is exactly why we need to work for equality. I cannot believe that any woman allows themselves to be treated in that manner. How dare he? I know I've got Thomas to look after, but I need to get back to the work that I should really be doing."

"He dares because he mistakenly thinks he has a right to treat his wife like that. It makes me as sad as angry. Sarah doesn't deserve that. And to think I considered marrying his brother." Molly shook her head finding it hard to comprehend what Sarah's life must be like. "I know it's sad, but I think Joe sees us as a threat to his control of Sarah. There's nothing much we can do about it right now. You're right about the work that needs doing. You shouldn't be working in the dairy with me, you should be working in the office with William and I plan to tell him so. Now let's go to see that new office."

Cecilia's face lit up and it was clear to Molly that Cecilia needed to find a way to combine bringing up a family with not losing sight of her calling. She needed to give it some thought. They moved the cart further along the road until they came to the new offices of Dixons.

"Do you think we could go in?" Molly climbed down from the cart and went across to the door. She went to peer through the glass and jumped when, with a flourish, William opened it from the other side.

"Ladies," he said bowing to them.

"Oh, you silly man." Cecilia laughed and looked so happy to see him.

"Well now, brother of mine, it's time you showed me around. And when you've done, we need to discuss an idea which has just this minute occurred to me."

CHAPTER 43

"Well, it's hard to know what to think." Miss Ellie was telling them about the strange events of the last few days in New York. "I don't rightly know what's going to happen. Some of the women are arguing that the 15th Amendment shouldn't go ahead as it only covers race. As far as I can see it's a step in the right direction, though I grant it might make our struggle the harder if the two things become separate."

They were all sitting in the new parlour of The Red House and, with so many guests to take care of, Cecilia was positively blooming. Molly felt less comfortable here than she would have done back at the farm, but as all barring Miss Ellie were staying at the house it had made sense to be here.

"I don't hold with suffrage being based on education," Mrs Hendry said. "Either we're all born equal or we're not. Just because someone isn't given the same opportunities in life shouldn't affect their right to be treated with the same respect."

Mrs Hawksworth nodded and looked across to Daniel and William. Molly presumed she was having the same thought about the contrast in the education of the two men and there being no reason for them to be treated differently.

"What I've been wondering," Mrs Dixon was looking out of the window as she spoke, "is what it's going to mean for our local associations. With such a split of views there's going to be a lot to talk about."

"If I'm permitted to speak?" William grinned around the room, with disarming charm, before he continued. "I don't think the linking of women's rights and rights based on race was ever going to get very far. Our current politicians don't see them in the same way. Oh, they feel threatened by both, but for completely different reasons and they'll give up power in their own homes far less easily than any other. Slavery has already been abolished, so the South can't hold to that as a reason to deny men the vote based on skin colour." He sighed. "I need to understand what's going on here in Pierceton, too. Most of my business so far is coming from the Association here. I don't think the more traditional thinking businesses of Pierceton have quite forgiven me for being your brother." He looked at Molly and she laughed.

Molly looked across to Daniel who was sitting on the floor playing with Mary. She really did consider herself one of the lucky ones. Her marriage was an equal partnership and she hoped she would never take that for granted.

"Daniel and I have been thinking of bringing one of the orphans into our own home, the next time the trains come this way, bringing them off the streets of New York or Boston." Molly said when there was a gap in the conversation. "We've seen the best and worst of what it can be like and hope we might be able to help a child who's going through some of what we experienced."

"I think that's a mighty fine idea." It was Mrs Hawksworth who spoke up. "I'm not so young as I used to be, but it makes me think that's something I could be doing. I'd have to talk about it with my sister, but it would feel as though I were making amends for all the things I couldn't fix for Daniel when he was young." She wiped a tear from her eye.

Daniel looked up. "You and Ben were the only people who were kind to me through those years. You've got nothing to make up for." Cady barked at him. "I said 'people', Cady, I'd have been lost without your father too." The dog seemed mollified and she went off to find her brother who was keeping well out of the way of the busy room.

With Mrs Hendry and Mrs Hawksworth travelling back to Iowa, and Mrs Dixon returning to Dowagiac, life around the farm seemed quiet. They fell into a routine of Grandma Ellie, as she was now more often called, taking care of both Mary and Thomas. Cecilia was still spending her mornings working in the dairy, sometimes alongside Molly and at other times being able to take over the work while Molly attended to other things.

In the afternoon Molly would undertake other work around the farm while Cecilia was getting involved in activities in the town, sometimes with Thomas in tow and sometimes with Grandpa James caring for both children. On the afternoons where there were no meetings to attend Cecilia had quietly returned to her studies and was making what steps she could towards a career in law.

It was the times that Cecilia and Miss Ellie went into town to the women's meetings that Molly minded most. She chided herself for the slight jealousy she felt, but tried to hide her disappointment.

"Why don't you go?" Daniel asked when he came into the yard and found her in with the chickens.

"Why don't I go where?" Molly painted on a smile and

tried to pretend everything was all right.

"Molly Reilly, I've known you an awful long time and I can tell when you're sad even if you are trying to hide it. Miss Ellie and Cecilia have gone into town and you'd like to be there too."

"But I've work to do here." She looked at Daniel and her smile was genuine as she saw the love in his eyes.

"There's nothing here that I can't do. If you want to make yourself feel better about it, then there's an order which needs dropping off up by the station. You could take that with you."

Molly threw her arms around her husband. How did she get so lucky as to be married to this wonderful man? Then she thrust the bucket into his hand and ran up to the house to tidy herself up ready to go into town. She would be a little late arriving, but if she were quick it would not be by much.

When she came out Daniel had prepared the horse for her. "The delivery is small enough to take in the saddle bag. You don't need the cart. You'll get there in plenty of time."

Molly didn't ride often, so she wasn't going to risk too much of a trot, but a brisk walk would still be faster than taking the cart. As they went along the lane on the beautiful summer's day, she found herself singing one of the old Irish ballads that Daniel used to sing so often.

The meeting was about to start when she arrived and Molly slipped quietly into a spare seat conveniently next to Miss Ellie. Her guardian said nothing, but simply slipped her hand into Molly's a tiny indication of both love and delight that she was there, which immediately made Molly feel foolish for her earlier jealousy.

They listened to women speaking about the 15th

Amendment and their views of whether the ratification of the Amendment would be a good or bad thing for the cause of women's suffrage. Molly could see good points in both sides of the argument. Certainly, she could see that more men able to vote might just serve to keep women further from the ballot box, but equally how could she deny others a right she felt so strongly should be given to all. In many cases the fact that those to whom it would be given had no education was not a fault of their own making and she thought of the life that Daniel had led and all that had been denied to him as a result.

The debate continued and she was glad that she was there, but was ready to be back out in the fresh air once it was over. She bid her farewells to Miss Ellie and Cecilia and went on toward the station to make the delivery. She dismounted to walk the last of the distance and as she did so, she saw a new poster affixed to a board at the station. In just another few weeks an orphan train would be passing that way. She took note of the details of where the meeting would be, her heart racing as she committed it to memory. It seemed a long time since her own train had arrived at the station and Miss Ellie had given a home to both her and Sarah. She could only hope that Daniel felt ready for them to do the same for the next generation.

Once her delivery was made, Molly remounted and rode home. Spurred on by the news she had for Daniel, she rode faster than she was used to and was breathless with excitement by the time she reached the yard.

CHAPTER 44

Though the night be as dark as dungeon,
not a star can be seen above
I will be guided without a stumble,
into the arms of my own true love.
I'm a Rover - Traditional

Daniel was thinking of another hall, in another place as they sat and listened to the introduction being given about the orphans. Molly was fidgeting and restless and he took her hand hoping it would help to calm her nerves. She clung tightly to him, and with her other hand dabbed at the corners of her eyes. The gesture made Daniel smile. He could still remember being surprised that so many adults around them were crying when their story was being told. To him, back then it was simply the facts of what had happened in his life and he saw none of the emotion. Now with the benefit of hindsight he could see the tragedy of the wasted lives.

This group included both boys and girls and he looked along their lines at the fake bravado and the unkempt appearances. Despite Molly's experience with Sarah, they planned only to bring one child home with them and the choice was to be his. He wanted to help a child much as he had been, younger, smaller, weaker; no one else's first choice.

The procedure had changed little in the intervening

fifteen years and the children were still regarded by most, much as cattle might be in a market. He could feel Molly tense and angry as they watched children having their muscles felt and having questions barked at them by those who would take them in.

"And I thought slavery had been abolished," Molly hissed as she turned and walked back to the other room. Daniel could understand her needing to get away, but he wanted to stay and watch the children, feeling protective and ready to stand up for any who looked as though they needed it.

Finally, the room began to clear and Molly came back to his side. There were still a good number of children standing bewildered and awkward in the room. There were a few who reminded him of William at that age, hiding their fear behind a mask of confidence and belligerence.

Molly took his hand and in silent agreement they moved towards a very pale and freckled boy, who was standing on one leg with his other ankle twisted around awkwardly as though ready to run the other way. His hair was as red as any child's could be and there was little need to wonder where he hailed from.

"Hello there," Molly spoke softly and the boy mumbled in return. Molly continued unperturbed. "And what's your name?"

The boy looked up at first Molly and then Daniel, his eyes wide, like an animal trapped with nowhere to run. "It's J-j-j…John, miss."

"Well, John, I'm Mrs Flynn and this is Mr Flynn." She held out her hand to shake that of the little boy. He looked up at her confused then gingerly stuck out his right hand after checking how dirty it was first.

"And where do you come from, John?" Molly spoke in a soothing voice and Daniel could see the boy starting to relax very slightly.

"I'm from New York, miss. F-f-f-f... from F-f-f-f...Five Points." He spluttered out the last word quickly and Daniel guessed his stutter was more nerves than a permanent impediment. The Irish accent was still clear even amongst his difficulty in answering.

"And where in Ireland are you from?" Daniel asked.

The boy's eyes widened. "How did you know I was Irish, sir?"

It wasn't the time or the place for Daniel to start to tell John their story, not yet. "Just a guess," he said smiling at the boy.

Molly caught Daniel's eye and he nodded.

"John," she said. "Would you like to come home with me and Mr Flynn and live with us on our farm?"

"Me?" the boy said, looking around as though assuming Molly might be talking to some other John.

"Yes, you." Molly held out her hand to the boy, but he moved away.

Daniel guessed that John's story would be a harsh and complicated one and that trusting might be a slow process. They'd give him time.

John reluctantly followed them as they went to sign the papers they needed in order to take him home.

"He's barely said a word to anyone. You'll have your work cut out there," the man who was supervising the children said. He looked dismissively at the child.

"I think we're going to be just fine, don't you, John?" Molly said gently to their new charge.

The little boy looked bewildered, but said nothing.

As they left, Molly continued to speak softly, more,

Daniel supposed, for the sound of her voice calming John than the words she actually said. "We've six cows on the farm, so we have and two calves at the moment. Then there are the chickens and of course our little dog, Junior."

On the cart journey home John was clearly tired and despite the bumping over the ruts in the lane he was soon asleep and leaning against Daniel.

Daniel felt a rush of warmth toward the boy and was determined that whatever had befallen the child until now, they would help him to live the best life he could have.

When the cart pulled into the yard, John was still asleep and Daniel gently lifted him down. As he held the boy he awoke and in panic started to kick out.

"It's all right. You're safe now."

As quickly, but carefully, as he could, Daniel put John down with his feet on the ground. The boy stood looking around with fear in his eyes. Daniel was uncertain what they should do next, but Junior took the lead. He ran up to John and sat in front of him, his tail wagging and a paw lifted into the air, begging for attention. For the first time, Daniel saw a small smile break across the boy's face and he got down onto the ground to be at Junior's level and let the dog lick him.

Rather than disturb this happy moment, Daniel stayed outside watching the child and dog, whilst Molly went to fetch a glass of milk and a cookie from the kitchen and brought them out to the yard to where John was still sitting.

If it had not been for the bond that Junior developed with John, those first few days would have been very difficult. As it was, Junior took the lead, sharing both the milk and the biscuit and never leaving John's side as he started to find his way around. Junior slept next to John at night and woke him with a lick in the morning. As John started to work out in the fields during the day with Daniel, Junior would always be by their side until little by little John began to forget to be scared.

Mary helped in getting him used to the farm as well. Daniel enjoyed watching as the toddler would waddle up to John and he held her hands as she tried to gain her balance. He suspected that at one time John had been used to being around a younger child, but the boy showed no sign of wanting to talk about his past.

It was harvest time once again and John was keen to work. Daniel stayed with him so that they worked side by side, rather than giving the boy an area of the field to do on his own. Daniel began to sing as he worked, something he had not been aware of doing for a while.

I'm a rover, seldom sober,
I'm a rover of high degree,
It's when I'm drinking I'm always thinking,
how to gain my love's company.

John just stopped and stared at him. "Me da used to sing that song."

"So did mine," Daniel said. "That's how I came to learn it."

"You're not like that though, are you? Me da was. He was always drinking, so he was." Then John went back to working and said no more.

Daniel was thrilled that the boy had felt able to open up, even to a small extent. He couldn't wait to tell Molly and he resolved to sing more often as they worked, hoping that in the music John would find the courage to talk about his early life.

Over the next days and weeks, Daniel learned a little more about John and the boy seemed to become more settled on the farm and stronger with it. "I think my name's O'Callaghan, but I can't write it," he said one day.

"I could show you how to if you'd like to learn." Daniel continued to pick the corn and didn't look at the boy. He'd soon learned that if he looked at John as they talked then the boy's stutter would return. He wondered how John would fare when he started school.

As Daniel walked with John on his first day of school in Pierceton they talked almost the whole way. Time and the security of a family had made so much difference to the boy and there was little sign of his initial stutter. Working in the fields had given him some strength and colour, as well as a new confidence. Daniel was determined that no farm work would keep the boy from his schooling and whilst they might still be working to harvest what remained, John would go to school and, despite his protestations, only help when he returned in the evening.

"There'll be time enough to help in the rest of the week," Daniel said as he parted from the boy, so he could get back to his own labours. For a moment he wondered if there'd be time for a leprechaun hunt and to keep alive some of the traditions of his own boyhood, but that would have to wait.

Junior was reluctant to leave the school gate and return with Daniel to the farm. Eventually, Daniel decided it would do no harm to leave the little dog where he was, keeping up his vigil over the boy. However, Junior decided of his own accord to follow, with his head down and his tail between his legs. Once back at Cochrane's farm, Junior sat by the entrance to the yard, watching the lane for the boy's return.

When Daniel heard Junior barking madly in the yard, he knew the dog's wait was over and that John was home. He could hear the noise even though he was working in the field and immediately left what he was doing to greet the boy.

By the time Daniel got to the yard, Molly and Mary were already there and John was sitting on the floor, his arms around Junior and tears rolling down his face. Molly looked at Daniel her face full of concern. He mouthed to her that she should bring milk and cookies once again, whilst he sat down on the ground next to John, put his arm around the boy and waited.

John said little as they sat there, the four of them and Junior having a little picnic in the yard. The crying had stopped, but when John had gone to speak his stutter was pronounced and he gave up. After a while, they got up and John went down to the field to help finishing the harvest with Daniel, while Molly took Mary back to the house.

John brightened as he worked beside Daniel and little by little Daniel felt the boy had relaxed enough to be able to talk.

"Why are people mean to me?" the little boy asked as he continued to work.

"What did they say?"

"They called me 'Paddy' and were rude about my hair."

"Was there anything else?" Daniel was thinking carefully about how to approach the bullying. He had not had to face the ridicule of children, but he knew Molly had and he'd seen the lengths William had gone to in order to avoid it.

"They said I should go back to the slum I came from."

As he talked, John continued to collect the fruit they were bringing in and put it carefully in the basket.

"When Molly was a child, she carried the rosary she had from her Mammy in a pocket of her skirt where no one would see it. Other children were rude to her too. It does get better with time."

"Were you bullied when you went to school?" John's eyes were filled with tears again.

Daniel chose his words carefully. "I didn't have the opportunity to go to school. I had to start my learning much later and that's much harder to do. Going to school is something I wished I could do more than anything." He didn't want to explain anything further, but he had an idea.

CHAPTER 45

And it's no, nay, never
No, nay, never no more
Will I play the wild rover
No, never no more
The Wild Rover - traditional

John was quiet as he and Daniel walked toward the school the following day. Junior trotted quietly at his side and Daniel watched as every so often the little dog would look to John and John would give the little dog a nod or a smile acknowledging the bond. Daniel could see that in the same way that Duke had been there for him when he was a child in a difficult situation, Junior was ready to take the same role, he could only hope that John's teacher would understand too.

"You and Junior wait here a moment," Daniel said when they got to the little school. "I'd like to talk with Mr Young before you come in. Is that all right?"

John nodded and sat on a step so he was nearer to Junior's level and could stroke the dog.

"Sir," said Daniel, after he had entered Mr Young's classroom. "May I speak with you?"

"Why, Mr Flynn, of course." The teacher got up from his desk and shook Daniel's hand.

"It's about John's stutter, sir." Daniel explained a little of what John had told him and how it had led to not only unhappiness but the return of the stutter. "I know this is an unusual request, but would it be possible for Junior to attend classes with him, until he is settled and a little more confident?"

"Well this is most extraordinary," the teacher, Mr Young said. "I really don't know if the School Board would permit it."

"Sir," Daniel said, "I know from your wife's involvement with the Equal Rights Association, that you are a fair man. There are more types of inequality than the ones based on skin colour or fairness of sex."

Mr Young, who had stood a little taller at the compliment which Daniel had paid him, now looked thoughtful. "Perhaps for a few days it can do no harm. Children often find it hard to settle into a new environment and the others that came into town with him have all been held back at their farms until harvest is over. I admire you for putting his need of education first. As long as the dog causes no trouble and stays quietly by Master O'Callaghan's side, he can stay for a week."

"Thank you, sir." Daniel took Mr Young's hand and shook it warmly once again, then went out to find John and Junior and tell the boy the news.

How Junior knew he was to stay with the boy, Daniel never could work out, but he did and the boy who came home from school that evening with his dog trotting behind was as different as Daniel could have hoped for.

Mr Young seemed to forget that he'd limited Junior's presence to a week and the little dog trotted to school every day and when the time came, happily padded home with his young master. No one needed to say that it was time for the arrangement to stop. The presence of the dog helped John to make friends. At break time, Junior sat with

John and, one by one, the other boys approached them, all eager to stroke Junior, or run with him in the playground. As John gained in confidence, Junior took to sitting first at the side of the class and then by the gate. Eventually he went home during the day, but wandered back to the school when it was time for John to come out.

Harvest was finished and the work on the farm was less strenuous. John still liked to help when he came in on an evening if that was possible, but there were fewer jobs needing doing and the daylight hours were shortening, making it hard for Daniel to find work he could do.

"Why did you call Mrs Flynn 'Molly Reilly'?" John asked Daniel one day when they were mending some fencing.

Daniel presumed the confusion was over her married name. "Because she was Reilly before she married me."

"But, I thought Mr Dixon was her brother, so I did."

Daniel could have jumped for joy. It was the first sign that John was rather brighter than they had feared. John had been with them now for a couple of months and Daniel decided that he was ready to hear a little more of their own background. "When we go in to eat tonight, Mrs Flynn and I will tell you a story." Daniel had no plan to tell the boy how he had been treated as a child, or to explain just what their own lives had been like in New York. That might come one day, but it would be many years hence before it did.

Over their meal that evening Molly explained how they too had come from Ireland and how they'd met in New York. Daniel told about how he and William had travelled on the very first orphan train and how William had taken the name of his new family and been adopted.

John looked up at Daniel, his eyes brimming with tears.

"I can't spell O'Callaghan, but I think I know the letters for Flynn." Then he looked away.

Daniel got up from his chair slowly and went to John. He lifted the boy up and then sat on his chair with John perched on his knee. Very quietly he asked, "Are you saying you'd like us to adopt you and make you properly part of our family?"

John looked first at him and then at Molly. He nodded solemnly. "And could I call you Ma and Da if I did?"

"Oh, John, you can call us Ma and Da in any case, but if you'd like us to adopt you then we would be very, very happy." Daniel could see Molly's eyes glistening as she spoke to the boy.

"Why don't I ask Uncle William to prepare the papers we need in order to do it properly?" Daniel said.

"Who is Uncle William?" John asked looking very serious.

"That's my brother, Mr William Dixon. He'll be your uncle now too."

It was as though the safety of a new family allowed John to speak about the past. "I don't rightly remember my first ma. She died when I was three, when Sinead was born. We were already in New York then. I don't remember leaving Ireland. Da looked after us, but he spent most of his time drunk. Sinead died when she was four. It was just me and Da then, but then one day he just didn't come back for me and I didn't know what to do. I was put in a home with lots of other boys, then I came here on the train. I can't really remember having a proper family before."

"Well, you've got a proper family now." Daniel looked at the boy in wonder. "You've a ma and da and a sister in our Mary." Daniel caught sight of Junior who was sitting with an ear cocked. "And, of course, you've got the best possible friend in the world in Junior."

By the middle of November John was officially part of the family and was only too proud to tell people his surname was Flynn. Whenever he was close to the house and yard, Mary would toddle after her brother and wherever he went Junior was at his heels.

John had no idea of when his birthday might be, no records had been made and no adults remained to tell him. They decided together that from now on they would celebrate his birthday on the day in August when he'd first joined their family. It was as good a point of the year to mark as any.

CHAPTER 46

"If the 15th Amendment is ratified without including votes for women then we will never be enfranchised."

Molly listened to the woman on the platform, but did not agree. Any and every step forward was important, as much in memory of Ben as for her own gain. She'd read of freedmen whose lives and safety may well depend on their ability to change the country's politics. Surely that was more important even than her own say in affairs.

"I wish my mother were here," Cecilia whispered to Molly. "Someone needs to get up there and put the other arguments."

"Perhaps you should do it," Molly said in return.

"Your brother might support the whole cause and for that matter be doing work for those involved, but I'm not sure he's quite ready for me to upstage his own fledgling political career."

They both grinned and Molly had to cover her mouth to contain a laugh.

"Besides," Cecilia spoke with a certain pride when William was the subject, "I think he plans to stand for office locally and try to change things from the inside. That has to be worthy of my support. I think working together, we could make a formidable team. What about you?"

Molly was taken aback by Cecilia's suggestion. It was certainly not something she could imagine herself doing. She shook her head. "Miss Ellie has spoken out in other places they've visited. I don't understand why she's reluctant to take the platform here." Molly fell silent as another speaker got to her feet. The two women sat attentively and listened as the woman suggested that despite not being directly enfranchised, they should proceed to vote in elections in any event and take legal action if they were denied. After all the constitution did not specifically refer to men rather than women, but to all being equal.

Cecilia sighed. "If we go down that path, I guess William's going to be working long hours and will have less time for politics." She grinned. "I suppose it might mean there is enough work for me to argue that I need to join him in the office, so it wouldn't be all bad."

Following the meetings she attended, Molly wrote long letters to Miss Ellie to tell her of all that occurred as well as updating her on the family's progress. She then waited impatiently for Miss Ellie's letters of reply.

"Daniel, Daniel," Molly called from the kitchen door.

Daniel looked up from the wood that he and John were chopping and wiped the sweat from his face.

"Everyone's going to be here for Christmas."

Mary started laughing at her mother's excitement, even though she had no idea what the occasion was.

"Oh, John, think of that. Your first Christmas with us and the whole family will be here together." Molly lifted Mary up and swung her around.

"Who's everyone?" John asked, looking more than a little concerned.

"Grandma Ellie will be here as well as Uncle William's parents and Aunt Cecilia's parents are coming too." Molly was now out of breath and put Mary down, whereupon her daughter promptly wanted to be picked up again.

Molly was aware that John was looking confused. He nodded slowly seeming to understand, but then asked the one question that they'd been avoiding talking about. "Who adopted Da?"

Daniel looked at Molly with worry etched across his face. They had both agreed that it wouldn't help John to hear the stories of what had happened to Daniel.

Molly smiled as an idea occurred to her. "He went to live with a lady called Mrs Hawksworth, so I guess she'll be your grandma too. She will be here at Christmas as well." She and Daniel could work out the details and maybe write to Miss Ellie and explain so it didn't come as a surprise to Mrs Hawksworth when the boy called her grandma.

"Families can be strange things. You choose to make them as wide as they need to be." Daniel grinned and then went back to the wood chopping.

Molly and Mary went back into the farmhouse and Molly began to make a list of what they would need to do in preparation. The Dixons and Hendrys would stay up at The Red House, but Miss Ellie's cabin would need to be made ready and she rather hoped that Mrs Hawksworth would stay with them there in the farmhouse. She would need to see both Cecilia and James to discuss all the plans. She presumed that Cecilia would have received a letter from her mother as well.

As Christmas drew nearer, John became more withdrawn. The more that Molly tried to involve him in the plans, the quieter he became.

"I thought we were doing really well with him, but suddenly I feel as though I don't know him at all." Molly said one night after both of the children were asleep.

"Do you think something has happened at this time of year that means he feels he can't be happy?" Daniel put more wood onto the fire to build it up for the rest of the evening.

Molly tried to think about her own early days with Miss Ellie. "I guess so. There's a lot we still don't know about him I suppose. It was a long time before I really talked about life before we came here. I don't want him to feel he isn't part of things, but I don't know what to do."

"You know." Daniel got up from the hearth and went over to the window, looking out into the darkness. "It might just be time for that leprechaun hunt. Could you do without us for a while after church on Sunday?"

"If you can get to the bottom of the problem then I shall be delighted to do so." Molly went over and kissed her husband.

At breakfast on the Sunday Daniel said, "I thought we might go out after church, just you and me."

John looked worried. "Have I done something wrong?"

"Why, no, of course not. It's just that I thought we might go on a leprechaun hunt."

The boy was wide-eyed. "What? Here? I thought they were only in Ireland."

"Well, I've been thinking. With so many ships bringing people from Ireland to America over the last few years, it wouldn't be very surprising to find some of the leprechauns had come too." Daniel winked at Molly.

She realised he'd worked out his story in advance and she quietly sat and watched the boy's reaction.

"When I was small, back in Ireland, I went on a leprechaun hunt with my father and one day we found one."

"Really?" John was out of his chair and bouncing up

and down.

"Well," said Daniel thoughtfully, "we found where the little fellow had been until just before we were there."

"Can we go now and not go to church?" John was clearly going to have difficulty sitting still for any length of time.

Molly wondered if they should have waited until afterwards to tell him. "Well, I think the leprechaun would want to be sure you'd been to church of a Sunday. Besides, I'm going to pack up some food for you to eat while you're looking and I'll need time to do that when we're back."

Later when they were back from church and the leprechaun hunt had begun, Junior was unhappy to be left behind. He sat by the door howling for his companion. As it was a fine afternoon Molly walked across to The Red House so that Junior could at least run around madly with Cady and not just drive her crazy. She had left a note for Daniel so that he and John could find her there on their return.

"Uncle William, Uncle William!" John came charging into the house later. "We found a leprechaun."

"He sounds just as I did when I ran back to tell my Uncle Patrick." Daniel looked wistful. "I wonder if we've still got family left back home."

Molly was glad that she'd explained the mission to the others and that William was happy to play along with the story, listening to John and making all the right encouraging sounds. Cecilia looked a little perplexed so William and John began explaining to her all about the little people and the luck they could bring, while Daniel spoke to Molly.

"It turns out it's rather simple really," Daniel whispered. "It was around Christmas that Sinead was born and his mother died. Whenever Christmas was talked about after that, his father would say what an awful time it was. I think that's when his drinking got out of hand."

Molly nodded. "Then I need to think of a way to help him include his mammy rather than let it spoil every Christmas he will have." Molly fell silent, watching the boy and thinking.

Later, when Molly was alone with John she asked, "John, do you believe in Jesus?"

He looked at her aghast. "Why, yes, Ma, of course I do. That's who my first mammy is with now, and Sinead."

Molly smiled. "Yes, John that's right. So that they could be with him now, Jesus had to live on earth for a short while, do you know that?"

He looked at her as though she were stupid. "Why, of course I do. I listen every Sunday in church."

Molly grinned, she often wondered how many of the children were actually listening and how many were just counting the minutes until it was finished. "At Christmas we celebrate Jesus being born here on earth. If that hadn't happened your mammy wouldn't be able to be with him now."

John's brow furrowed and Molly let the silence continue while he tried to order his thoughts. She had no way of knowing if her way of explaining things would have helped. Only time would give her the answer to that.

A couple of days later Molly was making garlands to decorate the house for when their guests arrived. Most of the celebrations would take place at The Red House, but Molly wanted Cochrane's Farm to look just as festive. John came into the kitchen where she was busy working.

"Can I help you?" he asked.

Molly wished she could rush and hug him, but did not want to make an issue of this sign of a change of heart, she smiled gently as she said, "Yes of course. If I move over, you can trim these branches ready to weave into the line. Here, let me show you." She took up the knife and showed him how she wanted the woody part of the stem to be cut, then keeping a watchful eye on what he was doing, she let him take over while she began to weave them one by one into the long green garland to go around the fireplace.

When they went to meet everyone at the station, Molly knew their letter to Miss Ellie had been related to Mrs Hawksworth. Her first words on seeing John were, "Now let me have a good look at my new grandson." Grandma Liza had tears in her eyes as she embraced the boy and the greeting she gave to both Molly and Daniel made Molly realise that far from being affronted by being asked to rewrite history, she was both honoured and delighted to become part of the family.

Mary was thankfully still too young to comment on the adjustment and happily adopted her new grandma with the same enthusiasm she had for Grandma Ellie.

"Such a change time has wrought," Daniel said, smiling at Molly, as they loaded all the cases onto the cart.

They might have been an eclectic family, but a family they were and when the fourteen of them sat down to Christmas lunch at The Red House, Molly couldn't remember ever being happier. She was sorry that Sarah could not be there, but Joseph had forbidden her from spending time with 'such women as Miss Ellie and Molly', which made Molly sad for her friend.

"Sing for us, Daniel," she said softly when lunch was drawing to a close.

Daniel looked around the table and Molly smiled as quiet fell and there were nods of acquiescence.

Daniel got up from the table and went to stand by the fire. "I think I should start with one I learned from Ben only a year or two ago and we should raise a glass to a man without whom we wouldn't be here."

They all raised their glasses and Molly wiped tears from her eyes as Daniel began to sing.

Go tell it on the mountain,
Over the hills and everywhere,
Go tell it on the mountain,
That Jesus Christ is born.

To Molly's surprise, John started to sing and Daniel invited the boy to join him by the fire where the two sang together. She wasn't the only one with tears rolling down her cheeks. The same was true of several around the room. As the song finished, Molly went to hug her son. She was so proud of how far he'd come in such a short time and so grateful that they had brought him into their home.

Daniel went on to sing other Christmas songs and whilst the rest of the family listened Mary began to clap her little hands together, already naturally following the rhythm of the song.

By the end of the day as they made their way back to Cochrane's farm it was James who said, "I think that's the happiest Christmas I have ever known."

Molly couldn't help but agree.

CHAPTER 47

Once Christmas was over, the family dispersed once again.

"Now, don't you look so sad, my girl," Miss Ellie said to Molly as they made their farewells. "There's work to do and no mistake. If we're to make sure that women aren't forgotten amongst the enfranchisement of the freedmen, then we need to make our voices heard. I'm trusting you and Cecilia to be working on our behalf here in Pierceton. There will be rallies all over that women need to attend. Mrs Dixon is returning to Dowagiac and I'm going with Liza and Mrs Hendry to Iowa to work with them there."

"I just wish you could stay here with us and see Mary grow."

"I spent enough of my life here fighting to be heard. You've got the farm running well enough and with the land from those Reese boys you should do pretty well without me watching over you. Those boys will be behind bars a while longer. Sheriff says they'll stand trial soon enough and no judge in his right mind is going to set those boys free. You've little to fear." Then Miss Ellie kissed her charge before picking Mary up and addressing her. "Now you look after your dear Mama for me. I'll not be away long and I want to hear about everything you've been up to when I return." She looked to Molly. "I could understand John not wanting to say goodbye. I guess, with his father going still feeling raw, goodbyes must seem strange. You're doing a fine job with him."

Once Miss Ellie put Mary down, she toddled straight into the arms of her other grandma, Mrs Hawksworth, who hugged the girl with unbridled affection.

"I'm only sorry about Sarah. I just hope she's happy." Miss Ellie shook her head. "Come now, Liza, we'd best be on our way."

Molly pecked Mrs Hawksworth on the cheek and then she and Mary stood waving as the train pulled away from the platform.

Miss Ellie had been right that there would be protests to coincide with the 15th Amendment being ratified. There were still a few weeks to go, but work was needed to encourage other women to get involved.

"I know William supports all we're doing, but I don't think I will be able to be out there as part of the march," Cecilia said as they talked about it later.

"You would have been if you were in Iowa." Molly was surprised by her sister-in-law's reaction.

"I know, but everyone accepts that Papa is just a little crazy and nothing Mama or I could do would affect that. William is trying to build the law practice and improve his standing in political circles. I'm worried that his reputation is too fragile so far for the damage I might do to it."

Frustrated as she was with Cecilia, Molly kept her thoughts to herself. She did understand, but if a cause was worth fighting for then surely that was what should come first.

There were a couple of meetings in the town ahead of the proposed rally and Cecilia did at least attend those. She also helped Molly to make a placard to take with her. Daniel supported Molly all he could, but for the most part was busy working on the farm and covered the work of hers that needed doing so she could be involved.

When the day of the rally arrived, Molly felt anxious. It would be the first time she had stood in protest and wondered what it would be like. She thought of all the tales Miss Ellie told and found strength in the thought that she was united with women across the country as well as in Pierceton.

It was a cold day to be out of doors, though she was used to it with the farm, but that rarely involved standing in one place for any length of time. She wrapped herself in warm clothing, took Mary down to James's cabin and then, armed with her placard, set off into town.

As she passed the general store, Sarah was at the window. Molly waved to her, but Joe ushered his wife away and Sarah did not respond. In her mind it was people such as Sarah that Molly was fighting for. The ones who didn't even realise what their lives should be like. She shook her head sadly.

By the time she got into town a group of women had already gathered. The rally itself was to involve speeches as well as the march which preceded them. Molly's placard said simply 'Votes for Women', but others had picked up the saying of 'No taxation without representation', as true of their cause as ever it was for others.

Their march was a peaceful one in terms of behaviour, though they sang the songs of the women's movement as they marched. Some families came out onto the street to see them. Others ushered children inside so that they didn't. What was worse was seeing husbands guiding wives indoors, preventing them supporting their sisters. Molly shook her head sadly.

The speeches were rousing and called for the Government to extend the vote to all adults regardless of race or sex. Molly felt empowered as she listened and shared the moment with other women around her.

As the women linked arms again and began to sing, the sheriff's men arrived and started to break the group up. Clearly, some of the men of the town had decided enough was enough and didn't like to see the strength of the womenfolk in plain sight. Molly would have left peacefully, had it not been for the goading by cousins of the Reese boys who had come out of Marsh's to see what was happening.

"Her man's too weak to keep her under control."

"She's stolen our cousins' farm, but we'll get it back."

"She should have burned in that fire. The place would be better without her."

Molly could have taken all of those and done so with dignity, but it was the last one that had her temper flaring: "I'm glad that nigger's dead, they're not fit to live around here anyway."

Molly turned to face the man who was standing with his beer in his hand. "What did you just say?"

"It's not murder when it's a nigger involved. It's a blessing for all of us."

Molly felt her nostrils flare as she answered. "Ben was a better man than any of you. He was brave and honest and did no one any harm."

She had done nothing but stand up for their dear friend in the face of unprovoked abuse, but within seconds she found her arms clasped by the sheriff's men and instinctively she tried to pull herself away.

The crowd outside the bar jeered as Molly was led away calling for the officers to let her go as she had done no wrong.

#

Daniel had finished working for the day and was back at the house when John came in from school.

"Where's Ma?" the boy asked.

"I'm not sure. I thought she'd be back by now. She went up to town to take part in the rally. Perhaps she's down at James's cabin collecting Mary, shall we walk down to see?"

The two were just leaving the farmhouse when William rode into the yard. Daniel frowned. "We don't normally see you at this time of day, is everything all right?"

William shook his head. "Molly's got herself arrested. I've just come from the courthouse. I'm not absolutely sure what she's supposed to have done, they seem to have arrested a few of the protestors. I think it's as much a statement as anything. Trying to put them off doing something like this again."

"It's not right." Daniel felt a depth of anger rising up. "Molly is equal to any of us and always has been. I'm going into town. John, you go down to Grandpa James and tell him where we are. I'll be back for the two of you as soon as I find out what's happening."

With that Daniel marched across to the stable and saddled the horse to speed his progress into town with William.

"I have to call into the office to collect some papers," William said as they came to a halt a little way from the courthouse. "I'll be back as soon as I can."

There was a crowd standing around as Daniel dismounted. These were no longer the protesters of earlier, but those who'd come out to see what gossip was to be had. Daniel was still fuelled by anger on behalf of his wife. He pushed his way through the crowd and went into the courthouse to ask when Molly would be released. There were a number of family members waiting for news and no one willing to tell them what was happening. After half an hour or more William came in to join him. Daniel shrugged.

"I think it's all part of making a point," William said, when he was able to get no information either.

Daniel couldn't bear to stand there any longer and decided to go outside and make his own demonstration. James, John and Mary were waiting outside when he got there and Mary toddled toward him.

He picked his daughter up and in full voice took up one of the songs of the women's movement.

Down with all barriers that prevent
Her culture, growth, and a'that -
Her rightful share in Government,
In Church and State, and a'that!...

As Daniel continued to sing, he moved forwards to the steps of the courthouse, apart from the crowd who were jeering at him. It wasn't just the menfolk, that he might have understood. They sought to protect their way of doing things. It was the actions of other women he failed to comprehend. Oh, he knew that Sarah was driven by her husband's views, but how could she, of all people, desert her childhood friend.

His voice was strong and clear even above the noise as he stood with Mary in his arms. He had no idea if Molly could hear him from her cell, but he would go on singing for as long as they kept her in that place.

As he came to the end of *Human Equality*, he turned to face the crowd. He felt the tension of the situation almost as though the arm he was trying to raise was at the same time being pulled back to his side. He did raise it though, and used it to silence the crowd. Heart pounding against his daughter's coat he began. "Fellow citizens of Pierceton…" He had never tried to address them before and, after a quiet murmur, silence fell.

Daniel cleared his throat and continued, "As God hears me now, I will come here every day until my wife is released. I will tell my daughter how proud I am of her mother and I will do whatever I have to do to make sure that my daughter is treated fairly and equally and is not persecuted for her sex."

He began once again to sing.

Amazing grace, how sweet the sound,
that saved a wretch like me…

As his voice rang out clear across the square, Sarah left Joseph's side, separated herself from the crowd around her and moved forward to join him on the steps. Lifting her voice with his as she did so.

Thro' many dangers, toils, and snares,
I have already come…

As they continued, Daniel turned to see William coming out of the courthouse once again. This time he was leading a group of women with Molly at the front. She came forward and linked her arms through Daniel's on one side and Sarah's on the other and sang the rest of the hymn with them.

'Tis grace hath brought me safe thus far,
And grace will lead me home.

THE END

PLEASE LEAVE A REVIEW

Reviews are one of the best ways for new readers to find my writing. It's the modern day 'word of mouth' recommendation. If you have enjoyed reading my work and think that others may do too, then please take a moment or two to leave a review. Just a sentence or two of what you think is all it takes.

Thank you.

BOOK GROUPS

Dear book group readers,

Rather than include questions within the book for you to consider, I have included special pages within my website. This has the advantage of being easier to update and for you to suggest additions and thoughts which arise out of your discussions.

I am always delighted to have the opportunity to discuss the book with a group and for those groups which are not local to me this can sometimes be arranged as a Skype call or through another internet service. Contact details can be found on the website.

Please visit http://rjkind.com/

SOURCES OF INFORMATION

In addition to the reference sources listed in The Blight and the Blarney and New York Orphan, the following additional information has been consulted:

Women's Suffrage

http://www.michiganwomenshalloffame.org/womens_hi story_timeline1.aspx

https://en.m.wikipedia.org/wiki/Timeline_of_women's_s uffrage_in_the_United_States

https://constitutioncenter.org/timeline/html/cw08_12159. html

http://www.thelizlibrary.org/suffrage/

https://votingrights.news21.com/static/interactives/voting hist/timeline.pdf

https://en.wikipedia.org/wiki/Women%27s_suffrage_in_t he_United_States

https://en.wikipedia.org/wiki/American_Equal_Rights_A ssociation#1868_annual_meeting

https://www.womenshistory.org/resources/general/wom an-suffrage-movement

The American Equal Rights Association, 1866-1870: Gender, Race, and Universal Suffrage - Thesis submitted for the degree of Doctor of Philosophy at the University of Leicester by Stuart Galloway School of Historical Studies University of Leicester - June 2014 https://lra.le.ac.uk/bitstream/2381/29034/1/2014gallowaysj phd.pdf

US History and Politics

http://sageamericanhistory.net/gildedage/topics/gildedag
epolitics.html

https://en.wikipedia.org/wiki/History_of_the_United_Sta
tes_(1865–1918)

https://en.wikipedia.org/wiki/39th_United_States_Congre
ss

Udemy.com courses
  US History 201
  US History 202
  United States History - Prehistory to Reconstruction

Pierceton

http://www.pierceton.us/history/

A History of Pierceton, Indiana - George A Nye 1952

Biographical & Historical Record of Kosciusko County,
Indiana. Chicago: The Lewis Publishing Company, 1887.

Iowa

University of Iowa Digital Library
http://digital.lib.uiowa.edu/browse/cat.php?subject=Cam
pus+%26+Iowa+History

http://dailyiowan.lib.uiowa.edu/

https://icfirstchurch.org/visit_history/

State Historical Society of Iowa
https://ir.uiowa.edu/annals-of-iowa/

https://archive.org/details/historyofjohnson00iowa/page/
n9

ALSO BY ROSEMARY J. KIND

New York Orphan (Tales of Flynn and Reilly 1)

Orphaned on the ship to New York in 1853, seven-year-old Daniel Flynn survives by singing the songs of his homeland. Pick-pocket Thomas Reilly becomes his ally and friend, and, together with Thomas's sister Molly, they are swept up by the Orphan Train Movement, to find better lives with families across America. For Daniel, will the dream prove elusive and how strong are bonds of loyalty when everything is at stake?

The Blight and the Blarney (Prequel to Tales of Flynn and Reilly) – *see Free Download information for how to obtain the ebook, including additional material on the series absolutely free*

Ireland has suffered from potato blight since 1845. Friends and neighbours have died, been evicted or given up what little land they have in search of alms. Michael Flynn is one of the lucky ones. His landlord has offered support.

With the weakening brought about by hunger, there are some things he is powerless to protect his family from. Is it time for the great Michael Flynn to take his family in search of a better life?

The Appearance of Truth

Her birth certificate belonged to a baby who died. Her apparently happy upbringing was a myth. Does anyone out there know – who is Lisa Forster?

The Lifetracer

Connor Bancroft is more used to investigating infidelity than murder, and when he's asked to investigate a death threat he's drawn into a complex story of revenge. He uncovers a series of, apparently, unlinked murders. He is nowhere close to solving the crimes but now his eight year old son, Mikey's life is in danger and Connor has little time left to find out – Who is The Lifetracer?

Alfie's Woods

Alfie sets out to befriend a money-laundering hedgehog when he is recaptured following his escape from the Woodland Prison. Hedgehog is overwhelmed that any other creature should care about him, finds the strength to change his life. Alfie's Woods is a story of the power of friendship and the difference it can make to all of us.

Embers of the Day and Other Stories

From the movingly beautiful, to the laugh-out-loud funny. This collection of short stories covers the breadth of Rosemary J. Kind's fiction writing in her usual accessible style.

Lovers Take up Less Space

A humorous review of the addictive misery of commuting on London Underground.

Pet Dogs Democratic Party Manifesto

Key political issues from a dog's point of view by self-styled political leader Alfie Dog.

Alfie's Diary

An entertaining and thought provoking dog's eye view of the world.

From Story Idea to Reader

Whether brushing up your writing skills or starting out, this book will take you through the whole process from inspiration to conclusion.

The Complete Entlebucher Mountain Dog Book

This book provides a complete insight into the Entlebucher Mountain Dog. Whether you are looking to add an Entlebucher to your family, get the best out of your relationship with a dog you already own or are interested in the story of the breed itself and its development in the UK, this is the book for you.

Poems for Life

A collection of poems by prize winning poet Rosemary J. Kind, including the inspirational 'Carpe Diem'.

You can find out more about the author's other work by: visiting her website http://www.rjkind.com

ABOUT THE AUTHOR

Rosemary J Kind writes because she has to. You could take almost anything away from her except her pen and paper. Failing to stop after the book that everyone has in them, she has gone on to publish books in both non-fiction and fiction, the latter including novels, humour, short stories and poetry. She also regularly produces magazine articles in a number of areas and writes regularly for the dog press. As a child she was desolate when at the age of ten her then teacher would not believe that her poem based on 'Stig of the Dump' was her own work and she stopped writing poetry for several years as a result. She was persuaded to continue by the invitation to earn a little extra pocket money by 'assisting' others to produce the required poems for English homework!

Always one to spot an opportunity, she started school newspapers and went on to begin providing paid copy to her local newspaper at the age of sixteen.

For twenty years she followed a traditional business career, before seeing the error of her ways and leaving it all behind to pursue her writing full-time.

She spends her life discussing her plots with the characters in her head and her faithful dogs, who always put the opposing arguments when there are choices to be made.

Always willing to take on challenges that sensible people regard as impossible, she set up the short story download site Alfie Dog Fiction which she ran for six years. During that time it grew to become one of the largest short story download sites in the world, representing over 300 authors and carrying over 1600 short stories. Her hobby is developing the Entlebucher Mountain Dog breed in the UK and when she brought her beloved Alfie back from Belgium he was only the tenth in the country.

She started writing *Alfie's Diary* as an internet blog the day Alfie arrived to live with her, intending to continue for a year or two. Thirteen years later it goes from strength to strength and has been repeatedly named as one of the top ten pet blogs in the UK.

For more details about the author please visit her website at www.rjkind.com For more details about her dogs then you're better visiting www.alfiedog.me.uk

ACKNOWLEDGMENTS

As always, my sincere thanks go to my writing buddies, without whom my writing would be much the poorer: Patsy, Sheila and Lynne. Also, to my husband, Chris Platt, for reading everything I write, and arguing with me when necessary.

Thanks go to Liz Hurst for her proofreading of the final book and to Katie Stewart, of Magic Owl Designs, who has once again brought my story to life on the cover.

Alfie Dog Fiction

Taking your imagination for a walk

visit our website at www.alfiedog.com

Lightning Source UK Ltd.
Milton Keynes UK
UKHW021358150919
349822UK00013B/565/P

9 781909 894433